DEDICATION

This book is dedicated to the memory of Alice S. Hogg
January 8, 1932 to September 3, 2017

She lived her life with an abundance of joy, compassion, integrity and most importantly love.

CONTENTS

Dedication iii

Contents v

Acknowledgements vii

Glossary of UK police ranks viii

Glossary of Liverpudlian phrases x

Fazakerley Family Tree xii

Plan of Park View Care Home xiii

Staff of Park View Care Home xiv

Residents of Park View Care Home xv

1. Pilgrim way 1

2. Down by the riverside 14

3. My happy home 23

4. We think and speak 33

5. We meet again 43

6. Many waters cannot quench love 49

7. The fret of Care 56

8. I love my love 64

9. Cast Care aside 76

IN MY LIVERPOOL HOME

A BERNIE FAZAKERLEY MYSTERY

JUDY FORD

Bernie Fazakerley Publications

In My Liverpool Home

Published by Bernie Fazakerley Publications

Copyright © 2017 Judy Ford

All rights reserved.

This book is a work of fiction. Any references to real people, events, establishments, organisations or locales are intended only to provide a sense of authenticity and are used fictitiously. All of the characters and events are entirely invented by the author. Any resemblances to persons living or dead are purely coincidental.

No part of this book may be used, transmitted, stored or reproduced in any manner whatsoever without the author's written permission.

ISBN: 1-91-108335-X
ISBN-13: 978-1-911083-35-1

10. Old folks at home 84

11. Home sweet home 93

12. Breaking bread 109

13. Too soon we rise 119

14. Eventide 126

15. Slow watches of the night 132

16. I stand at the door, and knock 139

17. Beloved physician 155

18. For whom the bell tolls 170

19. Tender care 179

20. The darkness deepens 188

21. Hail Mary 194

22. Come into the garden 204

23. Sitting in the shade 221

24. Will you walk into my parlour? 232

25. A hammer in her hand 241

26. Untangling the web 243

27. The Leaving of Liverpool 251

Epilogue 262

Thank You	265
Disclaimer	266
More about Bernie and her friends	267
About the Author	269

ACKNOWLEDGEMENTS

As many readers will have guessed, the title of this book was inspired by the popular song *In my Liverpool Home*, originally written by Pete McGovern, but with many additional verses added since.

I would like to thank the authors of a wide range of internet resources, which have been invaluable for researching the background to this book. These include (among others):

- Spinal Injuries Association (http://www.spinal.co.uk/page/living-with-sci)
- Diabetes UK (https://www.diabetes.org.uk)
- Diabetes.co.uk (http://www.diabetes.co.uk/)
- Wikipedia (https://en.wikipedia.org/)
- Google Maps (https://www.google.co.uk/maps)
- Police Oracle (https://www.policeoracle.com)
- The Disabled Police Association (http://www.disabledpolice.info/)
- The Care Quality Commission (http://www.cqc.org.uk/)
- The Crown Prosecution Service (http://www.cps.gov.uk/)

I would like to thank Gillian Gilbert and Revd Lyn Kenny for reading the manuscript, giving helpful comments and pointing out typographical errors.

Members of the *PeskyMethodists* and *The Apostrophe Protection Society* Facebook groups provided valuable opinions on correct grammar and punctuation.

Every effort has been made to trace copyright holders. The publishers will be glad to rectify in future editions any errors or omissions brought to their attention.

GLOSSARY OF UK POLICE RANKS

Uniformed police

Chief Constable (CC) – Has overall charge of a regional police force, such as Thames Valley Police, which covers Oxford and a large surrounding area.

Deputy Chief Constable (DCC) – The senior discipline authority for each force. 2nd in command to the CC.

Assistant Chief Constable (ACC) – 4 in the Thames Valley Police Service, each responsible for a policy area.

Chief Superintendent ('Chief Super') – Head of a policing area or department.

Police Superintendent – Responsible for a local area within a police force.

Chief Inspector (CI) – Responsible for overseeing a team in a local area.

Police Inspector – Senior operational officer overseeing officers on duty 24/7.

Police Sergeant – Supervises a team of officers.

Police Constable (PC) – 'Bobby on the beat'. Likely to be the first to arrive in response to an emergency call.

Crime Investigation Unit (CID) – Plain clothes officers

Detective Superintendent (DS) – Responsible for crime investigation in a local area.

Detective Chief Inspector (DCI) – Responsible for overseeing a crime investigation team in a local area. May be the Senior Investigating Officer heading up a criminal investigation.

Detective Inspector (DI) – Oversees crime investigation 24/7. May be the Senior Investigating Officer heading up a criminal investigation.

Detective Sergeant (DS) – Supervises a team of CID officers.

Detective Constable (DC) – One of a team of officers investigating crimes.

These descriptions are based on information from the following sources:

[1] Mental Health Cop blog, by Inspector Michael Brown, Mental Health co-ordinator, College of Policing. https://mentalhealthcop.wordpress.com/, accessed 31st March 2017.

[2] Thames Valley Police website, https://www.thamesvalley.police.uk , accessed 31st March 2017.

GLOSSARY OF LIVERPUDLIAN PHRASES

For those unfamiliar with the dialect spoken in Liverpool, some of Bernie's language may be difficult to understand. Here are just a few frequently-used words and phrases.

Ace– Excellent (e.g. 'He's dead ace, he is!') It may also be used to congratulate someone: 'Ace!' means, 'Well done!'

Across the water– On the Wirral side of the Mersey (e.g. in Birkenhead or Wallasey).

Boss!– Good! Marvellous! Wonderful!

Chocka– Full, busy

Cracking the flags– Very hot (literally, hot enough to make paving stones crack)

Dead– Very (e.g. 'dead good', 'dead awful', 'dead handy')

Footy– Football (i.e. soccer)

Flags– Flagstones (i.e. paving stones)

Givin' it bifters– Doing your best, making an effort, working enthusiastically.

Gorra– Got a

Gorra cob on– Fed up, in a bad mood.

Lavvy– Toilet

Me 'ead's chocka– Literally, 'my head's full'. This indicates mental overload or disquiet.

Our– Used to indicate that a person is a member of the family or a close friend. E.g. 'Our Bernie', 'Our kid', 'Our Dad'. May be used when speaking of someone or when speaking to them.

Our kid– Brother, often, but not always, the youngest of the family.

Over the water– On the Wirral side of the Mersey (e.g. in Birkenhead or Wallasey).

Ozzy– Hospital

Proddy– Protestant

Scouse– Used as a noun, this means either a type of stew, usually eaten with hunks of bread, or the dialect spoken in Liverpool. Blind Scouse, is scouse without any meat in it. Used as an adjective, it indicates that a person or object comes from Liverpool or is associated with Liverpool.

Scouser– Someone originating from Liverpool – a Liverpudlian.

FAZAKERLEY FAMILY TREE

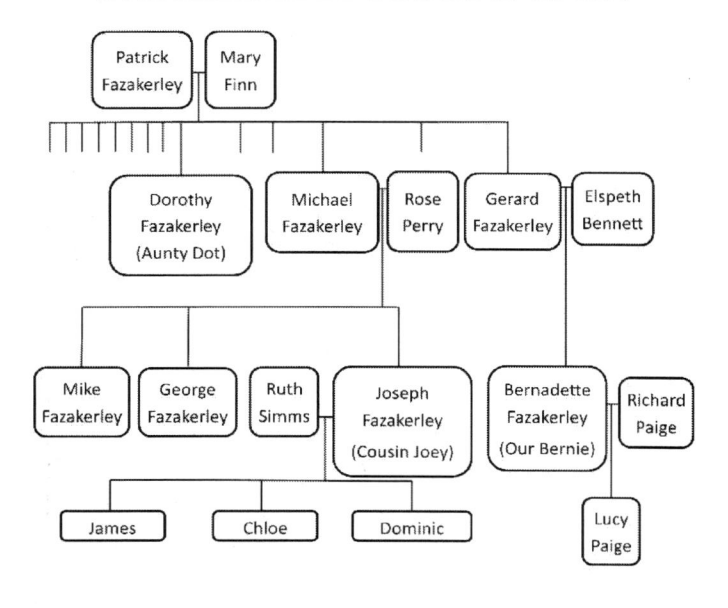

```
Patrick Fazakerley — Mary Finn
    │
    ├── Dorothy Fazakerley (Aunty Dot)
    │       ├── Mike Fazakerley
    │       ├── George Fazakerley
    │       └── Ruth Simms
    │
    ├── Michael Fazakerley — Rose Perry
    │       └── Joseph Fazakerley (Cousin Joey)
    │               ├── James
    │               ├── Chloe
    │               └── Dominic
    │
    └── Gerard Fazakerley — Elspeth Bennett
            └── Bernadette Fazakerley (Our Bernie) — Richard Paige
                    └── Lucy Paige
```

PLAN OF PARK VIEW CARE HOME

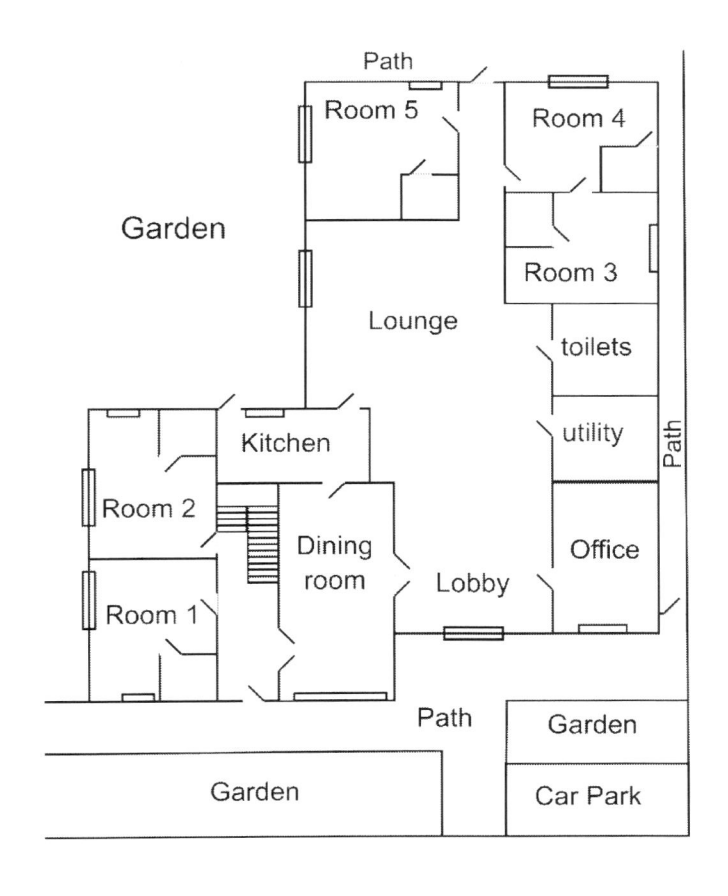

STAFF OF PARK VIEW CARE HOME

Fiona Radcliffe (Manager)

Rebecca Anderson (Care Assistant)

Jonathan Bates (Nurse)

Julia Freeman (Care Assistant)

Scarlet Jones (Care Assistant)

Maxine Shaw (Nurse)

Ian Wilton (Care Assistant)

Hector Bayliss (Caretaker)

Oonagh Conlon (Cleaner)

Grace Massey (Cook)

RESIDENTS OF PARK VIEW CARE HOME

Room 1. Frances Ray

Room 2. Eric Martin

Room 3. Charlotte Goodman

Room 4. Charles Melling

Room 5. Olive Carter

Room 6. Margery Cooper

Room 7. Betty Hunter

Room 8. Dorothy Fazakerley

Room 9. Kathleen Lowe

Room 10. Joan Pickles

1. PILGRIM WAY

Also, when he shall return again to the City, you shall go too, with the sound of the trumpet, and be ever with him.
John Bunyan: "The Pilgrim's Progress".

'I can't believe you talked me into this,' Peter grumbled, turning round in his seat to speak to Jonah, who was in his hi-tech electric wheelchair, safely strapped into the back of their specially adapted car. 'What makes you think that we'll be able to solve a murder case that the local police can't fathom?'

'Bringing a fresh eye to a situation often helps,' Jonah replied, smiling complacently. 'And I could hardly refuse an appeal from Bernie's favourite Aunt.'

'You keep me out of this!' Peter's wife protested from the driver's seat. 'I agree with Peter. I'm sure that Merseyside Police are quite competent to deal with it. Aunty Dot just has unreasonable expectations. She doesn't realise that these things always take time. Plus, she's determined to prove everyone wrong about this young man she's got fond of. You shouldn't encourage her. I only went along with it all because I'd already been thinking I ought to pay the family another visit, and getting you to take any leave at all has been like trying to get blood out of a stone.'

'But if this Jonathan that Aunty Dot's talking about really *is* innocent,' her daughter Lucy chimed in, from the seat opposite Jonah, 'shouldn't we be doing everything we can to prove it? I mean, it's not fair, is it? If they never find out who did do it, he'll have it hanging over him for the rest of his life.'

'There you are, Peter! Lucy agrees with me,' Jonah said triumphantly. 'It's our duty to help DCI Latham and her team to get to the bottom of things; and it's not as if I haven't gone through the proper channels. After Dot rang, I got on to Sandra Latham and she jumped at the idea that we might be willing to come up and give her the benefit of our experience.'

'Only because she's got this bizarre idea that you are some sort of superhero,' Bernie retorted. 'She still sees you in terms of those tabloid headlines when you first came back to work after you were shot: *Police hero back in the saddle after near-fatal shooting, Inspirational cop returns to the frontline…*'

'*Criminals beware! He's back! And he's on your trail!*' Lucy added with a giggle.

'I suppose she thinks she's getting Ironside to help her,' Peter muttered.

'I doubt it,' Bernie said, laughing. 'She's too young to have much idea who Ironside was. You're starting to show your age, Peter. Even I can only just remember when it was on the telly; and I never watched it. I was more of a *Cagney and Lacey* girl myself!'

'You're all talking nonsense,' Jonah said, when the hilarity died down enough for him to be heard. 'She simply recognised the benefits of having an independent mind to look at the evidence. And, of course, we did put her on the right track last year with that murder that you all got yourselves mixed up in.'

The summer before, Bernie had made a rare visit to her home city of Liverpool to introduce Lucy and Peter to her few remaining relatives. During their stay, they had witnessed the killing of a Roman Catholic priest aboard one of the iconic Mersey Ferries and Bernie, in particular, had been involved in identifying the perpetrator of the crime.[1] DCI Sandra Latham had been the Senior Investigating Officer and Jonah had struck up a friendship with her, based, as Bernie had rightly indicated, on her deep respect, verging on adulation, for the way in which he had refused to allow a disabling spinal injury to curtail a highly successful career in Thames Valley CID.

When Miss Dorothy Fazakerley had rung her niece, three days earlier, to say that there had been a suspicious death among the residents of the Care Home where she lived, Jonah's immediate reaction had been to contact Sandra to get a police perspective on the incident. To his delight, it transpired that she was in charge of the investigation and she confided to him that Merseyside Police were making very little progress towards finding conclusive evidence to establish how, and by whom, a lethal dose of insulin had been administered to 79-year-old Mrs Olive Carter.

Thus it was that the whole family was making the journey from their home in Oxford to spend a week in Liverpool, visiting Bernie's cousins – and her aunt, of course – and *helping the police with their enquiries.*

'If you're so against the idea, why didn't you stay at home?' Jonah demanded of Peter, 'instead of just sitting there complaining all the time.'

'What? And leave you lot alone together with a killer on the loose?' Peter exclaimed. 'Not bloody likely! You can't any of you be trusted to take care of yourselves. You need me around to exercise a restraining hand and stop you barging into things without thinking and getting yourselves

---

[1] See *Mystery over the Mersey* © Judy Ford 2016, ISBN 978-1-911083-19-1, 978-1-911083-24-5 (e-book) or 978-1-911083-29-0 (Large Print)

killed!'

He spoke jokingly to hide the real reason that he had insisted on joining the expedition: he was determined not to allow his wife and stepdaughter to shoulder the entire burden of caring for their friend in unfamiliar surroundings. The large house in Oxford, which they had shared with Jonah since the death of his wife three years previously, had been extensively modified to suit his needs. It also contained many labour-saving devices to assist them in various activities of daily living. A hotel, even one that boasted *full accessibility*, could not be expected to provide all the equipment that they were accustomed to having. Apparently simple tasks, such as giving Jonah a shower, were likely to involve heavy lifting, probably in awkward confined spaces, which would be much easier if Peter were there to help.

'But it's only what Mam and Jonah do all the time,' Lucy pointed out, taking her stepfather's words at face value and wondering why he should be concerned about a murder investigation in Liverpool, when he was sanguine about such things closer to home. 'I mean, that's their job, isn't it – investigating murders?'

'As part of a proper police team,' Peter insisted, 'with all the proper safeguards in place.'

'Tiredness can kill. Take a break,' Bernie read aloud from one of the roadside signs, hoping to distract them from a fruitless argument. She knew exactly why Peter had come, and shared his desire to avoid voicing his concerns in front of Jonah. 'We must be coming up to Keele Services. We'll stop there for a drink and to stretch our legs, and then we should be able to get to Liverpool in one more stage. Peter! You can drive on the last leg, while I navigate.'

They pulled in at the motorway service station and parked in a disabled bay close to the entrance of the building. Bernie and Peter got out, while Lucy leaned forward and started undoing the straps that held Jonah's wheelchair in place. By the time she had finished, Bernie and Peter had the back of the car open and were engaged in attaching the ramp that would allow Jonah to descend. Soon all four of them were together on the tarmac, looking around to get their bearings.

'Let's get off the road,' Peter suggested. 'There are some tables and chairs just over there,' he added, pointing towards a small paved area, cordoned off from the main concourse by green barriers.

Jonah expertly manoeuvred his electric wheelchair across the carpark and up a gentle slope to the patio that Peter had indicated. The others followed.

'I'll get us some coffee,' Bernie said. 'Everyone having their usual?'

'Yes please,' Jonah answered, while Peter nodded his agreement.

'I'll come and help carry,' Lucy volunteered.

They disappeared into the building, leaving Jonah and Peter sitting looking at one another. Jonah pressed a button on the arm of his chair, which made it recline slowly until he was lying on his back. Peter smiled approvingly, glad that Jonah had not needed reminding that the chief purpose of the break in their journey was to allow him to change his body position to avoid developing pressure sores or circulation problems as a result of being strapped into his wheelchair for too long.

Jonah manipulated the controls to make the surface upon which he was lying tilt, first to the right and then to the left, shifting his weight to relieve the pressure on his body. After a few minutes, he brought it back into a horizontal position and looked towards Peter.

'Would you mind strapping me in so I can stand up? Now that I've got the new chair, I might as well make the most of it.'

Peter carefully fastened wide bands of fabric around Jonah's legs and across his chest, just beneath his armpits, so that he was attached firmly to the chair, which now resembled a narrow bed or a hospital trolley

'OK,' he said, after double-checking that each strap was secure and that the wheelchair's brakes were applied. 'You're good to go.'

Jonah pressed another of the controls on the keypad beneath his left hand and the surface on which he was lying began to pivot as a hydraulic cylinder extended, bringing him into an upright position while leaving the wheelchair chassis standing firmly on the ground. His purpose-built chair made a large contribution, along with the support of his three friends, to Jonah's ability to carry on a normal life despite his extensive physical limitations. This vertical support mechanism was a new feature and Jonah enjoyed using it. As well as being beneficial to his physical well-being, it made him feel more normal to be standing up and viewing the world from his own natural height. Although he could not feel his feet, it gave him pleasure to know that they were now planted on the ground and supporting his weight, albeit still dependent on the straps to prevent his legs buckling.

He looked around and smiled to himself at the way that the crowds of people walking past them, on the way to the coffee shop, restaurant or toilets, were watching him while pretending not to. He caught the eye of a young man who grinned sheepishly and hurried on.

'Look at that man!' a young voice sounded behind him. 'What's he doing in that funny thing?'

Jonah turned his head and saw a woman pushing a baby in a buggy with a girl, whom Jonah estimated to be three or four, trotting along beside her, clutching a grey fur-fabric rabbit in her arms.

'Hello,' Jonah greeted them. 'Do you like my chair?'

The little girl drew back against her mother and clutched her rabbit closer to her. The woman looked embarrassed.

'I'm sorry,' she said, sounding flustered. 'I've told her not to stare at people, but …'

'Don't apologise,' Jonah put in quickly, smiling down on her. 'Children ought to take an interest in what's going on around them. How else are they going to learn? I'm Jonah,' he went on, 'and this is Peter. We're on our way to Liverpool. Do you have far to go?'

'We're going to stay with my mum in Clitheroe,' the woman answered. 'I'm Janice and this is Emily.'

'I know Clitheroe. My late wife came from Horwich,' Jonah told her. 'We used to go over there sometimes when we were staying with her family. We used to take our two boys up Pendle Hill.' He turned his head to address Emily. 'That's a nice rabbit you've got there. What his name?'

'*She*'s called Woffles,' Emily answered in a tone that suggested that the gender of her soft toy should be obvious to anyone with a modicum of intelligence.

'I do beg her pardon,' Jonah said hastily, favouring Emily with a lopsided grin. 'Is she looking forward to your holiday?'

Emily nodded. Then she plucked up her courage to ask, 'why are you in that thing?'

'Because I can't move my arms and legs anymore. This chair helps me to get about.'

'It doesn't look like a chair to me,' Emily observed with a frown.

'That's because it's a very special chair. Some very clever friends of mine designed it for me. It can be a chair or a bed or it can stand me up like this.'

'What happened to you?' Emily wanted to know.

'Someone shot me in my neck and it broke most of the nerves in my spinal cord. That's the thing that takes messages from my brain to my muscles to tell them what to do,' Jonah started to explain. 'It-'

'We'd better be going,' Janice interrupted, still embarrassed at her daughter's interest in Jonah's disability. 'Come along Emily! Olivia needs her nappy changing.' She started pushing the buggy towards the entrance to the services building. Emily looked Jonah up and down again before turning to follow her mother.

'Goodbye, Emily!' Jonah called after them. 'It was nice talking to you.'

Bernie's eyes lit up with pleasure at the sight of Jonah in his upright position when she and Lucy returned with the drinks. Like Peter, she worried that Jonah did not always take as much care over his own welfare as he could have done and she was pleased to see him making full use of the versatile new wheelchair's advanced features, designed to keep him healthy. She put down the two paper cups of coffee, which she was carrying, on one of the tables and busied herself with inserting a long drinking straw into the lid of one of them. Jonah raised the right-hand arm-rest of his chair into a horizontal position so that the small table attached to it was ready to receive the cup. Bernie placed Jonah's cup on it taking care to ensure that the straw was within his reach.

'Tell me more about this Care Home where your Aunty Dot lives,' Jonah urged her, as soon as they were all settled with their drinks. 'What sort of place is it?'

'Well, you've been there, haven't you?' Bernie reminded him. 'So I don't know what else I can tell you.'

'I mean: what sort of people live there? How many of them are there? And how many staff? Do they get out much? Or are they all stuck in there all day?'

'I don't know,' Bernie shrugged. 'It's quite small, I think. It's privately owned and, I *think*, it's independent – not part of a big chain, I mean. The residents are all elderly and need help with activities of daily living, but it doesn't offer nursing care, so they can't be really ill. They are a mixture of people like Aunty Dot, who have their fees paid by the local authority, and better-off ones who pay their own way. That's been a bit of a bone of contention, I gather. The ones who pay for themselves get charged more, ostensibly because they have the better rooms, but everyone "knows" that it's really just that the Home can only survive financially if the paying residents are subsidising the others. I don't know how true this is, but that's the perception, according to Aunty Dot.'

'And was Olive Carter, the victim, a local authority resident or paying her own fees?' Jonah asked.

'She was paying for herself. According to Aunty Dot, she owned a house in Mossley Hill, which meant that her assets were way over the limit for Local Authority assistance. She was going to have to sell it to raise the cash to continue paying the fees.'

'Aaaah!' Jonah nodded thoughtfully. 'And Dot said that it was her family who pointed the finger at this Jonathan, because she'd left him something in her will. But they must have been set to inherit a lot more than he did, assuming that she left the house to them.'

'Are you suggesting that *they* could have killed her?' Peter asked.

'I'm merely pointing out that they have a motive – two motives in fact: the straightforward financial one and possibly an emotional desire to prevent the family home being sold off. The way Bernie describes it, it sounds as if Olive's death occurred at the crucial moment to prevent that happening. They – or some of them – may even have been living in it. Did Dot say anything about that?'

'No.' Bernie shrugged. 'I didn't ask.'

'I'm sure Sandra Latham will have found out about all that,' Peter said. 'You'll just have to wait and let her brief you properly.'

'The Care Home management must suspect Jonathan,' Bernie said thoughtfully. 'When Aunty Dot rang last night, she said he'd been suspended from work. She didn't know whether that meant the police had told them he was a suspect or–'

'Sandra would have rung me if they'd got evidence of that,' Jonah interrupted confidently. 'It'll just be to reassure the residents that they're taking it seriously and aren't going to allow them to be murdered in their beds.'

'But that's awful!' Lucy exclaimed. 'What if they never

find out who did it? Will he lose his job?'

'I'm afraid he probably will,' Peter admitted. 'They'll say that his position would be untenable because the residents have lost confidence in him.'

'Which is why it's so important that we get to the bottom of what really happened!' Jonah added triumphantly. 'You see Peter? It's our duty to help. If this Jonathan is guilty, he needs to be stopped from going off somewhere else and doing it again; and if he's innocent then he shouldn't have to suffer for it.'

'The thing I'm most concerned about is making sure that Aunty Dot isn't left living somewhere where there's a serial killer on the loose,' Bernie commented. 'Don't forget: the main reason for suspecting Jonathan was that another old dear, who had also left him a legacy, also died recently. If it *is* Jonathan who bumped them both off for their money, she's probably safe because she doesn't have a bean as far as I know, but if another member of staff is doing it, who knows?'

'Dom says nobody thought anything was wrong when the first one died,' Lucy said. 'He got roped in to take Aunty Dot to the funeral, and everyone was saying how well she'd done getting to ninety-eight, especially when she'd had a heart condition for twenty years.'

Dominic Fazakerley was Bernie's first cousin once removed — the youngest of her Cousin Joey's three children. He and Lucy had become friends during their visit the previous year and regularly conversed via Facebook.

'Did he know what it was exactly that this other woman had left to Jonathan?' Jonah asked eagerly. This was the first that he knew that Lucy had access to inside information about the case. 'And did she have any family who might have resented her leaving it to him?'

'Just some ornaments off the shelves in her room, as far as Dom knew,' Lucy answered. 'He thinks it's bonkers to think anyone'd kill for them. I don't know about any family. Dom said Aunty Dot wanted to go to the funeral because she was afraid there wouldn't be anyone much there, so maybe not.'

'She told me that there was a daughter,' Bernie said. 'But Dot reckoned she was happy for Jonathan to have some of her mother's stuff.'

'But she would say that wouldn't she?' Jonah argued. 'To your Aunty Dot and the other people at the Care Home, I mean; but she may have warned Olive's family to keep an eye on Jonathan in case he worked his charms on her too. And the ornaments may have been valuable antiques, which it would have been worth Jonathan's while killing for.'

'Hardly worth bothering when the woman was ninety-eight,' Peter pointed out. 'He might as well have just waited for nature to take its course.'

'And maybe he did,' Jonah agreed. 'Or maybe he discovered that the daughter was working on her to change her will and decided to cash in his investment right away.'

'Or maybe he wasn't thinking about it at all,' Lucy said indignantly. 'Aunty Dot says he's just very nice and kind and helpful, and all the residents like giving him little presents. If her daughter wanted to have all her money after she died, why didn't she look after her herself, instead of putting her in a Home?'

'Maybe she couldn't,' Peter suggested. 'If the mother's ninety-eight, the daughter may well be well into her seventies and unwell herself.'

'Stan and Sylvia are in their seventies and they could do it,' Lucy argued. 'I don't understand why anyone would not look after their family themselves. It's-'

'Stan and Sylvia are remarkably fit for their age' Bernie cut in, 'and even so, Stan's arthritis would prevent him from looking after someone who needed a lot of lifting. We can't possibly know the circumstances, so you shouldn't judge.'

'The mother may have preferred to live in a Home,' Peter added. 'It may have made her feel more independent; or the daughter may have other caring responsibilities. We just don't know, do we?'

'I suppose so,' Lucy agreed reluctantly, still convinced that she would not have allowed anything to get in the way of her becoming the main carer for her mother under such circumstances. She had been involved in caring for their friend Jonah ever since his disabling injury when she was only nine years old; consequently she saw the idea of putting a loved one into the hands of professionals as something unnatural and incomprehensible.

'Mike says that insulin is a stupid thing to use to kill someone,' Lucy said, seeing that her parents did not want her to continue pursuing her argument. 'He says that it might well not have worked, because it depends so much on things like what she'd eaten before it was administered.'

Dr Mike Carson was a forensic pathologist and a longstanding friend of the family. Lucy, whose ambition was to follow in his footsteps, had discussed the case with him in some detail.

'I expect it was a copy-cat killing,' Peter opined. 'There was a case a few years back, which hit the headlines. Several hospital patients were killed or injured by someone putting insulin in their saline drips.'

'That's right,' Bernie agreed. 'And it wasn't so very far from Liverpool, so it may have been covered even more extensively up there. It was Stepping Hill Hospital in Stockport. A nurse was accused and then acquitted, as far as I remember.'

'No. She was never brought to trial,' Jonah corrected her. He had been researching the incident, having already concluded that it could well have been the inspiration for Olive Carter's killer. 'The charges were dropped. They discovered that another similar death had occurred after the first nurse had been suspended from duty. It turned out to be a different nurse altogether. It was nearly three years before he was convicted. And Mike is right: twenty-two people were poisoned, but only seven of them died.'

'Wow! I hope it doesn't take three years to clear Jonathan,' Lucy gasped.

'And I hope nobody else gets poisoned while the police are investigating,' Bernie added. 'But, it may not be the same sort of thing at all. I mean, it may not be a serial killer. Surely, it could even be an unfortunate accident.'

2. DOWN BY THE RIVERSIDE
*Gonna lay down my burden
Down by the riverside.*
Traditional American Spiritual

DCI Sandra Latham met them down at the Pier Head, after they had checked in and deposited their luggage at their hotel. They sat together on the concrete plinth beneath one of the *Lambanana* sculptures, which could be found at various locations across the city, and shared a picnic lunch.

'Tell me exactly what evidence you have so far,' Jonah urged. 'Start from the beginning. We've had bits and pieces from different people and I'm not sure how much is true and how much may just be hearsay and speculation.'

'OK.' Sandra thought for a moment before going on. 'We were called in a week ago yesterday. That was two days after Olive Carter was found dead in her bed when the Care Assistant went to help her up in the morning.'

'So she died overnight Tuesday to Wednesday ten days ago?' Jonah queried.

'That's right. They called the doctor, and he said that it looked like natural causes. He thought it might have been a stroke or a heart attack, but he warned them that he had to inform the coroner and there might have to be a post-mortem.'

'Did anyone object to that?' Jonah asked.

'None of the staff raised any objections. I rather fancy one of Mrs Carter's sons may have been unhappy about it, but I don't think he ... well, yes! I remember now. It was John: the younger son. He did try to stop the post-mortem. He said that it was unnecessary and a desecration of his mother's body.'

'That's interesting.' Jonah filed this piece of information away in his mind, making a note to follow up on whether or not Mr John Carter had had any opportunity to administer an overdose of insulin to his mother. 'Now go on, what do you know about how she died?'

'Olive Carter had type 2 diabetes. It had got to the stage where it could no longer be controlled purely by diet and oral medication. She was on a regimen of once-a-day injections of slow-acting insulin, which a member of staff would bring to her just before she went to bed each night.'

'So couldn't it just have been an accidental overdose?' Lucy asked.

'Apparently not. There was far too much insulin still in her blood for that and, even if she had accidentally given herself too much, because it was what they call intermediate-acting, it shouldn't have sent her into a coma as quickly as it seems to have done. It was supposed to last through the night and just stop her blood sugar rising while she was asleep. The pathologist reckons that she must have been given a large dose of rapid-acting insulin, which lowered her blood sugar very quickly, and catastrophically. Her blood also contained evidence that she had taken a larger than normal dose of her prescribed sleeping tablets that evening. She was in the habit of taking them, because she was in a lot of pain from arthritis and found it difficult to sleep.'

'So, you think that someone dosed her with sleeping tablets and then injected her with insulin?' Peter asked, becoming interested despite having promised himself that he was going to have no part in what he saw as Jonah's interference in the investigation. 'Or is the idea that the member of staff who gave Olive her insulin injection used a different dose of a different sort of insulin without her knowledge?'

'That's what we don't know,' Sandra replied. 'And that's why we haven't arrested Jonathan Bates yet.'

'But the Home has suspended him from work,' Bernie pointed out. 'That suggests that he's more under suspicion than any of the other staff, doesn't it?'

'That wasn't our doing,' Sandra told her. 'I think the manager felt she had to act because Olive's family were openly accusing him of killing her. She wanted to be seen to be doing something and she was afraid that other residents might not like having him around while there was a cloud hanging over him. He was the person who put Olive to bed and gave her both her sleeping tablet and her slow-acting insulin. He wrote it all up in the medicines book, which they keep in the office. What we can't be sure of is whether anyone else might have come into Mrs Carter's room later on and given her the fatal overdose.'

'Where did the rapid-acting insulin come from?' Jonah asked sharply. 'If Olive didn't use that kind, how did the murderer get hold of it?'

'Again, that's something we don't know for sure. There's another resident who has type 1 diabetes and has to inject several times a day. The Home insists that all residents keep their drugs locked away in a cupboard in the office. Any member of staff could have got the key and taken some.'

'Well, did they or didn't they?' Jonah asked impatiently. 'Was there any missing when you checked?'

'Unfortunately we can't tell for sure,' Sandra sighed. 'Their records aren't exactly ... Well, to be honest, they were a mess! The staff are supposed to record every dose that they administer, and update the stock list every time drugs are used or replenished, but it's very clear that this often doesn't happen. It's impossible to tell for sure whether the insulin – and the sleeping tablets for that matter – came from the supply in the drugs cupboard or were brought in from outside.'

'And this Jonathan Bates gave Olive her insulin and sleeping tablets that night,' Jonah mused. 'What about this other woman – the one who died a while back? Is he in the frame for that too?"

'Edna Lomax? Well, again, it's difficult to tell. We don't even know if she *was* killed, or if it was natural causes, the way everyone thought at the time. She was cremated, so there's no chance of going back and re-examining her body now, and nobody thought it was necessary to do toxicology tests on her because the doctors were confident that there was nothing wrong.'

'But presumably Jonathan Bates was around the day she died?'

'Yes. He was on duty that evening and he told the doctor that she'd been complaining of a headache and went to bed early that night. He could have been setting the scene to make it more likely that it would be accepted that the death was natural.'

'Or he could have been telling the truth and she really was ill,' Lucy pointed out forthrightly.

'Indeed,' Sandra agreed with a smile. 'That's why we haven't charged him with anything.'

'Aunty Dot said that people were pointing the finger at Jonathan because both women left him something in their wills,' Bernie said. 'Was that sufficient motive do you think? I mean, it seems rather unnecessary when they were bound to die within a few years anyway. How much exactly was he going to get from them?'

'Mrs Lomax – the first death – left him a collection of Wedgewood china, which he'd admired. She didn't actually name him in her will; she just asked her daughter to pass them on to him when she passed away. Mrs Carter, on the other hand-'

'Hang on a moment!' Jonah interrupted. 'You're saying that Edna Lomax's daughter was actually the one who gave Jonathan the china?'

'That's right. Her mother told her that she wanted it to go to someone who would appreciate it and look after it. Jonathan, as I said had admired it and he'd also been particularly kind to Mrs Lomax and she wanted him to have something to remember her by.'

'So the daughter can't have thought there was anything wrong with Jonathan,' Jonah said thoughtfully. 'If she suspected him of applying pressure on her mother to leave him something – or if she had any idea that he could have hastened her death – she could have kept it all for herself and not given him anything. Now what about Olive? What did she leave to Jonathan?'

'Five hundred pounds and a watercolour of the lake in Sefton Park. She added a codicil to her will just over a year ago, in which she set out a list of small legacies to friends. It was mostly personal effects – pictures, ornaments, jewellery and so on – but one or two of them, Jonathan included, also got cash.'

'Five hundred pounds isn't much to risk murdering someone for,' Bernie observed, 'especially if they were likely to drop dead spontaneously fairly soon anyway.'

'Well, Olive was the youngest resident in the Home and in comparatively good health,' Sandra told her. 'I agree that the gain was hardly worth the risk, but according to her GP, she could have lived for a good few more years.'

'OK,' Jonah conceded, 'Let's assume for the time being that this legacy does provide Jonathan with a motive for killing Olive. Is he the only person with something to gain from her death? Presumably her children must have been set to inherit something too?'

'Yes,' Sandra agreed. 'She had two sons: Desmond, the

older, is unmarried; his younger brother, John, has a wife and a grown-up daughter. The two brothers are Olive's residual legatees and executors. Her estate includes a house in Mossley Hill, which has been valued at between two and three hundred thousand.'

'Which they were set to lose if Olive lived for long enough for all the equity to be swallowed up in Care Home fees,' Bernie put in. 'That's what my Aunt told us. She said that the house was up for sale, because Olive didn't qualify to have her fees paid for her.'

'That's right,' Sandra agreed. 'Which is another reason why we have to consider other possibilities apart from Jonathan Bates when it comes to who might have killed Olive. Both brothers – and arguably John's wife and daughter – have a motive, but would they really kill their mother just to get hold of her house?'

'I suppose it depends how much they needed the money,' Jonah mused. 'How were they off financially?'

'Fairly comfortable,' Sandra answered. 'They're both secondary school teachers, and so is John's wife, Valerie. They're all coming up to retirement soon, with final salary pensions to look forward to; and they've both paid off the mortgage on their houses. There isn't any real reason why they'd be desperate for cash.'

'It could have been more the principle of the thing,' Peter suggested. 'They might not like the idea of their family home being sold in order to save the Local Authority the cost of Olive's care in her old age.'

'A bit drastic, though, to bump her off, just to spite the Council!' Bernie commented.

'The one member of the family who *might* be desperate enough to commit murder for money is Mrs Carter's granddaughter,' Sandra went on. 'She's an unemployed single mum with two kids. And they're all currently living with her parents, which I suppose might also give them a reason for wanting to cash in their inheritance sooner rather than later.'

'OK,' Jonah said. 'We've established that the family have a motive. Did any of them have the opportunity to administer the fatal dose? Presumably whoever it was would have had to be there during a fairly short time window?'

'Not as short as all that,' Sandra told him, 'but you're right: most of the critical time was during the night, when the only people who would have had access to Mrs Carter were the Care Assistant on duty and the live-in caretaker. However, it's possible – although unlikely – that the insulin was administered as early as the middle of the afternoon. Desmond Carter took his mother out for the day, returning in time for her evening meal; and John and Valerie called in to see her shortly after she got back. So they could have done it. The only thing that militates against that is that they would have found it harder to obtain the fast-acting insulin, since they wouldn't have access to the drugs cabinet in the Care Home office.'

'How can you be sure about that?' Jonah asked. 'They are presumably familiar with the Home, having visited their mother there over a number of years, and keys can be stolen or borrowed and copied. If the drugs records are in a mess then it may be that the staff are equally careless about the keys to the office and the cupboard.'

'Mmmm,' Sandra murmured. 'Yes. That's perfectly true. We did check the drug cupboard for fingermarks, but there were so many that it was difficult to distinguish who they belonged to. The manager of the Home is adamant that the cupboard is always kept secure, but she would say that, wouldn't she? And she is one of the staff who were on duty during the period of time when the drug was administered, so we can't rule out the possibility that she was responsible. If you come back to the Station with me, I'll show you the list of staff who were there at the crucial time.'

'Good idea!' Jonah declared enthusiastically. We've finished eating and Bernie has promised her cousin that she's going to call on them this afternoon. So I suggest that I go with you while the others socialise.'

'Hold on!' Peter protested. 'It's all very well for you to decide that you want to spend your holiday interfering in someone else's murder investigation, but Sandra's family may be hoping that she'll be able to come home for at least part of her weekend!'

'Don't worry about that,' Sandra said with a little laugh, which made Peter suspect that all was not completely well with the Latham family. 'My girls are staying with their dad until Monday evening, so nobody's going to be worrying about what I'm up to. I would be really grateful if you'd come and have a look at the case files,' she added, turning to Jonah. 'I'm really not clear where to go from here.'

'That's settled then!' Jonah smiled round with an air of satisfaction. 'We'll go through the evidence while Bernie hobnobs with her relations, and we'll meet back at the hotel for dinner.'

'I think one of us ought to go with you,' Lucy objected. 'In case you need anything.'

'Rubbish!' Jonah said decisively. 'It'll only be for a couple of hours. I'm sure Sandra will be able to cope, and we can always ring you if there's an emergency – not that that's at all likely.'

Lucy pursed her lips and looked towards her mother, still dissatisfied. She felt a proprietorial interest in Jonah and did not trust any stranger, however well-intentioned, to know how to look after him properly. What if his urine bag needed emptying? Or if he suffered a bout of autonomic dysreflexia[2]?'

'OK,' Bernie said, giving her daughter a look that told her not to make any more fuss about the matter. 'We'll drop you off at the police station and go on to Joey's.

---

[2] A condition, common in people with high-level spinal cord injuries, where there is a sudden and potentially lethal rise in blood pressure.

We'll give you until four-thirty, which will probably be as long as Joey and Ruth will want to put up with us, and then collect you and take you back to the hotel. No arguments,' she added firmly, seeing Jonah opening his mouth to speak and anticipating that he was about to protest that there was no need for them to curtail his session with Sandra so early. 'It's been a long day and we're all tired. Not to mention the importance of allowing time for you to do some physio before dinner.'

'Yes miss,' Jonah said meekly. Then he grinned up at Sandra and winked. 'You see how it is? We'd better keep on the right side of Nanny, or she won't let me go out to play with you again!'

3. MY HAPPY HOME
Jerusalem, my happy home, when shall I come to thee?
Joseph Bromehead: "Jerusalem, my happy home"

Bernie's first cousin, Joseph Fazakerley, 'Cousin Joey', lived only a few streets away from the row of terraced houses where they had both grown up. His wife, Ruth, was also a native of the Toxteth area. Their two sons, James and Dominic, still lived with their parents. Joey's mother, Rose, also shared their modest semi-detached house, now that she was too frail to live alone. With such a large family to accommodate, their small front room felt very crowded when Joey ushered them in.

'I don't think you've met Chris, have you?' Ruth said, gesturing towards a young man in jeans and a tee-shirt, who had jumped up from his seat as they walked in, and was standing rather self-consciously in the middle of the room. 'He's Chloë's boyfriend.' She looked towards her daughter, who got up from the sofa and smiled towards the guests. 'They've got a flat in West Derby.'

Bernie and Peter nodded towards Chris and Chloë and shook hands with them both.

'Chris works at Alder Hey too,' Ruth went on. Bernie remembered that Chloë was a play-specialist at the famous children's hospital. 'So the flat is handy for them both.'

Bernie got the impression that she was apologising for her daughter's behaviour in moving in with a man without the preliminary formality of a wedding ceremony, and trying to find reasons to justify it. She remembered that Ruth was a strict Roman Catholic and had brought her children up to be regular attenders at Mass. Did she approve of Chris? Or did she believe that he was leading her daughter astray?

'What is it that you do then?' she asked, turning to address the young man.

'I'm an orthoptist. I work with kids who have squints and stuff.'

'I get it,' Bernie nodded. 'Eye patches and that sort of thing.'

'That's right. And exercises and stuff, to promote binocular vision.'

'Sit down everyone,' Ruth urged, in an attempt to fill the silence that followed, 'and I'll make us all a brew.'

'Not for us, thanks Mum,' Chloë said quickly, as her mother turned to go out to the kitchen. 'We can't stop. We only came round to say "hello" to Bernie. We need to get back. We're in the middle of decorating the flat and we won't get it finished this weekend if we don't get the next coat of paint on today.'

'That's alright, princess,' Joey said, before his wife could express her disapproval of this discourtesy towards their guests. 'You two run along. They're going to be here for a week, so there'll be plenty of time later. We'll give you a bell and maybe go out for a meal one evening.'

'Thanks Dad,' Chloë said with evident relief. 'I'm sorry we can't stay. It's just …'

'It's quite OK,' Bernie assured her. 'You'd only be bored listening to me and your dad reminiscing about the good old days. Much better to wait until we've got that out of our systems and won't be making you feel like a spare part in the conversation.'

Chloë smiled round at the guests and then took Chris

by the hand and led him out of the room. Ruth watched them go, with a slight frown on her face.

'Chris looks like a pleasant young man,' Peter ventured.

'Yes,' Joey agreed. 'Chloë says he's very good with the kids, and he was very helpful when Rose was ill last winter and needed to get to doctor's appointments and that.'

'Yes,' Ruth agreed, a little reluctantly, Bernie thought. 'He's a good lad. I just wish Chloë had waited until he put a ring on her finger before agreeing to live together. I never know what to say when Father Nat asks after her. I can't help feeling that he thinks I'm hiding something from him.'

Father Nathaniel Milton was the parish priest at the church that the Fazakerley family attended each Sunday. It was the same church where Bernie and Joey had taken their first communion together fifty-odd years earlier and where Joey and Ruth had been married.

'Of course he does,' Dominic declared. 'He's bound to, the way you always look so guilty about it. All you need to say is that she's fine. He's not expecting a full account of her movements since the Sunday before.'

'And I daresay he wouldn't be the least bit shocked if you did tell him about her sharing a flat with Chris,' Joey added. 'That's just the way youngsters do things these days.'

'Well it's not the way I brought our Chloë up to behave,' Ruth insisted. 'But never mind! I suppose it'll all work out in the end. Now I'd better get the kettle on or we'll none of us be getting any tea.'

She bustled out, and soon they could hear the clink of china coming from the kitchen as she set teacups and plates on a tray and measured tea into the pot. Joey shook his head in mild exasperation at his wife's uncompromising attitude and grinned towards Bernie.

'Well, now we've got that out of the way, tell me what you've been up to this last year – not got mixed up in any more murders, I hope!'

'Oh yes!' Bernie replied cheerily. 'Lots! And plenty of muggings and burglaries as well, but then that's all part of my job, remember.'

'Of course!' Joey exclaimed. 'I keep forgetting you're not at the university any more. How's the police work going? But I suppose you're not allowed to tell me about any of it.'

'Well no, I probably ought not to,' Bernie agreed. 'There is one case, though, that Peter was involved in from the other side, so to speak. You'll have heard about it on the news, I expect. His baby granddaughter was snatched from her pram in the park.'

'Of course!' Dominic burst out with great excitement. 'I saw you on the box, appealing for witnesses. It must have been awful!'

'Yes,' Peter agreed, unsure how to expand upon this simple statement.

'It must have been terrible for your daughter-in-law,' Ruth declared forcefully, bustling in with a loaded tray. 'I simply couldn't imagine what she must have been going through.'

'It was awful for Peter and Eddie too,' Lucy said loyally, remembering the anguish that her stepfather had experienced, seeing his son's distress and being unable to do anything to alleviate it.

'It was traumatic for all of us,' Bernie agreed, seeing Peter's discomfiture and regretting that she had mentioned the incident. 'It only lasted for a few days, as it turned out, but it felt more like a year.'

'But Jonah solved the case in the end,' Lucy added, 'and got Abigail back safe.'

'Jonah? That's your friend in the wheelchair, right?' James asked. 'Where is he? I thought he was supposed to be coming too.'

'He's at the police station, giving DCI Latham the benefit of his superior knowledge and experience,' Bernie explained, with a grin. 'He thinks he'll be able to sort out this mysterious death at Aunty Dot's Care Home.'

'I thought they'd arrested that male nurse, Jonathan,' James said in surprise. 'Wasn't that what you told us, Dad?'

'I said he'd been suspended from work,' Joey replied. 'I suppose I assumed that meant that the police thought he'd done it, but maybe it's just the management being cautious.'

'And you shouldn't call him a *male* nurse, like that,' Lucy informed James. 'You wouldn't talk about a *female* doctor, would you?"

'No. I'd say, "Lady doctor",' James answered promptly.

'Well you shouldn't,' Lucy insisted dogmatically. 'You should just say, "doctor". Otherwise you're perpetuating outdated gender stereotypes.'

'We were wondering if we ought to move Aunty to another Home,' Ruth intervened, trying to divert the conversation away from what appeared to her to be an aggressive feminist agenda. 'We didn't like the idea of-'

'But, as you'd expect, dear old Aunty Dot has been just lapping it up,' Joey cut in. 'She fancies herself as Miss Marple solving a murder mystery. The only thing that she got upset about was the way everyone seemed to assume it must be Jonathan. She likes him.'

'Which is exactly what you'd expect, if he's a con-man who preys on little old ladies,' James pointed out, smiling round at the others, evidently expecting some recognition for his clever thinking.

'He's on a hiding-to-nothing if he's hoping to get anything out of Aunty Dot,' Joey observed drily. 'Considering she hasn't a bean.'

'It'd be a bit of a giveaway if he was only nice to the old girls who've got enough money to make it worthwhile,' James insisted. 'I don't see why they haven't arrested him yet. It looks obvious to me.'

'Well, you'd better not let Aunty hear you saying that,' Joey said grinning round and winking at Bernie. 'She's convinced that he's innocent and it's all to do with Olive's family having it in for him.'

'Yes,' agreed Dominic. 'She was telling me about it yesterday. She says that one of Olive's sons has a down on him for some reason. She thinks that *he* may have bumped her off for her money and then blamed it on Jonathan because he's an easy target.'

'Are you talking about John Carter?' Ruth asked. 'I agree. He's a nasty piece of work. I've met him and he doesn't have a good word for anyone – not even his mum. There's an old lady in the Home, wouldn't hurt a fly, but getting rather confused, poor thing, and does rather odd things sometimes. He was all for asking the management to chuck her out, or else to reduce the fees for all the other residents, because he said she was causing a nuisance. And the other day he had a row with his wife in the car park and I'm sure he would have hit her if he hadn't seen me there. I'd noticed once or twice before, she had bruises on her face, but I didn't put two and two together until then.'

'But you have to admit, Jonathan Bates had the best opportunity for killing Olive,' James persisted, ignoring the looks that both his parents were giving him, which clearly indicated that they would prefer him to desist from his argument.

'Dom did very well in his university exams,' Ruth said, studiously ignoring James' remark. 'We were very proud of him.' She got up and went over to the windowsill, which was crowded with pictures and ornaments, and picked up a photograph in a gilt frame. She handed it to Bernie. 'Here he is at his graduation.'

Bernie looked down and saw a head-and-shoulders picture of Dominic, dressed in gown and mortarboard and holding a cylinder of paper tied with a red ribbon. She muttered something appropriate and passed it on to Peter, who did the same before handing it over to Lucy.

'I think the picture you posted on Facebook was better,' she said, looking up at Dominic. 'The one with you and your mates waving your hats in the air.'

'Dom's going to be training to be a teacher next,' Ruth continued. 'He's starting at college in September.'

'Oh?' Bernie turned to address Dominic, 'where are you going?'

'Liverpool Hope,' he told her.

'He'll be able to live at home,' Ruth said approvingly. 'And when he's got his teaching certificate, he'll have no difficulty finding a job in Liverpool. We're very pleased he got a place. And while he's waiting to start, he's volunteering at the hospice three days a week, and next week he's going to be helping Father Nat with the children's holiday club he runs every summer.'

'It sounds as if you're keeping busy,' Peter said, smiling across at Dominic, who had gone rather red during his mother's eulogy.

'Well, I thought I ought to do something,' he said, a little awkwardly, glancing towards Lucy, anxious to gain her approval. 'I mean, it'd be a bit selfish just to laze around all summer waiting for term to start.'

'Are you planning to come to Mass tomorrow?' Ruth asked, turning to Bernie. 'Father Nat said he's looking forward to meeting you again.'

'I'm not sure,' Bernie began slowly, thinking of Jonah, who was unlikely to relish such "popery" as he was accustomed to describing anything associated with the Roman Catholic Church.

'I'd like to come,' Peter said, to everyone's surprise. 'If that's OK?'

'Yes, of course it is,' Ruth said quickly, 'but I thought … I mean, last time you were here, Bernie said …'

'Peter's been visited by Our Lady,' Bernie said solemnly, but glancing across at Joey with a twinkle in her eye, 'and he's promised her that he's going to become a Catholic.'

'Really?' Ruth's eyes shone. 'I wish you'd told us before Chloë and Chris left. I've been hoping that Chris might convert, but Chloë just laughs and says, "You can't teach an old dog new tricks." Can I tell them about you, Peter? To show you're never too old?'

'I can't stop you telling them,' Peter shrugged, 'but, I'm not sure that it's a good idea ... I think there comes a time when parents have to stop giving advice and allow their kids to make their own decisions. You might even make it harder for Chris, if he thinks that you'll be congratulating yourself if he does convert and thinking it's because you wanted him to. Do you see what I mean?'

'I suppose so,' Ruth conceded reluctantly. 'I just don't like to see families divided like that. You know what they say, don't you? *The family that prays together stays together.* That's what I'd like for Chloë and Chris.'

'It doesn't necessarily follow that families fall apart when they have different ideas about religion,' Bernie pointed out. 'I know lots of couples who belong to different churches – or where one or other doesn't go to any at all – and they haven't split up. I don't even know what Lucy's dad thought about that sort of thing. We never discussed it. And you could argue that Peter becoming a Catholic is going to split our family up, because Lucy and I will most likely carry on going to our Methodist Church.'

Bernie's father, like the rest of the Fazakerley family, had been a cradle Catholic, but her mother had belonged to the Salvation Army and shared Jonah's suspicion of Catholicism. Bernie's upbringing had involved attendance at both the Catholic church and the Salvation Army citadel. As a student in Oxford, she had joined the John Wesley society, thinking that it was a compromise between the two extremes, and shortly after that had become a member of the Methodist Church in East Oxford where she had worshipped ever since. It was only after Lucy was born, that she had re-visited her Catholic roots in order to make her daughter aware of her family heritage.

'He's being instructed by Father Damien,' Lucy told her cousins. 'He's the priest who prepared me for my first communion. Peter's going to take his first communion at the Easter vigil next year.'

'If he stays the course,' Bernie added. 'He may decide it's not for him after all.'

'No,' Peter said quietly, feeling horribly self-conscious, but determined to stand his ground. 'I won't change my mind. I promised. I can't let her down.'

'Who?' James asked, with a puzzled frown.

'The BVM,' Bernie explained, poker faced. 'She spoke to him. And he promised her that he'd do it if Abigail came home safe.'

'Are you serious?' James asked, looking round in amazement. Although brought up within the church and familiar with stories of miraculous appearances of the Virgin Mary in distant places and earlier times, he had never come across anyone who claimed to have experienced something like that for himself. Moreover, he associated such things with simple peasants – usually female – and not with staid and solid ex-policemen.

'It looks like that's settled,' Joey said decidedly, seeing from the expression on Peter's face that he was embarrassed at having drawn such attention to himself. 'Let's all go together. If you come to us around half ten, we can all walk over there together – unless you'd rather meet us at the church?'

'We'll have to talk to Jonah,' Bernie told him. 'His dad was a Baptist pastor and he's never really come to terms with smells and bells. If he doesn't want to come, one of us will have to stay with him.'

'And I'll stay with Gran,' James volunteered, 'so you and Dad can both go,' he added, looking towards his mother, who had a disapproving expression on her face at the thought that her son was appearing less than enthusiastic about church attendance in front of their visitors.

'Or would you like to come too, Aunty Rose?' Lucy said suddenly, turning towards her great aunt, who up to now had taken no part in the conversation. She had learned, on their previous visit, that Rose had stopped attending church because she found walking, even short distances, difficult and painful. She spent most of the day sitting in her high-backed dining chair, her walking frame positioned across her legs, reading, listening to music or reciting the rosary. 'We could take you in our car. You could borrow Jonah's folding wheelchair.'

'That's very kind of,' Rose said, smiling back at Lucy and then looking round at Peter and Bernie, 'but I wouldn't want to put you to any trouble. Father Nat's very good about bringing communion to me here at home.'

'It wouldn't be any trouble, would it Mam?' Lucy appealed to Bernie. 'Jonah would be in his powered chair,' she added, turning back to Rose. 'We only brought the other one because sometimes it's easier indoors – for getting him into the shower and that sort of thing. There's plenty of room in the car for an extra passenger.'

'Or I could push you in the chair all the way,' Dominic suggested, 'if the weather's OK.'

'Well, if you're sure …?' Rose wavered.

'Absolutely! Bernie said emphatically. 'If you'd like to come, it's no bother for us to take you.'

'Then … thank you very much.'

4. WE THINK AND SPEAK
E'en now we think and speak the same, and cordially agree.
Charles Wesley: "All Praise to Our Redeeming Lord."

Sandra Latham held the door open to admit Jonah to the room where police officers investigating the murder of Olive Carter had their desks. It being Saturday, most of the workstations were unoccupied, but two or three faces looked up from behind computer screens, and watched as Jonah manoeuvred his bulky chair down the narrow aisle between two rows of desks.

A young woman in a light green trouser suit stepped forward and greeted them. Jonah recognised her as Detective Sergeant Charlotte Simpson (*Charlie* to her colleagues), whom he had met during his time in Liverpool the previous summer. At the time, he had classified her in his mind as 'quite bright, but a bit wet-behind-the-ears'. Now she appeared confident and self-possessed as she moved furniture to make space for his wheelchair and offered to take him through the main points of the case so far.

'This is Park View,' she said, bringing up a photograph depicting a large Edwardian house with a modern extension visible on its right-hand-side. 'It's a small Care Home, which takes up to ten residents, each with their own room. There's a live-in caretaker, Mr Hector Bayliss.' A man's face appeared on the screen. 'He's a retired woodwork teacher. He isn't involved in looking after the residents. His duties are all to do with maintaining the building and providing security. Like I said, he lives in, so he was on the premises during the night when Mrs Carter died.'

'Presumably, like everyone else, he will have had his criminal record checked before he was given the job?' Jonah asked.

'That's right. We re-checked everyone who works at the Home, and all the residents as well, and they're all completely clear – well, apart from one resident who'd notched up a couple of motoring offences. Absolutely no evidence of any of them using violence of any kind.'

'OK. Go on. Tell me about the other people who work there.'

'This is Fiona Radcliffe, 52, married but no children.' A movement of the computer mouse brought up a photograph of a woman with black hair – too black to be natural, Jonah thought – and striking dark brown eyes. 'She's the Manager. She has a nursing background, but she's allowed her registration to lapse now that she isn't working directly with patients anymore. Her husband is a property developer and the owner of the Home.'

'I think his idea is that this is a little project to keep his wife occupied and bring in a bit of extra cash,' Sandra added. 'He doesn't play an active role in running it – that's all down to *Mrs* Radcliffe.'

Jonah studied Sandra's face for a moment. Had he detected a hint of resentment in her voice at Mr Radcliffe's assumption that his wife's career was of only secondary importance? Could there be something more personal underlying that reaction? But there was no time to ponder on the state of DCI Latham's mind, he had only an hour or two in which to acquaint himself with the full facts of the case.

'She works nine to five,' Charlie was saying. 'Or rather,' she corrected herself, after consulting her notes, 'she gets in at eight thirty each morning, Monday to Friday, and leaves at about five in the afternoon. That makes it unlikely that she could have administered the insulin before she left, because Olive had her family visiting her until after five that day.'

'And the medical evidence suggests that it's more likely that it was administered later in the day,' Sandra added. 'Probably not until after she'd had her dinner.'

'She could have come back later,' Jonah suggested. 'I assume that she would have her own keys and could have let herself in without anyone else knowing?'

'There's nothing on the CC-TV,' Charlie told him. 'There's a camera by the main entrance that records anyone who goes in or out.'

'Any other doors?' Jonah asked. 'Do you have a plan of the building you can show me?'

'Here's a sketch of the ground floor.' Charlie expertly selected a slide showing a rough drawing of the layout of rooms. 'The original house has two floors, plus a flat in the attic where Hector Bayliss lives. The extension on the side is single-storey. The main entrance is there, because the front door of the original Edwardian house has steep steps that make it inaccessible to anyone with any sort of mobility issues. There's a fire door at the back of the new part, which is the emergency exit for residents. Several of the residents' rooms have their own personal sliding doors opening on to the gardens, and there's another set of sliding doors from the lounge.'

'And how many of these doors can be opened from outside?' asked Jonah.

'It's up to the residents to keep their own doors locked. The patio doors from the lounge are often left unlocked during the day. It's one of Hector Bayliss's jobs to make sure that they are secure at night. He says that he made his rounds as usual at eight fifteen that evening and they were already locked. He also checked that the fire door was properly fastened. Apparently, sometimes residents accidentally lean on the emergency release bar and then leave them ajar. You can't open those with a key. They are just for people to escape through.'

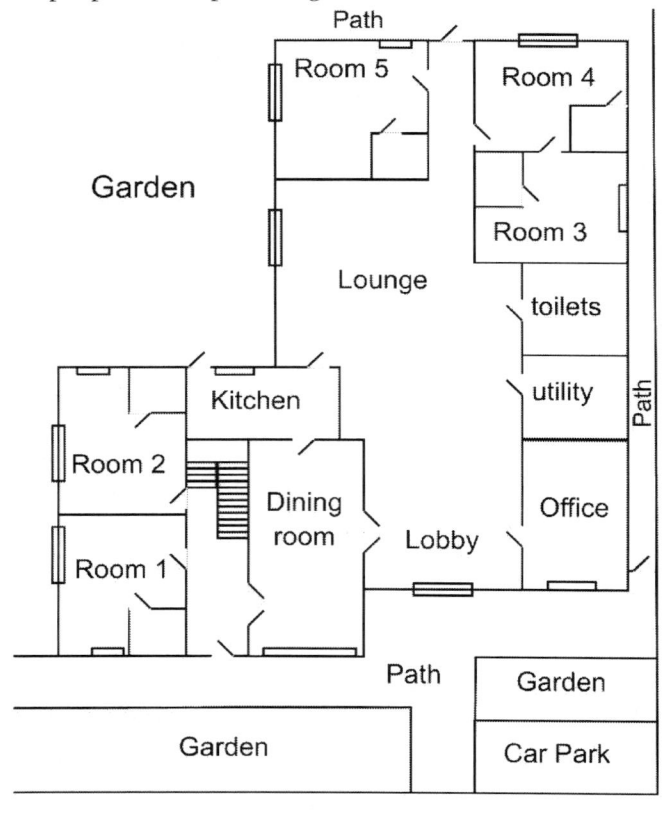

[Floor plan showing: Garden areas surrounding the building; Path along the top and right side; Room 5 and Room 4 at the top; Room 3, toilets, utility, and Office along the right side; Lounge in the centre; Kitchen, Dining room, and Lobby in the middle; Room 2 and Room 1 on the left; Garden and Car Park at the bottom.]

'And the front door?' Jonah asked. 'You said that isn't used any more, but is it possible to open it?'

'Yes. Mr Bayliss uses it as his front door, because it leads straight to the stairs up to his flat.'

'And Mrs Radcliffe would have a key to that too, presumably?'

'Yes. She has a full set of keys that she carries with her

and there's another set in the office, where there are also duplicate keys to all of the residents' rooms.'

'And would the CC-TV have shown her up if she'd come in through the front door or the fire escape?'

'Not directly, but unless she climbed over the wall from the road instead of coming in through the front gate, she would have had to pass in front of the one by the main entrance to get to the front door. The fire door, I'm not sure about. I *think* the camera covers the gate to the side path, but I'd have to check that.'

'OK. So Mrs Radcliffe *could* have come back after she clocked off, sneaked round the back, in through the fire door and lain in wait for Olive in her room. Or could she? Which room did Olive have?'

'She was in Room 5,' Charlie told him.

'Which is on the ground floor, right next to the fire exit!' Sandra continued. 'But we don't have any motive for her to want to get Olive out of the way. In fact, as the manager, she has a vested interest in keeping her clients alive: both because of the reputational damage if they keep dying in suspicious circumstances and because, when a resident dies they stop paying their fees.'

'She'd also have to get past the windows of Room 3 without being noticed,' Jonah observed, studying the plan carefully. 'Whose room is that? And were they in it on Tuesday evening?'

'It belongs to Mrs Charlotte Goodman,' Sandra told him. 'She went straight to her room after dinner finished at six fifteen, and the Care Staff helped her to bed soon after that.'

'But Fiona Radcliffe *could* have got in through the fire exit while everyone was eating dinner and hidden in Olive's room,' Jonah persisted.'

'Yes,' Charlie agreed, 'but why would she?'

'I don't know. I'm just trying to make sure we don't miss out any possibilities. Now, you said that Olive Carter had Room 5 and Mrs Goodman had Room 3; what about the other ground floor rooms?'

'Edna Lomax was in Room 4 – that's the one on the other side of the fire door,' Charlie told him. 'There's a new resident in it now, called Charles Melling. He only moved in the day *after* Olive was found dead, so he's completely out of the frame.'

'And that also means that there was only one window for anyone coming round the side path and in through the fire door to worry about,' Jonah mused, 'because the other room that they'd have had to walk past was unoccupied.'

'Yes I suppose so,' Charlie agreed. 'The other two ground floor rooms are in the old part of the house, beyond the Residents' Dining Room. They are Mrs Frances Ray and Mr Eric Martin. They've both lived there for over ten years – since the Home was opened, in fact.'

'Good. I think I'm getting a feel for the place now. We'll come to the other residents later. Carry on telling me about the staff. Who else was on duty the day before Olive was found dead, and who found her?'

'She was found by Scarlet Jones.' A new face appeared on the screen in front of them. It was a young black woman with a mass of frothy black hair piled up on the top of her head, held in place by a gaily-coloured scarf. 'She went to get her up on the Wednesday morning and found her dead in her bed, with a syringe and an empty insulin vial lying on the bedside table next to her. She'd died in her sleep.'

'Presumably the syringe and vial were checked for fingermarks?'

'Eventually,' Sandra sighed, 'but not until there had been plenty of opportunity for contamination by other people. Nobody even seems to have noticed they were there until hours later. It probably doesn't matter though, because there weren't any recognisable prints. Forensics say that the person who used them probably wore gloves.'

'And when did Jones come on duty? Did her shift cover any of the critical time for administering the insulin?'

'No. She works five seven-and-a-half hour shifts each week. Tuesday was one of her days off that week, and her Wednesday shift started at seven in the morning. So she had no possible opportunity for killing Olive.'

'The way the shifts work,' Sandra added, 'is that they aim to have one of the qualified nurses – they have two – on duty for the whole of the daytime, Monday to Saturday – that's eight in the morning to half-past seven at night. Bates worked a late shift on the Tuesday and a long day on the Wednesday. He does one short shift and three long ones every week. The other nurse did an early shift on the Tuesday and had Wednesday off.'

'OK. We've got the caretaker, who was in his flat upstairs all night, Jonathan Bates who could have administered the drug before he knocked off in the evening, and the Manager who may or may not have been able to come back to do it during the evening or night. Who else was around on that afternoon and evening?'

'They have one Care Assistant on duty overnight, in case any of the residents need help with getting to the toilet or that sort of thing. That Tuesday, it was Mrs Rebecca Anderson.' Another face appeared on the screen in front of them. 'She's 38 and divorced with three children. She lives with her father and likes working nights, because it means she doesn't need childcare.'

'She could easily have given the insulin to Mrs Carter,' Sandra added, 'but there doesn't seem to be any motive for her wanting to kill her. On the other hand, it could be one of those cases of Munchausen syndrome by proxy, where the only motive is satisfying some strange desire to cause harm to someone over whom you have control.'

'Was she also on duty when Edna Lomax died?' Jonah immediately wanted to know.

'Yes,' Charlie confirmed, 'and on that occasion, she was also the person who found the body and called the doctor out.'

'So she definitely warrants further consideration,' Jonah

mused. 'Is that it? Or are there any other staff who could have done it?'

'Julia Freeman worked a long day, starting at ten a.m.,' Charlie told him, displaying another photograph. 'She's another Care Assistant. She's fifty-seven, married with grown-up kids and a husband in the merchant navy. She helped to put the residents to bed. One of them wasn't well and she called out the doctor.' The picture on the screen changed to show a smartly-dressed man of South Asian appearance. 'This is Dr Amandeep Bhaskar. All the residents are registered with his GP practice. He was called at about eight, and came straight over. He treated the resident-'

'Who was?' Jonah asked quickly.

'A Mrs Kathleen Lowe. She has one of the rooms on the first floor. The doctor checked her over, decided there wasn't much wrong with her and gave her some paracetamol from the medicine cabinet in the Manager's office.'

'From which he *could* also have taken some of the fast-acting insulin,' Jonah observed. 'Did he have time to get down to Olive Carter's room, d'you think?'

'Hard to say,' Sandra told him. 'Mrs Freeman stayed with Mrs Lowe while he went to the office, and Jonathan Bates had already left by then, so there was nobody around to see whether he came straight back or not.'

'What about Rebecca Anderson?' Jonah asked sharply. 'When did you say she came on duty?'

'Eight,' Charlie said, after checking her notes. 'You're right. She was there by the time the doctor arrived. She let him in through the main door and showed him up to Mrs Lowe's room. Then she did the rounds of the other upstairs rooms, checking that the residents were all settled for the night.'

'So, you were right,' Jonah said slowly, 'when you said that there isn't anyone to confirm that Dr Bhaskar didn't give a fatal dose of insulin to Olive Carter while he was ostensibly getting paracetamol from the drugs cabinet. Where are we up to now? I make it five suspects from amongst the staff (if you include Dr Bhaskar): Jonathan Bates, Fiona Radcliffe, Rebecca Anderson, Julia Freeman and Dr Bhaskar. Any others?'

'No, I don't think so,' Sandra answered. 'As I said, the other nurse was on duty that day, but she was on an early shift and left before Mrs Carter got back from an outing with her son.'

'That's Desmond Carter, the older son?' Jonah asked. 'You said earlier that he took her out for the day; and you said that the other son came to see her after she got back.'

'That's right,' Sandra confirmed. 'Either of them *could* have given her the drug, always supposing that they had access to it, but it would have been right at the early edge of the window of opportunity.'

'Which brings the total number of suspects up to seven – or eight if you include the younger son's wife,' Jonah said in a tone that suggested that he was relishing the challenge, rather than becoming downhearted at the difficulties posed by the case.

'Plus all the other residents,' Sandra nodded. 'We can't rule them out, even though they *shouldn't* have been able to get hold of the insulin, because it's always possible that someone was careless with the keys.'

'And who knows what sorts of feuds and resentments may be going on within a closed community like that,' Jonah agreed. 'In many ways, it's the other residents who are like the victim's family in this case. They could easily have motives about which we know nothing. It's so easy to fall out with someone when you're living on top of one another all the time.'

There was a knock at the door. A young uniformed officer came into the room.

'There's a couple at the desk who say they've come for DCI Porter,' she announced.

Jonah looked at the time on the computer screen

attached to the right-hand arm of his chair and a resigned expression crossed his face. Then he looked up and nodded.

'That'll have to be it for today, I'm afraid.' He turned towards Charlie. 'Thank you for setting everything out so clearly.' Then, including Sandra as well, 'I'll give it some thought. It's going to be hard pinning the blame on any one person in particular because there isn't any forensic evidence and the drug could have been given at any time within a period of several hours.'

'Yes, that about sums it up,' Sandra agreed gloomily. 'If your friend's aunt is expecting quick results, I'm afraid she's going to be disappointed.'

5. WE MEET AGAIN
God be with you till we meet again,
Keep love's banner floating o'er you.
Jeremiah Eames Rankin

Father Nathaniel Milton, Parish Priest of Our Lady of Grace, in the Toxteth district of Liverpool, greeted them at the door and directed them to the space at the front of the church, where two rows of pews had been removed to make space for wheelchair users. As they followed in the wake of Jonah, in his powered chair, and Rose, pushed energetically along behind him by Dominic, Joey leaned towards Bernie and whispered, 'We've been trying for years to persuade Mum to try a wheelchair, but she wasn't having any of it. This could make a big difference to her, provided Dom doesn't get carried away and upset the applecart!'

There was a moment of embarrassment when a helpful usher attempted to hand a hymnbook and a mass card to Jonah, unaware that he was unable to move his hands to receive them. He smiled up at her and shook his head.

'I'll share with Mrs Fazakerley, thank you. That'll be alright, won't it?' he added, turning to Rose.

'Yes, of course.'

'And I'll need you to help me follow the service,' Jonah

went on, 'because I've never been to a Roman Catholic Mass before.'

Father Nat waited until they were settled in their places and then came to speak to them.

'When it comes to the communion,' he explained in a low voice, 'I'll come to you first, while the rest of the congregation is lining up to receive. That will save you getting mixed up in the scrum.'

'I'm not a Catholic,' Jonah said, sounding apologetic and then wondering to himself why he should feel the need to apologise for not subscribing to beliefs that his father had described as "full of ignorance and superstition". 'So it'll just be Mrs Fazakerley that you need to come to.'

'I usually give non-Catholics a blessing, but if you'd rather I didn't, that's fine too.'

Jonah hesitated. He considered himself to have an open mind and an ecumenical outlook. Nevertheless, his father's dogmatic insistence that the Roman Catholic Church was riddled with idolatry and false doctrines was difficult to shake off. He could just imagine how he would have reacted to the offer of a blessing from 'a popish priest'. He would have drawn himself up to his full height – a matter of only five foot six, which might have spoiled the effect – and looked Father Nat in the eye, demanding to know by what right he claimed to be able to bestow God's blessing upon one who was his equal, if not his superior.

'Thank you. I'd like that,' he said at last. After all, it could do no harm and it might please Lucy to see him making a gesture towards accepting the validity of the Roman ritual. And these people were all sincerely worshipping God in their own way, even if they had got Him all muddled up in their minds with a whole lot of saints and statues and ridiculous notions.

'I have to go now,' Father Nat apologised. 'I need to prepare for the Mass. If you need anything, Mrs O'Connor will be able to help you.' He tilted his head towards the usher, who smiled back self-consciously and nodded in agreement.

'You've not thought of following your friend's example then?' Rose asked, leaning on the arm of his wheelchair to speak to him in a low voice. 'I was so pleased to hear that Our Bernie's young man is becoming a Catholic. I'd been praying for them both, you know, ever since their visit last summer.'

'I'm sorry. I think I'm too set in my ways to change now,' Jonah whispered back.

'We're just behind you,' Bernie's voice came over his shoulder.

He turned his chair round just sufficiently to be able to see that the Fazakerley family were all ranged along the front pew. There was a gap between Bernie and Lucy. Where had Peter got to? He turned the chair back to face front and saw, to his surprise, that Peter had stepped forward and was standing, gazing at a statue, which stood a short way to the right of the altar. Jonah recognised it as a depiction of the Virgin Mary. It stood about three feet tall on a plinth of similar height, so that Peter's eyes were level with those of the image. She was dressed in white, with a blue cloak about her shoulders. Her arms were outstretched in a gesture of welcome. Somehow sensing that he was being watched, Peter dropped his eyes suddenly and hastily turned round and hurried back to sit beside his wife. In doing so, he passed close to Jonah and their eyes met. Jonah raised his eyebrows questioningly. Peter looked back, a little defiantly, Jonah thought, but said nothing.

Ruth insisted that they should all go back to their house for Sunday lunch after the service. As they crowded into the small front room and squeezed together round the dining table, Bernie reflected that it was a good thing that Chloë had moved out.

Determined to give the best to her guests, Ruth treated

them to a traditional Sunday roast, followed by a treacle pudding, which Bernie remembered had been a favourite of Joey's when they were children. She offered to help with the washing up afterwards, but Ruth waved her away.

'You'd best be getting over to Wavertree,' she said. 'Aunty Dot's expecting you. It's all she's been talking about ever since you said you were coming. She seems to think that you'll work some sort of miracle and get that lad Jonathan reinstated just as soon as she gets the chance to tell you all about it. We've tried to convince her it isn't as simple as that, but she's got this idea that your DCI Porter is some sort of detective genius.'

'Now I wonder who can have given her that idea?' Peter murmured to nobody in particular.

Peter, Bernie and Jonah were to visit Aunty Dot, leaving Lucy in the hands of Dominic, who had persuaded her to come with him for a walk in Princes Park.

'We kids used to have a great time playing there,' Bernie told them. 'Did your dad ever tell you about the time Our George fell in the lake?'

'Yes,' Dominic grinned back at her. 'And he said you were a right bossy boots and made him strip off down to his pants. And then he had to sit there with Dad's blazer on while the rest of you ran about trying to get his clothes dry.'

'It was a good thing someone was there with a bit of nouse to see he didn't catch his death of cold,' Bernie retorted.

'Yeah, but it was the *way* you went about it,' Joey chipped in, 'and the fact that you were the youngest of us. *We* were supposed to be looking after *you*!'

'No chance!' Bernie chortled with laughter. 'What on Earth made you think that?'

'Are you going to stand there all day chin-wagging,' Jonah complained, taking advantage of a brief lull in the conversation. 'Like the woman says, we need to be making tracks.'

It was not long before they were pulling up in the small car park in front of the Park View Care Home. Bernie released the straps holding Jonah's wheelchair in place, while Peter set up the ramp that would allow him to descend from the car.

They followed the sloping path that led up the incline from the road to the main entrance and stopped outside the glass doors. Jonah looked up, taking careful note of the position of the security camera on the wall above. It was directed down on to the path from the road, which meant that anyone approaching the building would be seen, whether they were aiming for the main entrance, heading for the front door or intending to go through the side gate into the back garden. The only way of evading notice would be to climb up through the shrubs and flowers on either side of the path.

They pressed a button at the side of the door and a disembodied voice asked them for their names and that of the resident whom they were visiting. Bernie gave the required information; there was a click, and the doors slid apart to allow them inside. A middle-aged woman in a tunic and trousers, similar to a nurse's uniform, came out of a room on their right to meet them. Jonah recognised the auburn-dyed hair, suntanned complexion and blue eyes of Care Assistant Julia Freeman, whose photograph he had seen the day before.

She shook hands with Bernie and Peter and then looked down at Jonah with a hint of anxiety.

'Miss Fazakerley is in her room,' she told them. 'She said she wanted to be private, not see you in the lounge, but ...,' she paused, looking down at Jonah in his wheelchair. 'We do have a stair lift,' she went on. 'Will you be able to manage on that? Or would you rather wait here while your friends ...? Or I could ask Miss Fazakerley to let me bring her down after all.'

Peter and Bernie looked towards Jonah for a decision. On the previous occasion when he had visited Aunty Dot, they had met her in the lounge on the ground floor. None of them had realised that there was no lift to take Jonah, in his chair, up to her room.

'We'd better have a look at this stair lift, hadn't we?' he said, after a moment's thought.

They followed Julia through double doors into the dining room and then out the other side to the hall of the original old house, from which the stairs led to the first floor. Then they stood looking down at the seat of the stair lift, which was parked at the bottom of the flight.

'Do you think you can get me into there?' Jonah asked.

'Yes,' Peter said at once. 'If you bring your chair alongside it and we lower the arms on both, we can just slide you across.'

'What about when we get to the top?' Bernie asked. 'I don't think we can carry your chair up these stairs.'

'Get the folding one out of the car,' Jonah ordered. 'It's lucky we've got it with us. If it hadn't been for taking Rose to church, we'd probably have left it at the hotel.'

They got Jonah into the lift and Bernie accompanied him upstairs, while Peter returned to the car for the manual chair. Julia came with him as far as the sliding doors, so that she could let him in again on his return.

Eventually, they were all upstairs, with Jonah in the wheelchair and Peter holding the handles, ready to push him wherever they needed to go.

'It's Room 8,' Julia told them. 'Just down there, on the left. I'll come with you and check that she's ready for you and there's nothing else you need.'

6. MANY WATERS CANNOT QUENCH LOVE

Many waters cannot quench love, neither can the floods drown it
Song of Solomon 8:7

'There it is!' Dominic announced, pointing through the railings that stood beneath a line of trees running along by the path. 'That's the famous lake where Uncle George fell in and your Mum pulled him out and dried him off.'

They followed the path to the point where the railings ended, and then strolled across the grass towards the water. Dominic tentatively reached out his hand and took hold of Lucy's. He felt her hesitate before accepting the gesture by closing her own fingers around his. They walked on for a few minutes in silence, Dominic savouring the moment, and Lucy debating how long she should indulge him before pulling away, and wondering how to explain that she had at least five more years of education ahead of her before she would be ready to start thinking about romantic entanglements.

'Where's Uncle George now?' Lucy asked. 'Mam's never talked about us visiting him. The only Fazakerleys I know are your family and Aunty Dot.'

'Dunno,' Dominic shrugged. 'Down South somewhere, I think. He moved away years ago, like the rest of Dad's brothers. You've got to remember, Dad's the youngest of his family and I'm the youngest of mine. So practically everyone had either moved away or died before I was old enough to take notice. Apart from my Gran and Granddad, the only one I know is Aunty Dot.'

'Did you know her when she was younger - before she moved into the Home, I mean?'

'Oh yes. She used to live a few streets away from us. Dad would call round two or three times a week to check that she was OK. I used to like going with him, because she always had some new toy or puzzle or trick to show me. I remember she could roll up a handkerchief and turn it into a mouse, and she had a wooden box that you put things in and they mysteriously disappeared. And she used to tell me stories about when Dad was a kid. She told me all sorts of stories about your mum too, but I only half believed her, because "Aunt Bernadette" never came to see us, so I was never sure that Aunty Dot wasn't just making her up to tease me!'

Lucy laughed.

'Couldn't you tell that it all had to be true because it was so unbelievable? Or did she tone Mam down so she didn't sound too outrageous?'

'I did wonder sometimes if some of the stories were really about Aunty Dot herself, but she didn't want to admit to it. I mean some of the things that she wouldn't have wanted to encourage us kids to do.'

Lucy gave another laugh. Then she became serious again.

'And now, you visit Aunty Dot in the Home quite often, I suppose?'

'Yes. When I'm not at uni, I try to get over there at least once a week. It saves Dad having to make time when he's got a lot of work on.'

'So, you'd know the staff there quite well too?'

'I suppose so,' Dominic answered cautiously, wondering where this sudden interest in his aunt and her carers was leading.

'Including this Jonathan that she's so concerned about?'

'Ye-es.'

'Do you think she's right and he's being unfairly accused, or could he have killed that woman?'

'I was afraid that was coming,' Dominic sighed. 'I really don't know. He always seemed nice enough, and you never expect someone you know to be a murderer, do you?'

'But?'

'But he admits to giving her an insulin injection the night before she died and he did stand to gain from her death and there doesn't seem to be anyone much else who could have done it.'

'According to DCI Latham, practically anyone who was in the Home that night could have done it,' Lucy told him. 'What do *you* think? Did any of the other residents have it in for Olive Carter?'

'Well,' Dominic began. He hesitated, wondering whether he ought to go on. Then, his desire to impress Lucy overcame his caution and he continued. 'If I had to choose which of the residents was the most likely, I'd plump for Joan Pickles.'

'Why? Who's she?' Lucy asked excitedly.

'She's a disagreeable old bat who's got the room opposite Aunty Dot's. She spends the whole time complaining and criticising people. She told me off the other day for not wiping my feet properly on the mat when I came in from the garden. According to Aunty Dot, she and Olive didn't hit it off at all. I think it was a bit like the irresistible force meeting the immoveable object. They were both used to having their own way and ordering people about and they both thought they knew how things ought to be done and didn't like to be contradicted.'

'That's interesting.' Lucy thought for a few moments. 'Yes. I can see why she might want to get Olive out of the way. And who knows? She could have dementia coming on and not be thinking straight.'

'But how would she know what to do?' Dominic objected. 'I wouldn't have a clue how to inject someone with insulin.'

'You never know, she may have had someone in her family who needed injections,' Lucy said confidently, reluctant to give up on this new suspect.

'Don't you think it's far more likely to have been one of the staff?' Dominic asked. 'Not necessarily Jonathan, but someone who knew about giving injections and where the drugs were kept and stuff.'

'OK then. Who would you say is the most likely of them?'

'I have no idea! None of them seems at all likely. Aunty Dot doesn't have much time for the manager, but that's more that she doesn't think she's up to the job. And *that* probably only means that she doesn't do it the way Aunty Dot would have done. You know Aunty was a nurse at the Royal, don't you?'

'Yes, I'd forgotten, but I remember her telling me now. Oh dear!' Lucy gave a little giggle.

'What's so funny?'

'I was just thinking. If I was DCI Latham and I was trying to work out which of the residents killed Olive Carter, Aunty Dot would be right at the top of my suspect list. She must know all about different kinds of insulin and how to give them to people and what dose you'd need to kill them.'

'Probably just as well that she's making such a fuss about clearing Jonathan's name,' Dominic commented, joining in the joke. 'That must put her in the clear, mustn't it?'

'Unless it was all a plot to get rid of her deadly rival and run off with the dishy young man that they've both fallen for!' Lucy laughed.

'Now there's a thought!' Dominic chortled. 'If Olive was planning a midnight flit to Gretna Green with

Jonathan, that would definitely give her family a motive for bumping one or both of them off.'

'Yes,' Lucy agreed, suddenly serious again. 'However you look at it, they're the ones who benefit most from her death – especially if there was any hint that she was planning to change her will – to give more to people like Jonathan, for example, and less to her next-of-kin.'

'It's not for us to speculate though, is it?' Dominic's conscience smote him, as he remembered that they had been joking about a real woman's untimely death. 'Let's leave it to the police, shall we?'

'OK.'

They walked on, both struggling to think of a new topic of conversation.

'Your mum said you're working at a hospice three days a week,' Lucy said tentatively. 'What made you decide to do that?'

'Father Nat suggested it. I wanted to do something to justify my existence over the summer and Mum was against me just stacking shelves or serving in McDonald's. I really wanted work with children, because it would be better experience for becoming a teacher, but all the schools are closed, of course. I went to Father Nat to ask if I could help with the Holiday Club and he said, *yes* but wouldn't I like to do something else for the rest of the summer? And then he suggested the hospice. It's not as bad as it sounds. I mean, I thought it would be ever so gloomy, people all just lying around waiting to die, but it's not like that at all.'

'Jonah's wife, Margaret, was in a hospice after she got cancer. They were very good there too. We all went round a few days before she died – all her family and me and Mam and Peter – and said goodbye and sang *Abide with me* together.'

'I hadn't realised ... I mean, I never thought about what happened to his wife. So you knew her?'

'Yes, of course. We were bound to, after visiting him in

hospital for a year after he was shot. She was great. She used to dye her hair a different colour every week – well that's an exaggeration, but it was quite often – and she rode a motorbike. She was a trauma surgeon. I remember her showing me some X-rays of how they pin bones together to help them heal in the right positions. I wasn't there when she died.' There was a hint of regret in her voice. 'I was at school. But Jonah was – and my Mam – and Peter took me to see her as soon as I got home.'

'You actually saw her after she died?'

'Yes. It was a bit weird. It didn't feel like seeing a real person. I mean, I could see it was her, but it didn't really feel any different from the time Mike let me sit in on a post-mortem. It was just a body. She wasn't there anymore.'

Dominic was conscious of feeling irrational resentment that, once again, his young cousin was able to claim a wider experience of Life than he had himself. At the age of twenty-one, with three years at university under his belt, he had begun to imagine himself to be something of a man-of-the-world, and yet this schoolgirl of seventeen had already seen so much more than he had! She had been a witness in a murder enquiry, had watched a real post-mortem examination, and knew more than he cared to contemplate about the nitty-gritty of caring for someone with serious spinal injuries. When she asked him about his work at the hospice, he had been hoping to impress her with his newly-acquired knowledge about end-of-life-care and his empathy with the dying; but (of course) Lucy would go and turn out to have had personal experience of it all that his two weeks of voluntary work could never come close to matching!

'Do you think they'd let me come with you one day this week? I'd like to see what it's like. It'd be some more good experience to put in my Personal Statement for applying to Medical School – and I'd like to help too,' Lucy added hastily, realising that she had managed to make her offer of help sound merely self-serving.

'OK. I'll ask them tomorrow, and you could maybe come on Wednesday. That'd be a good day, because they have a sort of social in the afternoon, when all the patients who are well enough come to the lounge and have a bit of a sing-song and sometimes there's some sort of entertainment put on. It's always useful to have some extra helpers for that.'

'OK. Thanks.'

They walked on in silence. Dominic was unsure whether to be pleased that Lucy had spontaneously suggested spending more time in his company or disappointed that she had taken care to ensure that they were unlikely to have any time alone together. Lucy continued to wonder whether, when and how she should make explicit her determination not to allow any new relationship to interfere with her career plans. But was she reading too much into his behaviour? Could it be that he was simply under orders from his mother to make his young cousin feel welcome?

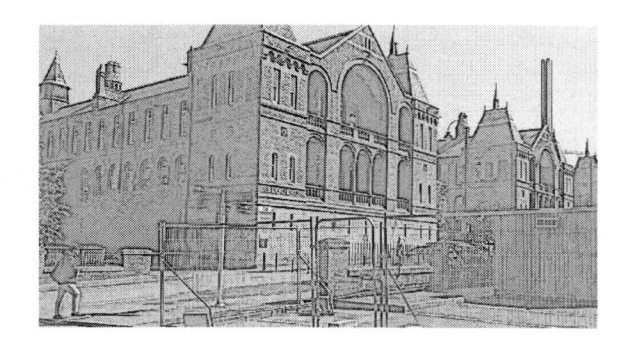

7. THE FRET OF CARE
Teach me thy secret; help me bear
The strain of toil, the fret of care
Washington Gladden: "O Master, let me walk with Thee".

'Bernadette!' Dot greeted her niece, as soon as they entered the bed-sitting room that now constituted her home. She held out both of her bony, twisted hands towards them, looking up at Bernie with piercing blue eyes. 'And Peter! And DCI Porter!'

'Jonah, please,' he protested, smiling broadly as Peter pushed his wheelchair across the blue, floral-patterned carpet and positioned it at a suitable distance from where Dot was sitting, so that they would be able to converse together easily. She leaned back into her pale green basket-weave chair, well-padded with cushions, and smiled round expectantly.

The room was bright with the afternoon sun shining in through the window. Looking round, Jonah took in a crucifix hanging on the wall over the bed and an array of religious pictures ranged on the walls. On the small table next to the bed, he recognised a black leather-bound Bible and another book, which he assumed must be a prayer book of some kind, together with a string of beads and a stubby candle in an ornate brass holder. Clearly, Bernie's aunt was another staunch Catholic, he concluded. It was surprising, with such a strong background on that side of the family, that Bernie had ploughed her own independent religious furrow – except, of course, that Bernie never liked to do what was expected of her!

He noticed that Peter had wandered over to look at one particular picture. As in the church that morning, he had homed in on an image of the Virgin Mary. It was a strange icon to Jonah's protestant eyes: there was the usual blue gown and pale face (this time in an expression of deep sadness with tears rolling down the cheeks), but in front of the bodice of her dress was a red heart with seven daggers protruding from it and drops of blood oozing out of it. Jonah wondered what anyone could find in it to admire.

'Our Lady of Sorrows,' Dot told Peter. 'Do you like it?'

'I'm not sure. That's not how I see her.'

'And thy own soul a sword shall pierce,' Dot quoted. 'That's what it's supposed to symbolise – and seven swords for the Seven Sorrows that Our Lady endured.'

'Yes. I get that. I just …,' Peter hesitated and glanced towards Jonah. 'I know it's all subjective, but when I see her, she's not blond and blue-eyed. I'm sorry. I'm not criticising. It's just …'

'She comes and talks to Peter,' Jonah explained, a little sarcastically. 'I suppose you won't find that surprising, being a Catholic.'

Bernie looked at Jonah with a puzzled frown on her face. It wasn't like him to speak with that slightly sneering tone in his voice.

'When you get to my age, young man,' Dot replied drily, 'very little in this world surprises you.'

'How are you keeping, Aunty?' Bernie asked, breaking the awkward silence that followed. 'Still wowing the Bingo Club with your inside information about the *Mersey Ferry Murder*?'

'Not so much of your cheek, young lady! Now sit down both of you. I don't want to have to keep craning my neck to talk to you.'

Bernie and Peter obediently arranged chairs so that they could all sit down together.

'Lucy not with you?' Dot asked, noticing for the first time that her visitors were depleted in number.

'She's on a date with Dom,' Peter told her in an amused tone.

'Seriously?'

'I don't know.' Bernie grinned at her aunt. 'I have a feeling it may be more serious on one side than the other. Lucy's still very focussed on getting into Medical School. I don't think she's ready to allow any such distractions.'

'Very sensible. Now let's get down to business.' Dot turned to speak to Jonah. 'You've had the basic facts. Do you have any ideas for new lines of enquiry?'

'DCI Latham has filled me in on where they're up to so far,' Jonah told her. 'I have to warn you that Jonathan Bates still looks like the most likely suspect. He had motive, means and opportunity.'

'Motive?' Dot snorted derisively. 'Five hundred pounds! The staff here aren't paid much, but even for them five hundred pounds wouldn't be worth risking a life sentence for. If you're looking for motives, Olive's boys are much more likely.'

'But they didn't have access to a supply of insulin and they weren't the ones who are known to have injected her with some the day she died and to have given her a sleeping tablet,' Jonah argued patiently. 'For any case against one of them to stand up, we need to find out how they got hold of the drug and when they administered it to her.'

'They could have paid one of the staff – not Jonathan, one of the others – to do it,' Dot suggested.

'That's a bit far-fetched,' Peter protested. 'How would they know which one to approach? They couldn't take the risk that whoever they spoke to might report them.'

'Well, whatever anyone says, I can't believe that it was Jonathan,' Dot insisted. 'He's such a nice lad – much better than some of the others. I can't believe that he's a killer.'

'I've met a few killers in my time,' Peter told her. 'And most of them were quite ordinary with nothing to make them stand out from the crowd. Some of them were extremely nice and well-liked by people around them.'

'I know you won't like me saying this, Aunty,' Bernie added, 'but if he's a con-man who makes money by ingratiating himself with old ladies and persuading them to leave money to him, you would expect him to be very nice to you and the other residents.'

'I'm not stupid you know, Bernadette.' Dot gave Bernie a withering look. 'I'm fully aware of all that. I suppose you think I've finally cracked and fallen for some personable young man who flatters me and makes me feel young again? Well, forget it. I've still got all my marbles and I still reckon I can tell the difference between genuine compassion and cynical smarm. Jonathan is *not* a gigolo. He's a happily married man and a very good and efficient nurse – unlike one or two of the staff here.'

'Are you suggesting that one of the other staff is a more likely suspect?' Jonah asked, picking up on Dot's hints that there were others whom she could not be so sure were not the type to kill one of their clients.

'If I had to name names, it would be Julia Freeman. She's the Care Assistant who showed you up just now. Olive had words with her the day before she died. She threatened to report her for not doing her job properly. She was right too. Julia wouldn't have lasted five minutes on my ward when I was a Sister.'

'You think she may have killed Olive, because she was afraid that she might make a complaint about her?' Jonah asked, excitedly. 'Do you know what it was about?'

'Lots of things, but the incident that sparked the row

was Mr Martin's fall. He's an amputee in a wheelchair. He called for someone to help him get to the toilet. Julia was on duty, but she couldn't be bothered to go to him. He tried to manage on his own and had a fall. When Olive heard about it, she tore Julia off a strip and told her that she was watching her and had a good mind to report her to the Manager. That was all on the Monday. Then, on the Tuesday night, Olive goes to sleep and doesn't wake up again. Makes you wonder, doesn't it?'

'It does indeed,' Jonah agreed. 'Have you told the police about all this?'

'No. Nobody asked. I think they reckon we're all gaga. As soon as I said I hadn't seen Olive since breakfast that day, they lost interest in anything I had to tell them.'

'Didn't you both have dinner together?' Jonah asked, remembering Charlie Simpson's account of Olive's last day.

'She was late down. I'd finished and come back up here before she got to the dining room. I only eat the main course. I never bother with the dessert. I wish I had that day. I'd have liked to have heard what she had to say about her day out with Desmond. I bet he was trying to persuade her not to sell the house. Both the boys were very upset about that.'

'But what did they expect her to do?' Bernie asked. 'If that was the only way she could afford to pay the Care Home fees, what else *could* she do – unless they were offering to pay for her?'

'Not on your nelly!' Dot snorted with laughter. 'No. They were angling for her to move back home and have carers coming in daily. Now that most of her savings are gone, she'd have got help from Social Services with that and they'd still have got the house when she died.'

'Mayn't they have genuinely thought she would be happier in her own house?' Peter suggested. 'It doesn't have to have been all about the money.'

'Not that house,' Dot insisted. 'She told me about it.

It's a big old rambling place with steep stairs and draughty windows and no decent heating. Olive admitted that she'd let it get in a bit of a state after her husband died. She said it was much more comfortable here – if only the staff would do their jobs properly.'

'So it wasn't just Julia Freeman?' Jonah leapt eagerly on this remark. 'She was critical of other members of staff too?'

'Oh yes! Mind you, that's partly just what she was like. She was always looking to pick holes in everything. She'd been a tax inspector, and I think she looked at the whole of life the way she used to look at income tax returns – always trying to spot things that weren't quite right and bring people to book about them, and never really trusting anyone to be telling the whole truth. *But not even Olive had a bad word to say about Jonathan*,' Dot concluded fiercely.

Jonah racked his brains, trying to remember which other members of staff were on duty during the critical period when the insulin must have been administered to Olive. He had the information stored on his computer, but that was attached to his electric wheelchair waiting downstairs for his return. What was the name of the Care Assistant who had worked the night shift that day? She had the greatest opportunity for committing the crime.

'Was there anyone else in particular, who might have been worried about Olive reporting them for neglecting their duties?' he asked at last.

Dot thought for a while.

'I don't think so,' she said in the end. 'I think she had something on practically everyone. She wrote it all down in a little book she had. She told me she was going to show it to the inspectors next time we had someone round from the CQC[3], but I don't know whether she would have done it really. However much we complain about the place,

---

[3] Care Quality Commission: the independent regulator of health and social care in England.

none of us would want to have it closed down. It would be too much of an upheaval moving somewhere else at our time of life.'

'But anyone whose name featured in her little book wouldn't know that,' Jonah pointed out. 'How many people knew about it? I mean, was it common knowledge?'

'She kept it hidden away from the staff, but most of the residents knew.'

'Interesting, very interesting,' Jonah mused.

'But I still think it's John and Desmond you should be looking at,' Dot insisted. 'They had much more to gain and don't you think it's a bit of a coincidence the way they were both here the day she died? And John was dead against having a PM. To be fair to Desmond, he was all for it, as I remember, but I always put that down to him wanting to pin the blame on Jonathan so that he wouldn't get his five hundred pounds.'

'So there was disagreement between the brothers as to whether their mother should have a post-mortem done?' Jonah asked.

'Yes. At least,' Dot paused briefly, 'that's what I heard. I have to admit I wasn't there, but that's what Kathleen told me. She was Olive's best friend, out of the residents here, and Olive had left her some of her things. Desmond and John came to talk to her about it and it came out then.'

'That's interesting,' Bernie said. 'It suggests that, if the sons had anything to do with Olive's death at all, it probably wasn't a conspiracy that they were both in on. If it had been, you'd expect them to have a united front on whether or not they wanted a PM.'

'I'm not so sure,' Jonah argued. 'If it wasn't something that they'd thought about and agreed on in advance, they may have had different ideas about how to appear innocent. One of them might have wanted to prevent the real cause of death being discovered while the other thought that opposing the post-mortem would throw suspicion on them – or he may have known that Jonathan had given Olive her insulin injection that evening and thought that he was bound to be blamed for killing her.'

'I'm sorry Dot,' Peter said, in the silence that followed while everyone digested this suggestion, 'I still think that you need to accept that Jonathan Bates *is* the most likely person to have given your friend an overdose of insulin. Couldn't it have been an accident? Couldn't he have used the wrong sort of insulin and the wrong dose? And then been afraid to own up?'

'If you'd ever met him, you'd see that he's not like that,' Dot said dogmatically. 'I think you ought to talk to him – get his side of the story. Are you doing anything this evening? I'll arrange for you to go round.'

She picked up a mobile phone from the table next to her chair and selected a name from the contacts list. Ignoring protestations from Peter and Bernie that it was unreasonable of her to expect Jonathan and his spouse to entertain three complete strangers in their home at a few hours' notice, she proceeded to make arrangements for them to visit.

'That's all settled,' she said briskly, as she put down the phone and reached for a pad of paper and a pen. 'I'll write down the address for you. It's one of those new apartments overlooking the waterfront. They chose it for the view. I suppose they can afford it, with it being just the two of them. Mark my words, you'll change your tune about Jonathan being a murderer when you meet him.'

8. I LOVE MY LOVE
Abroad as I was walking one evening in the spring
I heard a maid in Bedlam so sweetly for to sing.
Her chain she rattled with her hands and thus replied she:
"I love my love because I know my love loves me.
English traditional song.

'Come on in! Jonno won't be a minute.' The man who answered the door looked to be in his mid-thirties: tall with dark brown hair and eyes. He stepped back to make room for Jonah's wheelchair to enter. 'I'm Nigel – Jonno's husband,' the young man added, noticing the blank looks on the faces of his guests.

'We're very pleased to meet you,' Jonah said with a slightly exaggerated heartiness that betrayed his surprise at receiving this information. With a flick of his finger on the controls of his electric wheelchair, he crossed the threshold and entered the apartment in the shiny new tower block overlooking the Mersey.

'I'm sorry,' Peter added apologetically, following Jonah inside. 'Bernie's aunt told us he was married, but she didn't say ... We ought not to have assumed ...'

'Don't worry about that,' Nigel assured them. 'We're not offended.'

'I bet Dot did it deliberately.' Another young man emerged from a room on the right and pushed past Nigel to shake hands with Peter and Bernie. Jonah recognised his wispy blond hair and pale eyes from the photograph of Nurse Jonathan Bates, which Sandra Latham had shown to him the day before. 'She's a bit of a joker is Our Dot. Now come into the lounge and tell us what this is all about.'

Nigel led the way into a large airy room, sparsely furnished with a modern three-piece suite, upholstered in brown leather, grouped around a glass-surfaced coffee table and facing a large flat-screen television. The evening sun was shining in through large glass doors, which took up most of one wall. They stood open, allowing the perfume from night-scented stock and tobacco plants to waft in from a wide balcony. The other three walls were decorated with reproductions of paintings and sketches in a variety of styles, predominantly landscapes and industrial scenes.

Jonah manoeuvred his chair through the doorway and into the centre of the room, from which he looked round, taking it all in.

'Are those the pieces that Edna Lomax left to you?' he asked, looking towards a tall glass-fronted display cabinet containing an array of glass and china ornaments, including a dozen or more items in the traditional Wedgewood blue-and-white Jasperware.

'You've heard about that then?' Jonathan wandered over to the cabinet, opened the door and picked up an urn decorated with figures in classical costume and trees with delicate leaves and branches. He brought it over and held it for Jonah to admire. 'Yes. I was a bit uncomfortable about accepting it, but her daughter wouldn't take no for an answer.'

'She knew that Edna wanted you to have them,' Nigel said earnestly. 'And she didn't have any use for the stuff herself.'

'Edna knew I like nice things,' Jonathan explained.

'And she wanted them to go to someone who would enjoy looking at them. Now, how about a drink?'

He replaced the urn carefully on the shelf and closed the cabinet. Then he bent down and pulled open a door beneath the display shelves, revealing an array of bottles and decanters.

'Would it be really awkward of me to say I'd like tea?' Bernie asked.

'That would suit me too,' Peter added, 'I'm driving.'

'Let's make it tea all round,' Nigel said cheerily. 'I'll get it. Why don't you all go out on the balcony and make the most of the good weather?'

'Who's the gardener?' Jonah asked, looking round at the array of tubs and troughs of plants, which filled the balcony with scent and colour.

'This is Nigel's domain,' Jonathan told him. 'I'm better at looking after the indoor things. Plants always die on me.'

'He's got some lovely varieties here,' Jonah said appreciatively, wandering around, peering at the flowers. 'Those antirrhinums are an unusual colour! And what a magnificent camellia! I wouldn't have thought it would grow in a container. What a good idea to allow that rose to climb up through it, so that you get flowers for a much longer season. Camellias are wonderful when they're in flower, but it's for such a short time. This is a magnificent specimen for a balcony. We could do that with ours, don't you think, Bernie?'

'You're the boss!' Bernie smiled at her friend's enthusiasm. Jonah had been a keen gardener before his life-changing injury. Bernie, whose upbringing in a small terraced house in Toxteth had ill equipped her for managing the extensive grounds of their current house, was content to work under his instruction. 'Perhaps Nigel will tell you what sort of rose it is.'

'We've got a wonderful view,' Jonathan went on, leaning on the balcony rail and pointing out across the river. 'Those are the Welsh hills over there, beyond the

Wirral; and if you look to the right, you can almost see New Brighton.'

Bernie came alongside him and gazed down at the light from the setting sun glinting on the water and the dark hills silhouetted against the pink and orange of the sky.

'It's a lovely spot,' she agreed. 'Mind you, we used to be able to see the Welsh hills from my Aunty Bea's house in Dingle too. My dad used to work in the docks not far from here. It's all changed now – including the view from Aunty Bea's street. It used to look as if the river was just below the end of her road. Now the rooftops of your apartments are in the way!'

'Here we are!' Nigel's voice interrupted her reverie. She turned to see him stepping out from the lounge, holding a tray loaded with a willow pattern bone china tea service. He set it down on the table that stood in the centre of the balcony and started to set out the cups and saucers ready to pour the tea.

'I'll do it,' Jonathan said, stepping forward. 'Sit down everyone.'

'He doesn't trust me with his precious china,' Nigel told them with a smile. 'I was surprised that he let me get the tea.'

'Can you blame me? I don't know how he does it!' Jonathan gave an exaggerated shrug of incomprehension. 'Let him loose with anything breakable and you can be sure that he'll drop it or bash it into something or ...' He shook his head as if in despair at his spouse's clumsiness.

Bernie reached down into a bag that hung at the back of Jonah's chair and took out a plastic cup with a lid and a long straw protruding from the top. She took off the lid and put the cup down on the table.

'Could you fill this up for Jonah?' she asked. 'Just a dash of milk. No sugar.'

Jonathan poured in milk and tea, and then Bernie replaced the lid. Peter meanwhile went over to Jonah's chair and lifted a flap on the side of the right-hand arm-rest to form a small table. Bernie put the cup down on it and adjusted the straw so that Jonah could reach to drink from it. Nigel watched the proceedings with interest.

'That's a very neat arrangement,' he commented.

'Yes,' agreed Jonah. 'This chair is a real life-changer for me. I'd be lost without it. But we didn't come here to discuss me,' he added, turning to Jonathan. 'I want to hear your side of what happened to Olive Carter.'

'I'm not sure what I can tell you,' Jonathan answered, continuing to pour tea into the delicate china cups, 'apart from saying that I didn't do it.'

'Presumably you're absolutely certain that you couldn't have given her the wrong dose when you administered her insulin injection that evening?'

'Yes, I am – absolutely certain. I got her insulin pen out of the drugs cupboard, checked it was the right one, and then took it to her room. Afterwards, I took it back and put it away in the cupboard again. The syringe that was found by her bed in the morning was something different altogether. It was for another of the residents. He has type 1 diabetes and takes several shots a day of rapid-acting insulin. He administers it himself. I took it to him and he gave himself a shot before he had his dinner and then I put everything away again afterwards.'

'That's interesting. You're saying that, not only was the type of insulin different from what she usually took, but that it was administered in a different way?'

'Well, yes. Most diabetes patients prefer to use the pens, because they're easier to self-administer, but some still use the old method where you draw up the amount you need into a syringe.'

'And would it be easier to administer an overdose using a syringe?

'Do you mean accidentally or deliberately?'

'Either.'

Yes, I suppose it probably would. You could misread the graduations on the syringe and draw up too much from the vial, or you could deliberately draw up too much and the patient would be unlikely to notice.'

'But you might have expected Olive Carter to notice the difference between being given her medication through a pen and a syringe,' Jonah suggested.

'Yes. In any case, she usually did it herself. Just occasionally, when her arthritis was playing up, she'd ask a member of staff to help. It was a bit awkward, because only qualified nurses are really supposed to administer insulin. That's why it was usually me or the other nurse who took it to her. But there were times when it was unavoidable that a Care Assistant did it. So we always hoped she wouldn't ask for help then. We could be in trouble with the CQC if they found out that a Care Assistant was going beyond their competence.'

'Which all makes it much less likely that the overdose was given in place of her usual evening dose,' Jonah murmured. 'OK. Now tell me: how did she seem that evening, when you put her to bed and gave her the sleeping tablet and insulin?'

'I'm not sure what you mean.'

'Did she seem well? What sort of mood was she in?'

'About the same as usual.' Jonathan shrugged. 'I suppose she seemed rather tired, but I put that down to her having been out for the day.'

'But could it have been because she'd already been given sleeping tablets?'

'I suppose so.'

'Or even that she was feeling the effects of an insulin overdose?'

'I suppose so,' Jonathan repeated. 'But I'm sure that the syringe wasn't there when I put her to bed; so she must have been given that later.'

'Good. I think I've got things a bit clearer in my mind now.'

'Just hang on a minute,' Nigel said, taking advantage of a break in the conversation while Jonah thought through what he had just learned. 'Before you go any further with this inquisition, I'd like to know what this is all in aid of. Who exactly are you? And what right have you to come here asking all these questions? And whose side are you on?'

'It's alright Nige,' Jonathan said quietly, putting his hand on Nigel's arm and looking round at the others apologetically. 'He's Dot's friend. She's sent him here to help.'

'I'm on the side of justice,' Jonah said, slightly sanctimoniously. 'I want to get to the truth and see that nobody gets blamed for something they didn't do. Bernie's Aunt is convinced that Jonathan is innocent and she's hoping that I'll be able to prove it.'

'Aunty Dot was anxious that the police might never get to the bottom of things and people would carry on thinking that Jonathan was responsible,' Bernie added.

'I see,' Nigel still sounded suspicious.

'Come on Nige,' Jonathan urged. 'Don't be like that. Let them have a go. It can't make things any worse than they are already.'

'I suppose not,' Nigel sighed. 'It's so unfair!' he added bitterly. 'They've got nothing on Jonno at all, but now they've suspended him, everyone will be saying *there's no smoke without fire* and he'll probably never work again.'

'I suppose the management had to be seen to be doing something,' Jonathan said in a more conciliatory tone. 'After all, they've already had one resident moving out because she's afraid she'll be next!'

'Oh?' Jonah asked sharply.

'Betty Hunter,' Jonathan informed them. 'I'm surprised Dot didn't tell you about it. 'Her daughter came and took her away for an extended holiday with them. She made it quite clear that they were going to be looking for another Home and she'd be moving out permanently if this didn't get settled soon.'

'That same afternoon, they suspended Jonno on full

pay,' Nigel added. 'And now everyone's saying it must have been him. I almost hope whoever it was does it again, just to show them they were wrong!'

'Nige!' Jonathan reproved him. 'That's an awful thing to say. He doesn't mean it,' he added, looking round at the others. 'He's just angry about the way things have been going.'

'Angry? Angry doesn't even come close! What right have they to go round accusing you? It'll be that Desmond Carter at the bottom of it, I bet!'

'Why do you say that?' Jonah asked mildly.

'He never liked Jonno. Well, actually that's not quite true. He took against him when we got married. It was only then that he realised ...'

'Realised what?'

'He put in a complaint,' Jonathan explained. 'Well, more like a request really. He asked if I could be kept away from his mother. He said that it was unsettling for a woman of her age to have someone like me around her.'

'Because you're gay?' Bernie asked incredulously. 'I don't get that at all. Surely that would make you *less* of a threat – not that there's any rational reason for thinking you might be a threat at all – than if you were straight?'

'It was only an excuse,' Nigel broke in scornfully. 'He knew that his mother liked Jonno and he was afraid she'd disinherit him. Just because *he* couldn't be bothered with her himself! *She* gave us this tea service as a wedding present, and Desmond suddenly realised that he might be getting displaced.'

'Dot thinks that it could be one of Olive's sons who killed her,' Jonah told them. 'Do you think that's possible?'

'I absolutely do!' Nigel declared. 'The two of them were as bad as each other.'

'No,' Jonathan protested in his soft, mild-mannered voice. 'That's not fair. They were just doing their best for her.'

'Rubbish! You told me yourself they never visited her

for months on end. All they were interested in was her money – and buggering up your career!'

'They both visited her the day she died,' Jonah pointed out. 'And Desmond even took her out for the day.'

'And the next day, there she is, dead in bed!' Nigel said triumphantly. 'I rest my case.'

'But, what about the syringe on her bedside table?' Jonathan asked nervously. 'I'm sure it wasn't there when I put her to bed.'

'Hmmm,' Jonah mused. 'You're right. On the face of it, that does suggest that it must have been one of the staff – someone who was on duty *after* you put Olive to bed. And that means ...,' he looked down at the computer screen attached to his chair, consulting the notes that he had taken of his conversation with the police, 'Julia Freeman or Rebecca Anderson.'

'Or that doctor,' Nigel added. 'Remember, Jonno? You said they called the doctor out to one of the other residents that night. He could've done it.'

'I really don't think-,' Jonathan began.

'Did either Julia or Rebecca have any reason to want to kill Olive?' Jonah broke in, 'or have either of them been behaving oddly at all?'

'No – not that I know of.'

'What about the dodgy dossier?' Nigel said mysteriously. 'Tell them Jonno.'

'The day Olive died,' Jonathan began reluctantly, 'Fiona – that's the manager – called us all together for a staff meeting and told us that one of the residents had been keeping notes of adverse incidents, which they were threatening to show to the CQC at their next inspection.'

'And by *one of the residents* she meant Olive?' Jonah asked.

'She didn't say, but talking about it afterwards, everyone thought Olive was the most likely. She always did take an interest in everything that went on, especially with regard to the running of the Home. And she did have a habit of noting things down. She was in charge of organising the residents' Social Programme and she always wrote little reports about everything they did and pinned them up on the notice board. But we didn't have any other reason for thinking it was her – or if anyone else knew about it they didn't say.'

'What did the manager expect you all to do about it?' Peter asked. 'Why did she tell you?'

'It was just her way of giving us a kick up the backside after a particular incident the night before. One of the residents had a fall and he blamed it on the staff not getting to help him in time after he buzzed for assistance. It wasn't serious, but it shouldn't have happened. And, to make it worse, when Fiona looked, it wasn't in the accident book. So she was telling us all about how important it was not to let that sort of thing happen and to follow up any untoward occurrences properly. For all I know, she invented the story of the dossier, just to get us worried.'

'And did anyone appear particularly worried? Jonah asked. 'Who exactly was there?'

'Like I said, it was all the staff on duty that afternoon, which was: me, Maxine Shaw and Julia Freeman. Oh! And Dr Bhaskar was there too. He comes round alternate Tuesdays to see two or three of the residents who have conditions that need monitoring and any of the others who need to see him.'

'And that's the doctor who was called out later to see the woman who was taken ill that evening?' Jonah asked, remembering that Charlie Simpson had mentioned a doctor visiting during the evening.

'Yes, it will have been. I'd gone home by then, but it's bound to have been Dr Bhaskar. He's the GP for all the residents. It's easier that way.'

'OK.' Jonah thought for a moment or two. 'Now, tell me about this Maxine Shaw. That's a new name to me.'

'She's the other qualified nurse,' Jonathan explained. 'She worked the early shift that day, which means from seven in the morning to three in the afternoon. Our shifts overlap one day a week, which gives us a chance to do a proper handover, if there's anything that's changed with any of the residents' health. She's very good with the patients,' he added quickly, noticing that Jonah was taking notes of their conversation on his computer. 'She'd never harm any of them.'

'In any case,' Jonah replied, smiling up at him, 'she can't have given Olive a lethal dose of insulin, if she left at three and Olive didn't come back until an hour later.'

'No,' Jonathan agreed. He seemed to be about to say something more, but Jonah continued.

'So that leaves Julia. Did she have any particular reason to be worried about Olive's dossier?'

'Well,' Jonathan sighed before going on. 'She was the member of staff who should have got to Mr Martin quicker and who didn't write it all up in the accident book or tell Fiona about it.'

'Did Fiona suggest that she would apply any sanctions to members of staff whose names appeared in the dossier? Could Julia have been worried about losing her job?'

'Not really. It was more in the way of a general telling off and reminding us that we would all lose our jobs if the CQC close us down.'

'And do you think that Olive really intended to show her list of incidents to the CQC inspectors?'

'I doubt it,' Jonathan shrugged. 'She didn't want the Home closed down any more than the staff did. She was settled there. She was one of the youngest and certainly the most active and on-the-ball. She enjoyed organising them all – planning the Social Programme and so on – and bossing us all about. She used to be chair of the Women's Institute and the leader of some local community action group and all sorts. She was used to people doing what she said. She thought the staff needed better discipline and to pay closer attention to the rules, and I reckon she thought that just letting us know that she was watching us would be enough to keep us on our toes.'

'I still think you're barking up the wrong tree, looking at the staff,' Nigel said dogmatically, in the lull that followed. 'I don't pretend to know how they did it, but I'm convinced it was Olive's family who were responsible. And I reckon they deliberately fixed it so as Jonno would get the blame. They've had it in for him ever since we got married – complaining to the manager and telling the relatives of other residents that they ought to ask for him to be dismissed because it's not nice for them to have *someone like him* around the place – nod, nod, wink, wink, say no more!'

'Nige! Stop it. You don't know that.'

'What about what Mrs Ray told you? You know – about Desmond telling her grandson he ought to complain?'

'Frannie Ray always likes to exaggerate. I don't suppose he actually said half the things she said he did. Anyway,' Jonathan turned back to Jonah, 'you can't get away from that syringe on her bedside table. I'm sure it wasn't there at half past seven, and it was there in the morning. So she must have been killed overnight.'

'Or at least the syringe must have been put there overnight,' Jonah agreed.

9. CAST CARE ASIDE
*Cast care aside, lean on thy guide.
Lean and his mercy will provide.*
John S. B. Monsell: "Fight the good fight"

'Or possibly on Wednesday morning,' Jonah concluded, looking across at Sandra, who had joined the family for breakfast at the hotel, eager to hear news of what Dot had had to say to them about the case. 'Someone could have planted the syringe to make it appear that the insulin had to have been administered during the night. Do you have a record of when it was first noticed next to Olive's bed?'

'Not really,' Sandra said slowly, consulting her notes. 'Perhaps we should go back and ask the Care Assistant who found the body whether she saw it when she came into Olive's room first thing. As far as I can see, there's no mention of it anywhere in anyone's statement. The first person to pick up on it was PC Robert Thomas, who attended when the doctor called the police to report an unexpected death. He saw it there and asked about it. When Jonathan Bates told him it wasn't the sort that Olive usually used and nobody knew where it had come from, he bagged it up and took it away to check the contents.'

'And you say that it was also checked for fingermarks and there weren't any, if I remember correctly.'

'Well, more or less. We're fairly confident that whoever administered the insulin wore gloves, but then that would have been standard practice for the staff, so isn't in itself significant. There were some smudged fingermarks as if someone could have touched the syringe with bare hands at some point, probably after it had been used. There was some smudging on the vial too, more like marks from the palm of the hand than the fingers, nothing that could be used to identify anyone.'

'I suppose that makes it even less likely that Olive could have done it herself,' Bernie suggested. 'If she'd handled the syringe, you'd expect her prints to be on it.'

'And what time was this?' Jonah demanded, moving quickly on, now that the question of fingerprints was settled. '*Could* someone have put the syringe in Olive's room after she was already dead?'

'PC Thomas arrived at about eleven. Jonathan Bates met him at the main entrance and showed him to Olive Carter's room. He did a quick visual check and noticed the syringe.'

'That's very interesting,' Jonah said, nodding slowly as he thought through the implications of this. 'That leaves a gap of more than two hours between finding the body and finding the syringe. Who else went into the room before eleven that morning?'

'Scarlet Jones found the body. That was sometime between eight thirty and nine. She told Jonathan Bates and he went to the office and called the doctor.'

'But did he go into the room then?' Jonah asked sharply.

'I don't know.' Sandra looked rapidly through her notes. 'It's not clear, but I think that Scarlet Jones came out of the room and found Bates and told him that Olive was dead and then he went straight to the office to make the phone call.'

'OK. Carry on.'

'The manager arrived just after the doctor was called.

Bates told her about Olive's death and she went to see for herself, leaving Jonathan to let in the doctor when he came. However, before the doctor actually arrived, she came back to the office and telephoned Mrs Carter's two sons to let them know that their mother had died.'

'And did they come over that morning?' Jonah asked eagerly. 'Did they go into Olive's room before PC Thomas arrived and saw the syringe?'

'The older one – Desmond – definitely did. He got there about the same time as the doctor. According to Scarlet Jones, the doctor had just started examining the body when Desmond came in and started kicking off about how well his mother had been the day before and how there must be something wrong. She thought that the doctor might have simply certified cause of death as hypoglycaemia resulting from poorly-controlled type 2 diabetes and tried to avoid notifying the coroner or getting a PM done, if Desmond hadn't been so definite that there must be something more to it than that.'

'Interesting ... very interesting,' Jonah mused. 'That fits in with Nigel's idea that Desmond had it in for Jonathan and was trying to frame him.'

'Or maybe he was just knocked for six by his mother's sudden death and needed to know how it happened,' Peter suggested mildly.

'It also raises questions about the doctor,' Bernie added. 'I mean, if he really was reluctant to inform the coroner.'

'So, we've got Scarlet Jones, Fiona Radcliffe, the doctor and Jonathan Bates all around before the syringe is noticed. Was there anyone else? Were any of the other staff on duty before Constable Thomas arrived?'

'Julia Freeman started her shift at ten,' Sandra replied, after consulting her notes again. 'That was shortly before John and Valerie Carter arrived. I don't think she went into Mrs Carter's room, but I suppose we can't rule it out.'

'That makes eight people who could potentially have

planted the syringe that morning,' Bernie observed thoughtfully. 'The manager, the doctor, Scarlet Jones, Julia Freeman, Jonathan Bates and the three Carters.'

'But Jonathan and Julia were both on duty until late the previous evening,' Sandra pointed out. 'So planting the syringe to make it look as if the death occurred during the night would be pointless for them.'

'John and Valerie Carter opposed the post-mortem,' Jonah murmured to himself. 'That doesn't make sense if they've just planted the syringe to make it look like murder by one of the staff. That's a pity, because they are the ones with the best motive. I could well imagine them wanting Olive's money in order to get their daughter and her kids set up in her own home and out from under their feet. That's why I originally thought that they opposed the PM in the hope that it would all pass off as natural causes.'

'But hang about,' Peter objected. 'It's all very well talking about motives and people being around at the right time to give the insulin injection, but I still don't see how it was done. Whoever did it and whenever they did it, why didn't Olive stop them? At the beginning, I thought the idea was that someone injected her with the wrong sort of insulin while they were pretending to give her her normal dose. Now you're saying that it was a different sort of syringe and at a different time and that she normally administered it herself in any case.'

For a few moments, everyone was silent.

'Peter's right,' Jonah said at last. 'Whoever it was would have had to have some pretext.'

'The doctor would be the best bet for that,' Bernie suggested. 'He could have made out that she needed an injection of some sort and persuaded her to allow him to give it to her. But maybe that would be true of the Care Home staff too.'

'What you've just told me about that staff meeting and Olive's list of complaints makes me think that it's probably the Care Home staff who also have the best motives for wanting her out of the way,' Sandra added grimly. 'The Carters weren't desperate for money and Olive was bound to die eventually, but anyone who knew that they'd done something that would lose them their job if it got out might be desperate to make sure that nobody saw that dossier.'

'You're right,' Bernie agreed. 'And depending on what it was, it might mean they'd never get another job.'

'It could be even worse than that,' Jonah added, his eyes lighting up as a new idea struck him. 'What if Edna's death wasn't natural? What if Olive knew how it really happened?'

'You mean she could have been blackmailing Edna's murderer?' Peter asked.

'Not necessarily. Maybe her death was the result of negligence. Maybe the person responsible knew — or thought they knew — that Olive's dossier included stuff that would show up something that they did — or didn't do — that contributed to her death.'

'You mean Edna died of a stroke because someone forgot to give her her blood pressure pills, or something like that?' Sandra suggested.

'Yes. That's the sort of thing,' Jonah agreed.

'What I'd like to know is where this *dossier* is now,' Lucy said, speaking for the first time. She had been following the conversation closely, but had been nervous of expressing an opinion in case somebody decided that she should not be included in possibly confidential police matters. 'Isn't it important to know what is actually in it?'

'Lucy's right,' Peter agreed. 'If we don't know what's in it, we're only guessing about which members of staff could be worried about Olive telling on them.'

'Did you find anything of that sort in her room?' Jonah asked quickly.

'No. But I'm afraid that doesn't prove anything,' Sandra admitted. 'The room wasn't sealed. PC Thomas did lock the door before he left and he told them not to disturb anything, but that was all. For all we know, someone could have got the spare key from the office and then gone in and taken this dossier or list or diary, or whatever it really was, away before we examined the room.' She sighed. 'What we really need is to find out more about the people who live and work in the Home. We could do with having someone on the inside, whom we can be sure doesn't have an axe to grind, to tell us what's really going on there. Did anyone really have anything to fear from Olive's revelations? Does anyone actually have it in for Jonathan Bates? What do the-'

'I could do that,' Jonah broke in suddenly. 'I could be your spy on the inside. All I need to do is to book myself in for a week's respite care, to give Bernie and Peter a proper holiday for once. Presumably they must have a room spare. They can't have filled Olive's room yet, surely?'

'I'm not sure they'd take you,' Sandra said doubtfully. 'I think it's probably just older people that they cater for.'

'I could ask them to stretch a point because it would be so good for me to be in the same Home as Bernie's Aunt.' Jonah did not want to give up on this exciting new plan.

'But what if there really is a serial killer working there?' Lucy demanded to know. 'What if one of the care workers is killing off the residents one by one? You could be next!'

'She's right, you know,' Bernie agreed. 'And even if it isn't a serial killer, if whoever killed Olive *is* one of the staff, they might see you poking your nose into things and decide to get rid of you.'

'I can look after myself.'

'Sorry Jonah,' Peter was apologetic but firm. 'Actually, you can't. Once you're out of that chair of yours, you'd be pretty vulnerable to anyone who wanted to make sure you never got the opportunity to get to the bottom of what's been going on. We can't let you go in there on your own.'

Lucy, who was sitting between Peter and Jonah, took hold of her stepfather's arm and squeezed it gently to show her appreciation of his intervention.

'Yes, I see the problem,' Sandra said slowly. 'But I do think that this might be the only way of finding out who did kill Mrs Carter. What we need is some sort of backup to make sure that Jonah is safe.'

'No,' Lucy disagreed. 'We need you to do your job without getting Jonah involved. It's your case. He's only here in an advisory capacity.'

'Let's hear her out,' Peter said calmly, taking hold of Lucy's hand under the table and giving Jonah a look that told him to keep quiet. 'What exactly did you have in mind, Sandra?'

'I think we're going to have to be open with the manager about what we're doing,' Sandra said, after a few moments' thought. 'I know that technically it's not impossible that she let herself back into the Home after she left on Tuesday to give Olive a lethal dose of insulin, but on balance I think she's not a very likely suspect. So, how about we tell her that we need to put an undercover police officer in the home for a few days? We'll swear her to secrecy, so that none of the other staff know that it isn't just a disabled friend of Bernie's Aunt coming to stay with her. That way, we can insist that Jonah is given Olive Carter's old room, *and*,' she paused to give greater emphasis to the following words, 'we can arrange for a couple of other officers to be on hand, primed to step in if anyone attempts to prejudice Jonah's safety.'

'How?' Lucy asked suspiciously. 'How can they be there without anyone knowing about them?'

'I haven't thought out the details, but it should be easy enough, with the co-operation of the manager. They could pose as ... window-cleaners, say, or perhaps they could pretend to be builders carrying out repairs. Jonah would be wired up for sound, so that they would be able to monitor everything that was going on and intervene before anything happened to him.'

'That's no good,' Lucy argued. 'What about when the

staff undress him? He can't hide anything from his carers.'

'That's true enough,' Jonah agreed, looking round with his lop-sided smile. 'You'd do better wiring up my chair and bugging my bedroom and bathroom, in case the murderer strikes when I'm out of it.'

'And if you've got them cleaning windows,' Lucy persisted, 'how are they going to get inside in time to rescue Jonah if he needs them?'

'That's another reason why we need the manager on board,' Sandra told her. 'They'll need to have a set of keys and we'll have to work out quick and easy ways for them to get inside at any time of day or night.'

'I still don't like it,' Bernie muttered. She could see that Jonah had made up his mind and that nothing she said would deter him. Nevertheless, she did not want to give in without a fight. 'Aunty Dot's bound to have boasted to her friends that Jonah's a DCI, so they're sure to be suspicious of him.'

'On the other hand, that'll probably make them want to talk to me about Olive's death,' Jonah argued.

'Not if they killed her,' Lucy said sulkily. She too realised that it was pointless to argue further and was feeling all the more annoyed as a result. She turned to address Sandra again. 'I don't understand why you're letting him do this. Can't you see how dangerous it is for him?'

'I'm sorry,' Sandra coloured under Lucy's stare. She looked round at them all. 'Lucy's right. I shouldn't have asked you to-'

'You didn't,' Jonah interrupted. 'It was my idea, remember? And I'm a responsible – well, fairly responsible – adult and can decide for myself what sort of risks I'm willing to take. If you can fix up some sort of emergency response team to support me, then I don't see that there's any problem about me spending a few days checking out *Park View* from the inside.'

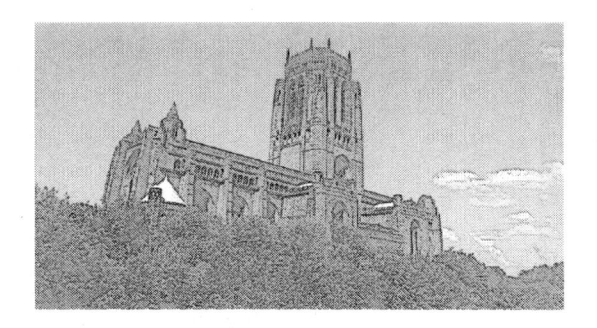

10. OLD FOLKS AT HOME
There's where the old folks stay.
S. C. Foster: "Old folks at home."

That afternoon, Bernie took Peter and Lucy on a sight-seeing trip around her home city – something that they had intended to do the previous year, but had been prevented by the unexpected circumstance of their becoming witnesses to a murder. Jonah meanwhile, persuaded Sandra to take him to see Edna Lomax's daughter to check out Jonathan's story that she had been delighted to give him her mother's Wedgewood collection.

At first, Lucy protested that, since Jonah was due to start his week in the Care Home the following morning, he ought to spend the remainder of that day with them. She was very fond of Jonah and resented having him taken away from them during one of his all-too-rare periods of leave. She was also distrustful of Sandra Latham's ability to care for him properly in their absence. However, a few words from her mother persuaded her to give way gracefully, and she contented herself with taking Sandra to one side and subjecting her to a lecture on the importance of ensuring that Jonah took regular rest breaks and the correct procedure for changing his urine bag.

When they were ready to go their separate ways, Lucy

insisted on being the one to strap Jonah safely in the back of the car, double-checking that he had everything he could need during the course of an afternoon stowed in the bag attached at the back. She put her arms around his shoulders and kissed him on the cheek before reluctantly getting out and closing the door behind her. Peter handed over the keys to Sandra and she got into the driving seat.

'We'll be back here by five,' she promised, switching on the engine and preparing to set off. 'And don't worry, we won't do anything silly.'

She closed the window and drove away, leaving the hotel, which was in the dockland area, and heading uphill away from the river.

'Your Lucy is quite a forceful character, isn't she?' Sandra observed with a smile. 'I feel very much that I'm on probation and she's going to be checking up that I've taken proper care of you!'

'Well, she's been doing it for eight years now, so she has a right to consider herself an expert.'

'Wow! And she's only seventeen. I can't see either of my girls wanting to be bothered – not even now, never mind when they were only nine.'

'How old are they?'

'Sixteen and fourteen: both going through the bolshie teenage stage. I suppose I should be glad they like going to stay with their dad, but ...,' she sighed. 'When they're with me I seem to be shouting at them all the time, but it still annoys me that they keep angling to spend more time with him and his girlfriend and their baby.'

'Is that far away?'

'Southport. We all used to live there. Gary has a garden centre and nursery there. It's a big old house with loads of grounds, which he uses for the business. The girls love the freedom. It's much better for them than sharing with me and my mum and dad. And Mel seems hardly any older than them, so she knows about the same music and clothes and stuff as they're interested in.'

'So you and the girls moved out when he ...?'

'There didn't seem to be any other option, at least ... well, Gary's idea was that we could all live there as one happy family: him, me, the girls, Melanie and the new baby. I ask you! Did he really think I'd agree to carrying on with me working full-time *and* helping out with the business and running the house, while Mel just sits around looking pretty and cuddling *his* baby?'

The awe-inspiring sandstone bulk of the Anglican Cathedral rose up ahead of them. Before they reached it, Sandra turned the car into a narrow side street and pulled up in front of a far less imposing single-storey brick building, which was the Senior Citizens Day Centre.

'He made me feel such a fool,' she continued. 'I'd known Mel for years. She'd been helping at the garden centre ever since she left school. Then one day, she was just leaving when I got home. I hadn't seen her for a while, so we stopped and had a chat. She was very obviously pregnant, so I said something about when was her maternity leave starting, and she giggled a bit and said she and Gary hadn't decided that yet. I still didn't twig, because I assumed she meant that she hadn't agreed it with her boss. Anyway, I mentioned it to Gary that evening and I said something about not having realised that she even had a boyfriend, and did he know who the father was. And he got a bit flustered and said that he'd been meaning to talk to me about that. And then of course it came out that it was him! I couldn't ask him to leave, because the house was part of the business, so I took the girls to live with my parents. Luckily, their house is big enough, but Sophie and Pippa have to share a room, which they never did before. It's been a real nightmare getting them to school this year. I couldn't move them right away because it was Sophie's GCSE year. If my dad hadn't been willing to act as chauffeur I don't know how we'd have managed. It'll be better when they go back in September.' She sighed again. 'But you don't want to hear about all that. I didn't bring you here to talk about *my* family. It's Edna Lomax's daughter who may be able to shed some light on this case.'

It took a little while to explain to the woman who met them at the door that Jonah was not a new client hoping to avail himself of the Day Centre's facilities. Eventually she understood that they had come to see one of her regulars. Sandra held up her police identification to establish their credentials. The woman nodded and smiled, looking a little anxious, however, at the idea of a visit by the police.

'Laura? Yes! She's here. You'll find her sitting in her usual place, by the window. Go on in.'

They looked round the large room. It seemed to be filled with high-backed easy chairs grouped in fours and fives around low tables. The far wall had three windows. One of the small tables was positioned beneath one of them, with three chairs arranged around it. One of the chairs was occupied by a small, white-haired woman, who sat motionless, apparently staring into the distance. Beneath the table lay a large black dog wearing a guide-dog harness.

'That's Laura Lomax,' Sandra whispered to Jonah. 'Come with me and I'll introduce you.'

They crossed the room. Sandra put out her hand and gently rested it on Laura's shoulder.

'Miss Lomax? It's DCI Latham — Sandra — do you remember me? I came to see you to ask you some questions about your mother.'

The woman turned her head towards the sound of Sandra's voice and peered up at her.

'Yes. I remember.'

'I've brought a colleague to see you,' Sandra continued. 'His name's Detective Chief Inspector Porter. He's visiting from Oxford and I've asked him to advise me on our investigation into the death of Mrs Olive Carter in *Park View* Care Home. He'd like to ask you about your mother's legacy to Jonathan Bates. Is that alright?'

'Yes,' Laura nodded, looking round vaguely as if

searching for something. 'Where are you? I can't see much anymore, even here by the window.'

'I'm just here,' Jonah told her. 'I'm afraid I can't shake hands, because my hands don't work anymore.'

'That's better,' Laura turned her head to face Jonah. 'Ah! I can see that you're there now. What was it you wanted to know?'

'I've been talking to Dorothy Fazakerley. She lives in *Park View* and used to know your mother. She's very concerned that people seem to think that Jonathan Bates could have killed your mother and Olive Carter because they'd left him things in their wills.'

'My mother didn't make a will. She said there wasn't any point, seeing as there was only me and she didn't have much to leave anyway. But she told me that she wanted me to give something to each of the staff in the Home as a *thank-you* for the care they'd taken of her.'

'*All* of the staff?' Jonah queried, 'not just Jonathan Bates?'

'That's right. She said she didn't want to cause any trouble so I was to let each of them choose something to remember her by from the things in her room. She said that some of the staff didn't deserve anything, but she didn't want them making trouble for the ones who did, so they were all to get something.'

'I see. That's very thoughtful of her.'

'She knew what people were like – always making trouble. That's why she said to let them choose what they wanted so nobody could compare with anyone else. The only thing she wanted different from that was the Wedgewood. She didn't want it split up, because it was a proper collection that belonged together. And she wanted it to go to someone who would treasure it and keep it, not sell it for the money. So she told me to give it to Jonathan. He'd been ever so good with it, cleaning it and that, although it wasn't his job to do it; and she knew he'd be pleased to have it. It's no good to me, and I've got nobody to leave it to when I go, so it seemed like a good idea.'

'And did Jonathan know that she was planning for him to have it?'

'No. He tried to turn it down at first. He was afraid of what the others would say. But in the end he agreed to have it, on condition that no-one else knew that he'd been treated any differently from everyone else. I never told anyone, but somehow it got out. Someone must have overheard us talking or else seen him packing the Wedgewood into a box.'

'Do you have any idea who it might have been? Who spread the word around, I mean?'

'Probably Frannie Ray. She's always wandering around poking her nose in everywhere; and as for chattering! She could gossip for England!'

'And was there anyone in particular who disapproved of Jonathan being singled out?'

'He said that Eric Martin made a lot of jokes about him having been Mum's fancy man. Eric always was a bit crude.'

'Eric's one of the residents, I take it. What about the staff? Did any of them express an opinion?'

'You'd have to ask Jonathan. He did mention to me that one of the night-staff asked him if he was going to sell it. He said she's very hard up and always looking for ways of making a bit on the side.' Laura sat in silence for a while, pursing her lips in thought. 'And there was one of the cleaners – I can't remember the name. Jonathan did tell me – who said what lovely pieces they were and offered to come round to his place to clean them for him.'

'So not really the resentment that he'd anticipated?'

'Or at least he didn't tell me about it,' Laura said drily. 'But he might have been wanting to spare my feelings, do you not think?'

Jonah thought about this for a few moments, impressed by Laura's insight. This observation fitted in very well with the reluctance that Jonathan had shown, when they visited him, to complain about the behaviour of Olive Carter's family towards him.

'Coming back to what your mother said about not all of the staff really deserving anything from her,' he said at last. 'Was there anyone in particular that she thought wasn't doing their job properly?'

'She didn't have much time for Fiona Radcliffe, the manager. *Couldn't organise a piss-up in a brewery* was how she put it. Mum ran her own business after my dad was killed in the war. She had a dozen people working under her. She could see that Fiona didn't have what it takes.'

'That's interesting. Anyone else?'

'She said that Julia Freeman was careless and it was a wonder she hadn't killed anyone yet.' Laura smiled grimly. 'She didn't mean deliberately, just forgetting to give them their tablets or … Did anyone tell you about the time Kathleen Lowe fell off the stair lift?'

'No?'

'Kath's got Parkinson's disease. She can get about alright with a walking frame, but she can't manage the stairs and she needs to be strapped into the lift when she uses it. Julia got her into the lift and set it off going down, but she didn't do up the straps and poor Kath fell out. Luckily it had nearly got to the bottom so she wasn't hurt, just a bit shaken up.'

'Did Kathleen or her family complain about it?' Sandra asked. This was an incident that she had not heard about before.

'I don't think so.'

'Did Olive Carter know about it?' Jonah enquired.

'I should have thought so. It was common knowledge among the residents.'

'And yet nobody reported it to the manager?'

'Nobody wanted to cause trouble,' Laura explained. 'It isn't that easy to get a place in one of these Homes, and it's very good in many ways. Most of the staff are pretty good. Jonathan did really stand out, but there were others who did more than they were obliged to, to make the residents comfortable. Even Fiona and Julia weren't doing it deliberately; they were just rather incompetent.'

'I see. And were there any others who were ... incompetent?'

'Mum used to complain that Becky Anderson was always on about her kids, instead of having her mind on the job. And ...,' Laura paused as if wondering whether or not to go on.

'Yes?'

'Hector Bayliss – the caretaker – the residents thought that he sometimes took things from their rooms.'

'Valuables, you mean?'

'Yes. Well, nothing worth an enormous amount. Little things – a pair of gold earrings, a Parker pen ... the sort of thing that easily gets mislaid. Mum was never convinced that the owners hadn't lost them themselves. It's just they often seemed to disappear after Hector had been in to fix something.'

'Thank you. That's very interesting information. Now, as Inspector Latham said, I'm here to help with investigating Olive Carter's death. You've obviously got to know the people in the Home quite well over the years. Is there anyone that you would think was capable of doing such a thing? Or anyone who might have wanted to?'

'I've been giving that a lot of thought, ever since the police started talking about how Mum's death might not have been natural after all. I can't really believe that anyone would have ... Couldn't it have just been an accident?'

'No. I'm afraid not,' Jonah told her quietly. 'Or if it was then it would have had to be an accident caused by quite monumental negligence.'

'Then I was wondering if it could have been Olive's own decision. She put a brave face on it, but she did suffer agonies with her arthritis. And she'd not long been diagnosed with macular degeneration. I know about that because she talked to me about it. She was very worried about losing her sight. I think she could well have wanted to go before it got so bad that she was dependent on other people.'

'There are question marks over whether she would have had the dexterity to inject herself with the insulin,' Sandra commented. 'And we also don't know how she could have got enough of it to give herself an overdose.'

'Getting the stuff wouldn't have been a problem,' Laura said scathingly. 'I've known that drug cupboard door to be left hanging wide open any number of times. She'd only have needed to bide her time and watch out for when all the staff were busy and she could easily have helped herself. But I was thinking more that she might have asked Dr Bhaskar to help her.'

'Why d'you say that?' Jonah asked eagerly.

'Mum was sometimes in a lot of pain. Dr Bhaskar was very good. He prescribed all sorts of different tablets for it and he arranged physiotherapy for her and got her a special chair that was more comfortable for her back. But she still worried that it might get so as the painkillers didn't work anymore. She told him that she'd had a good innings and wouldn't want to just go on and on, if she was in constant pain. He promised her that he wouldn't allow that to happen. I wondered if Olive might have said the same sort of thing to him too.'

'Are you suggesting that he was responsible for your mother's death too?' Sandra asked.

'No, no. There was no need. I'm quite sure she just passed away naturally. She was ninety-eight and she'd had chronic heart failure for years. But Olive?' Laura sighed. 'I'm not saying he did it; and if he did do it, I'm sure it was only because she wanted it; but if you're sure that it couldn't have been an accident or natural causes then ... Well, that just seems less impossible than the idea of that lovely Jonathan Bates doing her in for her money.'

11. HOME SWEET HOME
Be it ever so humble, there's no place like home.
John Howard Payne: "Home, sweet home."

'Mr Porter? Welcome to *Park View*!' The wide glass doors slid open to allow Jonah's wheelchair to enter the Home. 'My name's Ian. I'm one of the Care Assistants. I'll show you to your room and help you to get settled in.'

He ushered them through the open-plan lounge, where a dozen or so armchairs stood in a wide arc facing a large television screen, and headed for a corridor at the other side. There were no residents in evidence here; probably it was too early in the morning for them to be wanting to socialise, or perhaps they were outside, taking advantage of the fine weather to sit in the garden and enjoy the sunshine.

'It's a nice bright room,' Ian told them, 'especially round about mid-day. And these patio doors lead straight out on to the garden. You're lucky. The ground-floor rooms are very popular. We don't often have any available, but sadly, a resident passed away only a little while ago, which leaves this one free at the moment. The bathroom is fully accessible,' he continued, going over to a door on the other side of the room and opening it to show them a spacious room containing both a bath and a shower cubicle.

'Do you have a hoist?' Lucy asked sharply, 'for using the bath?'

'No, I'm afraid we don't. Not in this room.' Ian sounded apologetic. 'We've arranged to hire a mobile one. It should be here this afternoon, I think.'

'That's fine,' Jonah assured him. 'In any case, as a backup, I've got a manual wheelchair that can go in the shower, so long as you don't mind drying it off thoroughly afterwards. The toilet could be more difficult. You'll need two people for my bowel-management routine, I'm afraid.'

'Shouldn't be a problem,' Ian assured him. 'We'll just need details of exactly what your normal routine is. Now to get back to your room facilities: there's an intercom to enable you to speak to a member of staff if you need help,' he resumed, indicating a microphone attached to the wall over the bed. 'Since you won't be able to press the button to switch it on, we'll see that whoever puts you to bed leaves it connected during the night. Then, if you need anything, all you have to do is to call out and they'll hear you in the office.'

'What about during the day?' Lucy wanted to know. 'At home the doors are all voice-activated. 'How's Jonah going to get out if he goes to his room and closes the door behind him?'

'That's something we'll have to discuss with you, Mr Porter,' Ian answered. 'We could put the intercom on whenever you're in here or you could just keep the door open. I've got a checklist of questions about your specific care needs that I'll go through with you later,' he went on. 'But that can wait until after your family have left. Shall I leave you to get unpacked now or would you prefer me to show you all round first? Just to reassure you that he's going to be in good hands,' he added, turning to look at Bernie and Lucy, who were prowling round the room checking the facilities.

'I'm sure that everything will be fine,' Bernie assured

him. 'We chose this place because my aunt speaks so highly of it. And it means that we'll be able to pop in to see Jonah when we visit her.'

'Of course! I knew I'd seen you before. You're Dot Fazakerley's niece, aren't you?' Ian's face broke into a wide smile. 'She's always talking about you. You're an Oxford professor aren't you? She's very proud of your achievements.'

'Well, I never rose as far as professor,' Bernie laughed, 'and I've retired from the university now, but that's roughly right. I owe a lot to Aunty Dot. She was like a second mother to me when I was growing up. But I always thought I was a bit of a disappointment to her. She never let on she thought I was a success!'

'I suppose you must get used to residents dying,' Jonah said innocently, 'with most of them being elderly.'

'Yes, I suppose we do, in a way,' Ian answered cautiously, 'but it's still always a bit of a shock when it actually happens.'

'The person who had this room before me – had they been ill long?'

'Not really. I mean she had diabetes and arthritis, but lots of older people do.'

'Oh! So it was unexpected then, was it?'

'Well, sort of. I mean, when someone's in their eighties it can never be completely unexpected, can it?'

'No, I suppose not,' Jonah agreed, deciding not to press the subject any further. Ian was clearly intent on keeping to a party line that did not admit the possibility that any resident could have died an unnatural death. Was Olive really over eighty? Dot had said that she was the youngest resident in the Home, but then Dot was ninety-seven, so perhaps eighty did seem young to her.

'Well, anyway, if you've been to visit before, you'll have a good idea what the place is like; so if you haven't got any more questions, I'll leave you to settle in. Like I said, you can press the buzzer on the intercom if you need me, or you can come to the office and there'll be someone there to help you.'

'I don't need the intercom when I'm in my chair,' Jonah told him. 'It's got a mobile phone connection built into it. I can ring the office any time I like. Don't you worry! I can look after myself alright.'

'Yes,' agreed Bernie. 'Your main problem is going to be keeping tabs on him and not letting him get himself into trouble. He has this funny idea that this chair of his makes him invincible!'

Ian left. For a few moments, they stood there looking at one another. Then Bernie lifted the trolley case containing Jonah's clothes and equipment on to the bed and unzipped the lid. Lucy helped her to unpack, stowing everything away in the fitted wardrobes that lined the wall of the room on either side of the bed.

Peter wandered over to the patio doors and looked out. Then he tried the handle and slid them apart. Jonah watched as the doors glided silently open. Peter closed them again and seemed to be peering down at something. He flicked the catch up and down a few times, before opening the doors again and stepping out through them into the garden and examining the lock from the outside.

'What's up?' asked Jonah, intrigued by this performance.

'It's this door. The catch is broken. The lock doesn't work. I wonder how long it's been like that.'

'You mean: someone could have got in from outside and killed Olive during the night?' Lucy asked excitedly, looking up from the drawer where she was busily stowing Jonah's supply of clean socks and underpants.

'That's exactly what I mean,' Peter agreed. 'There's a keyhole on the outside and a latch on the inside. Olive could have put the latch down, thinking that she was locking the door, but it doesn't engage properly, so anyone could just pull the door open. They wouldn't need to have the key.'

'That certainly opens up the field,' Jonah mused. 'It means that any of the staff could have done it, not just the ones who were on duty that evening and overnight. All they would have had to do was to avoid the CCTV camera when they were sneaking in round the back.'

'Or it could have been one of the other ground-floor residents,' Bernie suggested, 'going out of their own patio doors and in through these.'

'Or *any* of the residents, in fact,' Jonah agreed,' because they could have gone out of the doors from the lounge or out of the fire door at the end of the corridor.'

'Except they'd have been more likely to have been noticed wandering round the house at night,' Peter pointed out. 'Anyone coming down from upstairs would have had to walk right past the office where the night-nurse was on duty.'

'It could even have been a complete outsider,' Jonah continued. 'One of the Carters, for example. They could easily have noticed that the catch was broken, and taken advantage of it to get into their mother's room during the night.'

'But how would they have got round the back?' Peter asked sceptically.

'They could have got hold of a key, or-'

'The side gate doesn't have a key,' Lucy cut in eagerly. 'I looked, while we were waiting to be let in just now. It's got one of those combination locks where you have to press the right numbers.'

'There you are then!' Jonah said triumphantly. 'I bet the residents all know the combination and Olive Carter wouldn't have thought twice about giving it to her sons.'

'I wouldn't have much difficulty climbing over that gate, anyhow,' Bernie added, 'especially if I had someone to give me a leg up.'

They were silent for a minute or two, contemplating this new theory.

'But aren't we forgetting something?' Peter said at last.

'What about the way the syringe seems to have appeared during the course of the morning – *after* Olive was already dead? We had said that it was put there to implicate Jonathan or … or whichever nurse it was who was on duty overnight.'

'It was Rebecca Anderson,' Jonah told him. 'And she's not a nurse; she's a Care Assistant. But go on.'

'If whoever killed Olive did it by sneaking in during the night, then they could have just left the syringe behind to be found in the morning, couldn't they? So why wasn't it there when the doctor went in?'

'Perhaps it was and he didn't notice it,' Lucy suggested.

'Hardly likely,' Peter insisted. 'It was his job to make an initial assessment of the cause of death. It should have been routine for him to look around for any signs that she had taken any medication.'

'I don't know,' Bernie mused as she wandered across to the bathroom with Jonah's toothbrush and toothpaste. 'Didn't they say that Desmond Carter arrived not long after the doctor? If he was pestering him, wanting to know what could have happened to his mother, the doctor could easily have got distracted.'

'Or perhaps,' Jonah said dramatically, thinking rapidly, 'the importance of the broken patio door lock is that it makes it easier for someone to get in during the Wednesday morning to plant the syringe in Olive's room. Suppose, for example, that John Carter gave Olive the insulin when he called to see her just before dinner. The broken lock would have given him an easy way in to plant the syringe without anyone noticing.'

'Only if the room was left empty during that time,' Peter pointed out. 'Didn't one of the staff stay in there while they waited for the doctor to come?'

'Yes, but I'm talking about after that, between the doctor leaving and PC Thomas arriving. Once the doctor had seen the body, there wouldn't have been any reason to hang around in the room.'

'I think we're done here,' Bernie declared, closing the case and stowing it inside one of the wardrobes. 'I'm going to pop up and call in on Aunty Dot. I can't go without seeing her. And then we'd better leave you to it.'

'Ask her to come down to the lounge. I'd like to have a chat with her, and she can introduce me to all my new neighbours.'

Dot was delighted to be invited to meet with Jonah and tremendously excited at the prospect of being part of an undercover police operation. She insisted on coming down to the lounge at once and hastily shooed Bernie and the others away, once she and Jonah were settled in a convenient position where they could observe anyone entering the building either through the glass doors from the garden or via the main entrance. They also had a clear view of the entrance hall, through which anyone visiting the office or moving between the old and new parts of the Home would have to pass.

'I can introduce you to everyone,' Dot told Jonah, once they were alone together. 'They serve morning coffee in here at eleven, but most of the residents tend to stay in their rooms until lunch time. Some of them may come down though, especially if they've heard that we've got a newcomer. They'll all want to size you up.'

'I suppose it's too much to hope that you won't have told them what my job is?'

'I didn't need to tell them,' Dot chuckled. 'Don't forget: you're famous! As soon as they heard your name, one or two of them worked out who you were, and I could hardly deny it, could I? It's caused quite a stir, having a celebrity staying with us!'

'You'd better tell me a bit about them all before they come for their coffee, so that I'm not at a disadvantage. Let's start with my neighbours. One of the rooms opposite me belongs to Charlotte Goodman. What's she like?'

'Loopy Lottie? Her mind's going a bit, poor old girl. She gets confused sometimes. If you leave your door open, she'll probably wander in thinking it's her own room. You won't get any useful information out of her. She can remember things from years back, but not what happened yesterday. If you ask her about how Olive died, she'll most likely get her muddled up with one of her patients from when she was a District Nurse back in the fifties.'

'She was a nurse? So she'd know about drawing up insulin into a syringe from a vial and injecting it into someone?'

'Oh yes! As I said, she hasn't forgotten anything she knew forty years ago. It's what she had for breakfast today that she wouldn't have a clue about.'

'And you said that she wanders about? So she's reasonably fit physically?'

'Better than most of us,' Dot agreed, with a smile, looking down at the walking frame that stood next to her chair.

'And the other room near to mine is occupied by a Mr Charles Melling, but I gather it belonged to Edna Lomax before that?'

'That's right. Charles is a bit stand-offish. I don't really know him. He hasn't been here long.'

'What about the other two ground-floor rooms? Who have we got in them?'

'Frances Ray and Eric Martin. I must introduce you to Frannie. If anyone can tell you what's been going on here, it'll be her. You can't so much as sneeze without her knowing about it. I should think she'll be here soon. She doesn't spend much time in her room; she'd rather be out gossiping and poking her nose into everyone's business.'

'She sounds like a very useful person for me to get to know,' Jonah agreed straight-faced. 'And Eric Martin?'

'He's another great talker. He used to be a traveling salesman. I'm not sure what he sold, but I'd guess it was housewares or lingerie or something like that. He fancies himself with the ladies. He's always full of smiles and compliments. I can't stick him myself, but – and here he is!' Dot broke off suddenly at the sight of a man in a manual wheelchair emerging from the dining room into the entrance hall. 'Come over here, Eric! Let me introduce you to my niece's friend, Jonah Porter. He's going to be staying with us until the weekend.'

'Ah yes! The famous policeman!' Eric called out jovially, propelling his chair across the carpet with his hands, to join them. 'Not investigating us, I hope?'

'Not unless you have any crimes you'd like to confess to me,' Jonah replied, trying to match Eric's bantering style. 'Not been sneaking double-helpings of pudding or pinching the young nurses' bottoms, I trust!'

'No, more's the pity! Being in this chair rather cramps my style.' Eric glanced down at his lower limbs with an exaggerated grimace. The left leg was a mere stump, amputated at the knee with its trouser-leg folded over beneath it. His right foot was also missing leaving a sock-encased stump dangling a little above the footrest of his chair. 'Diabetes,' he informed Jonah. 'I've had it all my life, but it only caused me any real trouble after I retired. I let myself go a bit, to be honest. Couldn't keep to a proper routine. Ate what I fancied whenever I felt like it – comfort eating they call it. Can't afford to do that with diabetes. But mustn't grumble,' he added cheerily. 'It's better now I'm in here. The nurses see to it that I test my blood sugar and take my insulin jabs like a good boy. And at least I got myself back on track before it affected my eyes, so I can still appreciate a pretty woman when I see one – and some of the younger nurses are very pretty. Take little Scarlet Jones, for instance; she's welcome to give me a bed bath any time she likes!'

More of the inmates started arriving in the lounge. Seeing Jonah in conversation with Eric, they nodded and smiled towards him and then went to sit down in other parts of the room. Jonah gathered that Eric was not as popular with the women as he liked to think.

A rattling of china heralded the arrival of a trolley laden

with two large insulated jugs (a tall one labelled *coffee* and a squat one bearing the inscription *tea*), a milk jug and piles of cups and saucers. A young woman wearing a brightly-coloured tabard over a blue uniform dress, pushed it into the centre of the room and started setting out the cups ready to serve drinks to the residents.

A tall woman wearing a floral-patterned dress wandered in from the corridor that led to Jonah's room and stood for a few moments staring round blankly, as if she were not sure where she was or why she had come there. Then she went over to the trolley and demanded tea, which the woman in the tabard poured for her.

'What's *he* doing here?' the tall woman asked in a loud voice, pointing towards Jonah.

'That's a new resident, Lottie,' the small woman said in a low voice. 'At least, he's visiting. He's going to be here for a week. He's a friend of Miss Fazakerley.'

'Miss Fazakerley? Who's she?'

'Oh Lottie! You're having me on! You know Miss Fazakerley. Look! Over there! She's been here longer than you have. Now, why don't you just sit down nice and quiet and I'll bring you your tea?'

Taking Lottie by the arm, she guided her to a chair and settled her there, carefully placing a cushion behind her back. Lottie muttered something about knowing that the woman in the corner had got to the lounge before her, but what had that to do with who she was?

'That's Oonagh Conlon,' Dot whispered to Jonah, indicating the woman who had brought in the refreshments. 'She cleans the rooms and makes the tea. She's not very bright – she's got what they call *Learning Disabilities* these days – but she's good-hearted and she handles poor Lottie very well.'

Oonagh returned to Lottie with a cup of tea in one hand and a plate of biscuits in the other.

'Here you are, love! I'll put the cup down here for you. Now, would you like one of these biscuits?'

It was not long before all the residents had cups of tea or coffee in front of them. When she came to Jonah, Oonagh became somewhat flustered at his request that she got out his own plastic cup from the bag at the back of his chair instead of giving him the china cup that she had ready for him. Then she had some difficulty arranging the straw conveniently for him to drink.

'I'm so sorry,' she apologised. 'I've never done this before. Is it OK now?'

'Yes. It's absolutely fine,' Jonah assured her. 'Don't worry about it. You can't expect to know what to do until I tell you.'

Oonagh smiled her gratitude. Jonah watched her anxious expression thoughtfully, wondering if some of the other residents were more demanding and less patient than he had been. Olive Carter, for example: might some of the enormities on her famous list be more to do with unreasonable expectations from the residents than incompetence or negligence on the part of the staff?

'It's good to have another man in the Home.' Eric interrupted his thoughts. 'There are far too many chattering women in this place. We could do with evening up the sexes a bit. Mind you, we've already made a start. Until a few weeks ago, it was just me and my harem of old biddies, but now we've got you and across the way from your room, there's Charles. Have you met him yet?'

'No. I don't know anyone – well, except Dot here, of course.'

'I think Charles is having difficulty settling in,' Eric confided. 'He doesn't come to any of the socials He just stays in his room most of the time. But I expect that'll all change when he gets used to things a bit more. I've got a few plans up my sleeve. We'll soon bring him out of himself! Now,' he continued, putting down his empty teacup and starting to turn his chair to face the open patio doors, 'let's leave all these lovely ladies to their gossip and I'll take you on a tour of the estate. Have you seen the gardens yet?'

'No, I haven't. I only arrived a few minutes ago. That's very kind of you – if you're sure I won't be taking up too much of your time.'

'It will be my pleasure. We men ought to stick together. And, as for taking up my time? Time is the one thing we've all got too much of in here!'

They made their way out through the glass doors and into the sunny garden. Jonah found himself on a wide paved area decorated with tubs of busy-lizzies and geraniums. There was also a rustic table and three benches, so that the residents could sit out in the sunshine admiring the flowers. Glancing to the right, he realised that this was the same patio as Peter had stepped out on to from his own room when he had been checking the door lock. Beyond the paving, there was a large lawned area, surrounded on three sides by a paved path, which separated it from wide beds containing a mixture of shrubs and herbaceous perennials.

Eric led the way, turning to the right and heading past Jonah's room towards the back of the house.

'That path goes right round to the front gate,' Eric told him confidentially, pointing at how the paving continued round the back of the building. 'It's handy if you want to slip out to the pub without that busy-body manager seeing you from her office. Now let me show you the rest of the garden. It's all been left to grow wild back here. They only really bother with the bit outside the lounge: the bit that all the visitors see. I keep telling them they ought to-' He broke off in surprise at the sight of two figures in overalls busily attacking the brambles and briars with secateurs and piling the cuttings into an already nearly full wheelbarrow. 'What have we here? Has Fiona finally agreed to spend some money on getting the garden in order?'

'Morning!' the taller of the two gardeners greeted them. 'It's a lovely day, isn't it? Better make the most of it; they say it's going to rain this afternoon.'

'I hope we're not in your way,' his companion added. 'I'll move the barrow if you want to get past.'

Jonah recognised the pair as Detective Constables Oliver Ransom and Bryony Foster, the officers who had been tasked with acting as his minders during his stay in the Home. Fiona Radcliffe had evidently used DI Latham's request that she find some suitable excuse for their presence to get some much-needed work done free of charge.

'A lady gardener!' Eric exclaimed in delight. 'I'm very pleased to meet you. 'You must call in and see us sometime – both of you, I mean,' he added hastily, seeing Bryony's expression change from affability to suspicion. 'How about a drink together this evening, out on the patio? I'm sure you could do with one after working out here in the sun all day.'

'Thank you,' Oliver answered. 'We'll look forward to it.'

Eric continued on his way, stopping eventually at the far end of the garden, beneath an overgrown pergola. Jonah could see a much-neglected climbing rose and the straggly remains of a clematis, but these were both obscured by a mass of bindweed. They sat together in the shade, watching the butterflies flitting from flower to flower on the many buddleia bushes springing up between the paving stones, and a group of starlings squabbling over the birdbath, which must once have been the central feature of this part of the garden.

'We won't be disturbed here,' Eric told Jonah. 'None of the old biddies ever make it this far. It's a good place for a bit of private … *conversation* with the nurses, if you get my meaning.'

'What are the staff here like?' Jonah asked casually. 'Are there any I should be steering clear of? I've had one or two bad experiences in other places.'

'Oh these are all OK,' Eric assured him. 'At least, they mean well. One or two of them are a bit careless and don't always have their minds on the job. The other day, for instance, I rang my bell for someone to help me to the lavvy. It was out of hours, so there wasn't anyone in the office, but Julia was supposed to have the bleep with her. I waited, but nobody came, so I decided to try to manage by myself. Well, to cut a long story short, I ended up falling over and giving my shoulder a nasty knock on the washbasin.'

'Did you complain to the management?'

'No. There was no real harm done and I didn't want to get her into trouble. She apologised and explained that she'd been trying to help Betty Hunter to find her glasses. Betty's always wanting them to do something for her, and her daughter is a right so-and-so: always complaining that something isn't right. So I expect Julia didn't like to leave her in case she claimed she was being neglected.'

'I don't think I've met Betty,' Jonah said innocently.

'No. You won't have. She's gone to stay with her daughter until this business with Olive Carter is sorted. We had a right to-do the other day, I can tell you! When Betty's Helen came and took her away, she gave poor Fiona a right rollicking. They were in the office with the door closed, but you could hear the shouting from the lounge. Anyway, to cut a long story short, Helen packed her mother off in the car and took her away, saying she wasn't coming back until the murderer was under lock and key.'

'Is she the only resident who's left because of it?'

'Yes. And I don't suppose it'll be long before Helen gets fed up with having her mother at home and brings her back – unless they decide to find another Home for her. I can't see Helen being prepared to interrupt her busy social life to look after her mother for long.'

'I heard they've suspended one of the nurses. Do you think he did it?'

'I doubt it,' Eric shrugged.

'But, why would they suspend him if they didn't think

he did?' Jonah persisted.

'Fiona Radcliffe just wants to be seen to be doing something. It doesn't matter what, just so long as it doesn't look as if she isn't bothered.'

'If it wasn't him, who else could it have been?'

'If you ask me, I'd say it's far more likely to be Olive's own family. They're the ones who benefit. Oh! I know poor Jonathan was supposed to have been left a few pounds, but that's peanuts compared with the value of that house of hers in Mossley Hill. There's no way it would have been worth the risk for him to bump her off. And the same goes for the rest of the staff. No. you mark my words, it's one of her sons – or, more likely still, that daughter-in-law of hers. She's a nasty piece of work, if ever there was one.'

'Oh?'

'I've seen her round here any number of times, always complaining, always with a sour look on her face as if there was a nasty smell under her nose.'

'What about the residents? Could it have been one of them? Someone that Olive had fallen out with, perhaps?'

'What? One of the old dears? Don't make me laugh! They're all far too scatty to work out how to murder someone – and get away with it too! No. Take it from me, it's the Carter family you need to watch. They're the ones who pointed the finger at Jonathan, but if you think about it, he had much more to gain from keeping her alive. All the old dears were sweet on him and kept giving him presents. He knew which side his bread was buttered alright.'

'Coo-ee!' Jonah was prevented from asking any more questions by the approach of Julia, who had come looking for them to call them in for lunch. 'Oh there you are! Fancy hiding yourselves all down here,' she scolded. 'If it hadn't been for those two new gardeners pointing me in the right direction I might never have found you. Come along now. Scarlet's waiting for you with your injection all ready.'

'I have to have insulin before each meal,' Eric explained to Jonah, as they made their way back through the overgrown garden. 'I can perfectly well do it myself, but they have a rule that all medicines have to be kept locked away in the office. It's a nuisance, but I suppose they can't risk having them getting into the wrong hands or one of us taking an overdose or something. And besides, if I had my own supply of insulin in my room, *I* might have been accused of killing poor Olive!'

'Now stop that, Mr Martin,' Julia said quickly. 'Let's not have any talk of overdoses and killing people. You'll be worrying our guest. Come along and have your lunch.'

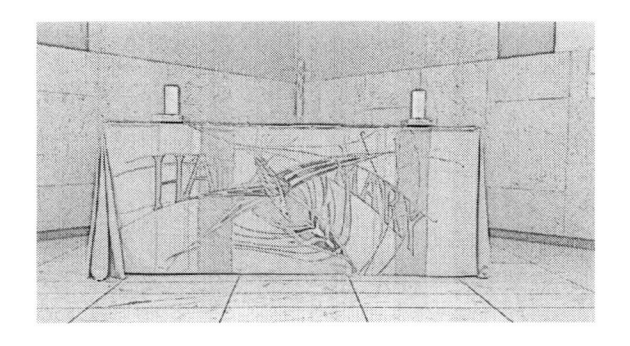

12. BREAKING BREAD
Be known to us in breaking bread
James Montgomery

'I've got your lunch all ready over here,' Julia told Jonah as they entered the dining room, gesturing with her arm towards a corner of the room that was hidden from view behind a tall woven bamboo screen. 'And Oonagh's put yours in your usual place,' she added to Eric, waving her other hand towards a table near the window.

'Can't you bring Jonah's food over to my table?' Eric asked. 'Then we can carry on talking.'

'Sorry. I've got it all set up now. It'll go cold if we start moving things about. Don't you worry! You've got all week to have your little chat.'

Seeing that she was not to be persuaded, Eric propelled his wheelchair in the direction of the window table. Julia watched to see that he had safely negotiated a path between the other tables, round which the residents of the Home were now seated. Then she turned and led the way behind the screen.

'This'll save you having everyone gawking at you being fed,' she said to Jonah in a low voice, once they were safely out of sight of the rest of the dining room. 'I'm sure you won't want them all staring at you and whispering about you – especially seeing as some of them can't seem to tell the difference between a whisper and a bellow!'

'Thanks.' Jonah gave her one of his lopsided smiles to indicate that he appreciated her thoughtfulness.

'Your daughter left us a long list of instructions,' Julia went on, returning the smile. 'I don't think she trusts us to know how to look after you properly.'

'Lucy? She's not my daughter. She's ... She and her mother are just friends of mine.'

'I'm sorry. She talked as if you all lived together and I just assumed ... So Miss Fazakerley's niece isn't your wife?'

'No. She's married to the tall, self-effacing chap with the fading red hair, whom you probably didn't even notice following along behind.'

'Oh.' Julia looked momentarily nonplussed. 'Well, let's get started, shall we?'

She tied a large napkin around Jonah's neck to prevent any spilled food from soiling his shirt, before starting on the task of cutting up his food and feeding it to him.

'I suppose relatives are often anxious that you won't know how to look after them,' Jonah suggested, in between mouthfuls. 'It must be hard for them, if they've been caring for someone for a long time, to trust someone else to get it right.'

'Yes. I suppose it must be,' Julia agreed non-committally.

'And, of course, if anything goes wrong, there must be a temptation for them to blame the staff. This business with Olive Carter, for example: I suppose it's only natural that the family should think it must be something to do with the nurse who gave her insulin injection to her that evening.'

'It may be natural, but that doesn't mean there's anything in it,' Julia said firmly. 'You shouldn't believe everything people tell you. I'm sure it'll be all sorted out soon and they'll find that it was all just an unfortunate accident.'

'I imagine you must get quite a lot of those – accidents, I mean – with all the residents being old and infirm in one way or another.'

'Well, I wouldn't want you to think that we get people dying every five minutes; but yes, we do get our fair share of little accidents,' Julia admitted as she carefully forked up mashed potato and peas and inserted them into Jonah's mouth. 'Very often it's the residents bringing it on themselves. They forget that they're not as young as they were and they try to do things for themselves instead of asking for help. We do our best, but we can't be everywhere at once. Our injury statistics are well below the national average,' she added defensively.'

'I know they are,' Jonah concurred. 'We checked the reports from the CQC before booking me in here. Bernie insisted on it, even though she knew her aunt was very satisfied with the Home. That's what makes this unexplained death so very strange, doesn't it?'

'I wouldn't know about that. I just know that none of the staff would ever dream of doing anything that might harm one of the residents.'

'No. Of course not. Miss Fazakerley told us that you're all very good indeed. She also said that one of the other residents who died recently was so grateful that she put it in her will that each member of staff should get a small gift from her room when she died. I expect that happens a lot – especially when people have been living here for a long time.'

'I wouldn't know about that,' Julia said perfunctorily. 'I haven't been here all that long, so there have only been two deaths that I know of.'

'And I suppose some people like to give gifts before they die, instead of putting it in their will,' Jonah mused, as if to himself. 'I think that's what I'd do. I'd rather be able to see people enjoying what I'd given them.'

'Yes. I suppose that's one way of looking at it. Now, are you ready to move on to your dessert?'

'Yes. Thanks.' For a few minutes, Jonah concentrated on eating. Then he cleared his throat and tried another avenue of enquiry. 'Tell me about yourself. Do you have family still living at home with you?'

'No. Our two boys are both grown up and moved out. Darren – he's the older one – followed his dad into the merchant navy, and Jake has got a job on the assembly line at Halewood.'

'Really? I've got two boys myself, and four grandchildren. I've got some photos here. Would you like to see them?'

Jonah pressed a button on the arm of his chair and the computer screen lit up. He expertly navigated his way to a page of photographs from which he selected a picture of three children looking rather self-consciously toward the camera.

'These are my son Reuben's three,' he told Julia. 'George is the oldest. He'll be nine in October. Then Carolyn is coming up to seven and Little Andrew is four. He'll be starting school next month. I can hardly believe it. It seems only yesterday that they brought him down to see us two weeks after he was born.'

'They all look like very bright kids,' Julia said politely, continuing to ply Jonah with spoonfuls of raspberry cheesecake.

'And this is my other son's little girl,' Jonah went on, flipping to a new picture. 'She's just six months. We had a bit of a scare back in June when she contracted meningitis, but she's fine now.'

'She looks lovely,' Julia said. 'Such beautiful dark brown eyes and pretty black curls!'

'I don't see as much of any of them as I'd like,' Jonah continued. 'But I suppose you must be used to that, with your husband and son being sailors?'

'Yes. I'm used to my own company, I have to admit,'

Julia laughed, a little sadly Jonah thought. 'But it gives us an excuse for a big celebration every time Jack's boat comes in, so it has its compensations, I suppose.'

'That's your husband? Is he at sea at the moment?'

'That's right. He's been gone nine weeks now, but that means only another three and he'll be back with a couple of weeks' leave due and I expect I'll take a few days off and we'll have a fine old time. You just learn to fit things around when he's at home and when he's away. Right! Now, would you like me to take you out to have your coffee with the others, or would you rather stay behind here?'

'Oh I think I ought to socialise, don't you? I don't want people thinking I'm standoffish.'

Emerging from behind the screen, Jonah looked round the dining room. Most of the tables were now empty. Evidently some residents had either declined coffee or had already finished theirs and returned to their rooms. He saw Eric sitting with Dot and another woman whom he did not recognise. Eric looked up and waved towards him, but Jonah pretended not to have noticed. He estimated that he had exhausted Eric as a source of information. It would be better to use coffee in the dining room as an opportunity to speak to someone else.

The only other resident still present was a thin, angular woman with permed white hair, who sat, very straight-backed, by the table closest to the door from the older part of the house, with a cup of coffee in front of her. She nodded briefly when Jonah went over and asked if he could join her. In response to his polite enquiry, she confided that her name was Joan Pickles and that she had been living in the Home for six years.

'You must have got to know all the staff pretty well in that time,' Jonah remarked. 'How d'you find them? They seem pretty good to me so far – compared with one or two that I've come across in my time.'

'I'm sure they mean well,' Joan sniffed a little

contemptuously, 'but most of them wouldn't last long if I were in charge.'

'Oh? Why's that?'

'Very slipshod. But that's what you get when you have weak leadership. I've seen it any number of times in school. I taught for forty-three years, ten of them as headmistress. If you don't have good, firm leadership at the top, standards always suffer.'

'So you don't think Fiona Radcliffe is up to the job?' Jonah asked innocently. 'She seems very nice to me.'

'Niceness isn't what you need in a manager,' Joan told him decidedly. 'You need to be firm, fair and consistent. Fiona is none of those. The result is that the other staff run rings round her and she's always fire-fighting and never strategic.'

Julia brought him his coffee, carefully adjusting the straw so that he could reach it easily. After she had left, Jonah resumed his conversation with Joan.

'*She* seems very kind and helpful,' he observed.

'On the odd occasion when she happens to have her mind on her job,' Joan conceded scathingly, 'which isn't often. You'd think by her age, she'd have learned a bit of sense, but she can be as scatty as any of my fourth-formers used to be. I had to pull her up sharp the other day when she brought me my blood-pressure tablets. She'd got me mixed up with one of the other residents and she was about to give me all sorts of stuff that had been prescribed for them, not me! It's a good thing I was on the ball, or it could have been me who was found dead in her bed, instead of Olive Carter!'

'Good gracious! Did you report it to the manager?'

'No. No point. I told you: Fiona's so ineffective she wouldn't have done anything, or else she'd have got into one of her autocratic moods and alienated the whole lot of them by imposing a string of new rules and spying on them to check they were doing their jobs properly. She can never get the balance right between respecting their professional judgement and having proper safeguards in place to see that standards are maintained.'

'Someone told me that Olive was keeping a log of incidents like that. They thought she was planning to hand it over to the CQC at their next visit.'

'I wouldn't be at all surprised. Olive was a bit of a busybody, if the truth be known. She was always interfering in things that weren't any of her business. She fancied herself standing up for people who don't have the courage to complain themselves, and she didn't have the sense to realise that often they just wanted a quiet life and to be left alone.'

'Do you think anyone resented her interference enough to have wanted to get rid of her?'

'Given her that overdose of insulin, you mean? I shouldn't think so. If you want my opinion, it was a mistake, not deliberate. As I was telling you, they're all very careless and sloppy. Practically any of the staff could have given it to her, thinking they were doing the right thing. Mind you, Jonathan Bates is a lot better than most of them. I'm surprised at him getting the dose wrong, but … as I said, if you haven't got good leadership at the top, everyone lets their standards slip.'

'So you think he's being made a scapegoat?'

'Yes, if you like to call it that.' Joan nodded. 'Fiona's under pressure to do something and he was the easiest target. Personally, I'd say it was more likely to have been one of the others: Julia maybe or Becky Anderson. She never has her mind on the job – always yacking on about her kids instead of thinking about what she's doing.'

'I don't think I've met her yet.'

'No. you won't have. She generally works nights – so she can look after the kids during the day. That's probably why she's so dozy: lack of sleep. That used to be a big problem when I was in school. I always used to say that if parents made sure their children got eight hours sleep every night they would learn far more.'

'I'm sure you're right,' Jonah agreed, hypocritically in view of his own propensity to work at all hours during an interesting case. 'Establish a routine and stick to it.'

'Exactly! And that's what young people nowadays don't seem able to do. Mind you,' Joan continued, pleased to have found a sympathetic audience for her grumbling, 'some of the older ones aren't much better. Take Hector Bayliss, the caretaker, for instance. They took him on because he's a retired woodwork teacher and told them he could do odd-jobs around the Home. I suppose Fiona thought it would save money not having to get people in to do repairs, but the time it takes! I reported a fault on the shower in my bathroom over three weeks ago and he still hasn't fixed it.'

'That's bad,' Jonah agreed. 'I did wonder about how you get repairs done here, because there's a problem with the lock on my patio doors and I wasn't sure who I ought to report it to.'

'You mean they still haven't got that sorted? You *are* in Olive's old room – number five?' Jonah nodded and Joan reacted with an exasperated sigh. 'She reported that fault three weeks before she died. So you see what I mean about having to wait for repairs to be done?'

'I do indeed. It doesn't sound as if it's worth me bothering to ask for it to be fixed, seeing as I'm only here for a week.'

'The trouble is: Hector only really bothers with the jobs that interest him. He spent weeks last year making a set of wooden chairs and tables for the garden. You've probably seen them. I have to admit they are very comfortable and attractive, but they could easily have bought some just as good. At the end of the day, it all comes back to weak management. Fiona should have seen to it that Hector got the jobs that really mattered done, instead of messing about with fripperies.'

'I suppose it may be fripperies that look good to potential residents,' Jonah suggested. 'I could imagine people coming round and seeing those chairs out among the tubs of flowers and thinking: *Mum would enjoy sitting out there.*'

'Yes. You're right. There *is* far too much concentrating on appearances these days,' Joan agreed, delighted to discover a kindred spirit who shared so many of her own prejudices. 'I always used to say, when people criticised our school buildings, that it was quality of teaching and firm discipline that mattered, not the state of the paintwork.'

She paused to allow Oonagh to collect their empty coffee cups, before continuing with her lecture.

'That's the key to running any sort of organisation: quality staff and firm leadership.' She waited until Oonagh had disappeared through the door into the kitchen, before continuing. 'And quality staff means having a rigorous appointment system and *not* giving jobs to people just because they're friends or friends of friends.' She tilted her head towards the kitchen in a manner that suggested that her remark was more than simply a general statement.

Jonah looked at her with interest, confident that she had more to say. He did not have to wait long.

'Take Oonagh, for example. She's pleasant enough and very willing, but nobody could call her *bright*. The only reason she got a job here is that her mother is a friend of Fiona's. And she's supposed to be a cleaner, but as you've seen, she gets asked to do all sorts. She shouldn't be serving meals without a Food Hygiene certificate; and it's no good telling me she's capable of getting one. I've seen her struggling even to read the menu. She's practically illiterate.'

'I suppose it saves money having someone who's just grateful for a job,' Jonah suggested, 'as well as Fiona feeling she's helping her friend.'

'Oh, no doubt about that. You can't fault Oonagh's willingness. She gets landed with all the unpleasant jobs, and the hours that she works sometimes! I don't doubt she does a lot more than she's paid for.'

'How's she taking this business with Olive Carter? I would have thought she might find it rather upsetting.'

'She did get very upset when Fiona suspended Jonathan Bates. She's had a bit of a crush on him ever since she started here last year. Of course she's on a hiding to nothing there, but I don't think anyone has had the heart to tell her the truth.'

'Oh?'

'Has nobody told you? I suppose we're all so used to it now that no-one thinks anything of it anymore. A couple of years ago, he got married — to another man. It caused quite a stir at the time. People talked about hardly anything else for weeks. I remember one of Olive's boys threatening to move her somewhere else, because he didn't like the idea; and Eric, of course, made a lot of rather crude jokes at Jonathan's expense. But, at the end of the day, it doesn't affect his work, so everyone stopped bothering about it.'

'So his sexuality is common knowledge in the Home?'

'Oh yes! Everyone knows — apart from poor little Oonagh.'

'Could that be why the Carters pointed the finger at Jonathan when they heard that Olive had been given an overdose, d'you think?'

'It could be.' Joan shrugged. 'Or it could just be that he was the obvious person, seeing as he admitted to having given her insulin that night. As I said before, it seems to me that an accident due to carelessness is a much more likely explanation than anyone deliberately setting out to kill.'

13. TOO SOON WE RISE
Too soon we rise; the symbols disappear;
The feast, though not the love, is past and gone.
Horatius Bonar, "Here, O my Lord, I see thee face to face."

After lunch, Joan Pickles returned to her own room. Jonah, finding himself alone in the dining room, made his way back to the lounge. It was deserted, apart from a small, auburn-haired woman reading a magazine. She looked up and smiled as Jonah entered.

'Good afternoon! You must be Dot's niece's friend. I'm Frances – Frances Ray. She's told us *such* a lot about you. I'm *very* pleased to meet you. We get so *few* new people here.' She spoke quickly and rather breathlessly, as if she were hurrying to get as many words out as she could before he lost interest and went off. 'How are you liking it here? I suppose it must be *very* quiet compared with your life as a policeman. It *was* a policeman that she said you were, wasn't it?'

'Yes,' Jonah confirmed. 'I'm a detective with Thames Valley CID.'

'That must be *very* interesting. I do admire the *boys in blue*, but I suppose *you* must be plain clothes. How do you manage? Being in a wheelchair, I mean. It must make it *very* difficult, but I suppose there's probably a lot of deskwork involved in being a detective. Have you ever had a *really big* case – a murder or something like that? But I suppose you mainly get burglaries and vandalism and that sort of thing.'

'Yes, I have investigated quite a few murders,' Jonah answered when Frances paused for breath. 'And we've only recently solved a child-abduction case[4]. You may have heard about it – there was a national appeal for people to look out for the missing baby.'

'Oh yes!' Frances gushed. 'I remember *all* about that. Dot told us she knew the policeman who was in charge. She pointed you out when we were watching the news. She *said* she knew the baby's family too, but then she acted surprised when the parents were black and some other relative – was it the grandfather? I can't remember – was white. So I don't think she knew as much as she wanted us to think she did. She's like that, Dot is – likes to think she's in the know about things.'

'The baby's father is Dot's niece's stepson,' Jonah explained. 'Dot hasn't met him, but she does know his father, of course, because he's married to her niece. Peter's first wife was black, which is how he comes to have a black son and a white granddaughter.'

'It all sounds very complicated. I'm glad *my* family isn't all mixed up like that. It would be *so* confusing. My cousin Derek married a Chinese girl, but when you look at their kids, you wouldn't know the difference. Not that I've got anything against other races; it just makes it *so* confusing having them mixed up in one family like that. Do *you* have any family? But I suppose perhaps you couldn't, being …

---

[4] See *Sorrowful Mystery* © Judy Ford 2017, ISBN 978-1-911083-23-8 (paperback), 978-1-911083-25-2 (e-book), 978-1-911083-26-9 (Large Print)

well … the way you are.'

'I have two sons and four grandchildren,' Jonah told her, taking advantage of the gap in her flow of words as she trailed off in embarrassment. 'And I haven't always been paralysed. It was the result of a bullet wound eight years ago.'

'Oh yes! Dot did tell us about that. She showed us some news reports on that funny computer thing she has. We all thought you were *very* brave, going back to work in the police force after that. All except Margery, that is. She said it was ridiculous and they shouldn't use tax-payer's money to keep someone in a job that they couldn't possibly do anymore. But that's Margery all over: she always has to see the bad side of everything. Eric said how pleased he was that *all you girls* – he calls us that,' she tittered, 'he always calls us *you girls*. He's a *terrible* flirt. He said he was pleased to see us all falling for a man in a wheelchair, because it gave him hope for his own chances!'

'I don't think I've met Margery yet.'

'No. She didn't come to lunch. She's not well at the moment, so they took it up to her room. You haven't missed much. I'm the *last* person to say anything against another resident, but I'm afraid Margery isn't an easy person to get on with. She's always got to be right about *everything*! And that usually means telling everyone else that they're wrong. I remember her and Joan having a real set-to one evening over something. I can't think what it was now. But don't you worry,' she added, smiling reassuringly at Jonah. 'Mostly we rub along *very* well together. We have a *great* time! Let me show you some of the things that we do.'

She got up from her chair and crossed the room, walking slowly and holding on to the chairs to steady herself. She went over to a bookcase that stood against the wall beneath the television screen and leaned down to inspect the contents of the top shelf. She pulled out a large photograph album and returned slowly across the room to where Jonah was sitting.

'Here we are! This has got pictures of some of the things we've done over the past year.'

She opened the album and turned the pages slowly, giving a commentary on each picture as she did so. Jonah looked at the photographs with interest.

'This is the trip we went on to Blackpool to see the illuminations. Joan organised it all – hired a minibus to take us and everything. Look there's Dot, wearing a kiss-me-quick hat. She only bought that to annoy Margery. She brought it back with her and wore it around the Home for days afterwards. The ridiculous thing is that Margery's sight is so bad that she didn't realise what the writing on the hat said until Eric started making a big thing of chasing Dot and trying to kiss her. Margery didn't come on the trip. She said Blackpool was full of low-life and she couldn't see why we would want to go there; but it was only because it was Joan's idea. Margery always has to disagree with any of Joan's ideas.'

'It sounds as if Margery is someone I'd want to avoid,' Jonah commented when Frances eventually paused for breath. 'Or is it just Joan that she doesn't like?'

'It's anyone that she thinks is telling her what to do. Mind you, Joan's quite good at putting people's backs up without any help from Margery, if she thinks they're wrong about something. She doesn't mince her words, you might say.'

'Yes. I was speaking to her just now. She doesn't seem to think much of the management here.'

'Thinks she could do better herself,' Frances agreed. 'Now here's a happy photo – if only half of them weren't dead now. That's the trouble with this place – we're all just waiting to go, in a manner of speaking.'

She placed the album on Jonah's lap and pointed with a bony finger at a photograph of a group of four people sitting on a bench. Three smiling faces looked towards the camera, while the fourth, sitting slightly apart from the main group, appeared to be gazing rather wistfully at the merry trio.

'That's Jonathan Bates, in the middle there,' Frances went on. 'He's one of the nurses. He came with us even though it was his day off. And that's Edna, who died a few weeks back, and Olive, who used to have the room you're in now.'

'What about the other woman?' Jonah asked. 'The one at the end, next to Olive?'

'That's Kathleen. She and Olive were thick as thieves. She's been *ever* so cut up about this poisoning thing. She made a big fuss about going to the inquest, even though Fiona told her – and she was right about that, for once – that nothing was going to happen there. They just opened it and then, what's the word? The coroner said he was …'

'Adjourning the inquest pending completion of the police investigation?' Jonah suggested.

'That's right. And he released the body for the funeral, which was a big relief to the family by all accounts. He gave permission for a cremation, which is what they wanted, but ordered some tissue samples to be retained in case they need to do any more tests later. But let's not dwell on all that. Have a look at these pictures of the Christmas Party. Look at Eric! He rigged that up on his wheelchair so that he had a sprig of mistletoe hanging right over his head all the time; and then he chased all the ladies round the room demanding kisses. He's dreadful like that – a real flirt! And there's everyone in the dining room having Christmas dinner. They put all the tables together and we sat round like a big family – all except Betty who went home to her daughter's and Edna who was in bed with a virus. There are Olive and Kathleen again, sitting together the way they always did, and Jonathan's just pulling a cracker with Olive.'

'You certainly all seem to be having a good time,' Jonah commented, thinking to himself that Kathleen appeared less happy than the others around the table did. Would she have liked to be the one chosen to pull her friend's cracker, instead of the ever-popular young nurse? Or was she jealous of the attention that Jonathan was giving to Olive?'

'Do you mind if I clean in here?'

Jonah looked up at the sound of Oonagh's voice, speaking in apologetic tones.

'No, no, please, go ahead,' he said quickly. 'Would you like us to go outside, so we're not in your way?'

'No, you're fine,' Oonagh assured him. 'So long as you don't mind me working round you. I'll leave the hoovering to last, so you can carry on talking.'

'Don't worry about that. We were only looking at some photos. Frances was telling me about all the things the residents get up to here: outings and parties and so on. Do you get a chance to join in?'

'Sometimes. Well, not the trips, but I usually help with the food whenever there's something special on here.'

'I think I'll go back to my room,' Frances said, getting to her feet and reaching for her walking stick. 'I've got some letters I ought to write and I can't stand the noise of that hoover. It's been nice chatting to you. I expect we'll see each other again at dinner.'

Jonah watched her slow progress towards the glass doors that led out of the lounge to the garden. Seeing his puzzled expression, Oonagh explained, 'Mrs Ray's room is on the ground floor. It's quicker going through the garden and in at the patio doors than all round through the dining room. Mr Martin goes that way too, whenever it's not raining.'

Jonah nodded understanding, mentally noting that this habit that the ground floor residents had of accessing their rooms via the garden could increase the significance of the faulty lock on Olive's patio doors. Nobody would think anything of one of them approaching her room from the outside, either before her death or even during the morning after, when the incriminating syringe could have been planted there. They would just appear to be nosy neighbours wanting to get a slice of the action.

'Mrs Ray showed me some pictures of the nurse who's been suspended – Jonathan, I think she said his name was. Did you know him?'

'Oh yes!' Oonagh said softly, her eyes lighting up. 'He's ever so kind. He sometimes helps me with the cleaning, when I get behind, so I won't be in trouble with Mrs Radcliffe. He shouldn't really, but sometimes I just can't get it all done in the time and the residents complain if their bins haven't been emptied and that sort of thing. It's awful the things they're saying about him. He's not like that at all. He'd never hurt a fly.'

'So everyone tells me,' Jonah agreed, speaking gently and looking earnestly into Oonagh's wide eyes. 'But he *was* the one who gave her an insulin injection the day she died.'

'I think she did it herself,' Oonagh said defiantly. 'She was always complaining about her aches and pains and how she couldn't see properly anymore. I think she did it herself – or else she got that foreign doctor to do it for her. I heard her talking to him one time. She said she needed more painkillers and he said he couldn't give her them, because they were dangerous and too many could kill her, and she said she wasn't that fussed if they did. I think she *wanted* to die. But I can't stop here talking,' she added hurriedly, recollecting herself. 'I've got to get on with this cleaning.'

14. EVENTIDE
Once more 'tis eventide, and we
Oppressed with various ills draw near.
Henry Twells: "At even ere the sun was set"

'Jonah! How are you?' Lucy burst into Jonah's room and strode across to put her arms round his shoulders, hugging him to her possessively, as if she feared that he might have suffered some accident or neglect during the few hours since they had left him there.

'Making progress – slowly,' he told her. 'But I can't tell you about it yet. Peter's the official go-between, so you'll have to give us a few minutes on our own for me to brief him. There are a number of things that DCI Latham may want to follow up on.'

'I warned Lucy that there wasn't much point in her coming,' Bernie said, 'but she insisted she had to see you. I don't think she trusts anyone else to look after you properly.'

'Well, as you see, I'm still here and still alive and kicking. Sorry, Lucy. I'd love to hear all about what you've been up to, but there's not a lot of time before they'll be along to get me ready for bed. The residents all have to go to bed early because most of the staff knock off at seven-thirty, to avoid having to pay unsocial hours supplements. They've promised that I'll be the last, because I'm the only one who's physically unable to get out of bed on my own, but even so …'

'We'll go up and see Aunty Dot,' Bernie said. 'I promised her we'd come again. And I'll be able to get a report on what the others think of you,' she added with a grin. 'I hope you've been behaving yourself!'

Lucy gave Jonah another hug and then followed her mother reluctantly out of the room. Jonah waited until the door had closed completely and then turned to address Peter.

'Right! Now, let's see … Where shall I begin? Ah yes! Ask Sandra what she knows about Oonagh Conlon. She's one of the staff, but I don't remember Sandra mentioning her, so she may have escaped under the radar. She's nominally a cleaner, but she does other odd jobs around the place, including serving meals to the residents.'

'Oonagh Conlon,' Peter repeated, taking out a notebook and writing down the name. 'Do you have any reason for suspecting her, or is this just a general query?'

'She seems harmless enough, but there could be something going on between her and Jonathan.'

'Hardly likely,' Peter commented, 'considering.'

'It could be only on her side,' Jonah explained. 'But she may have read more into his kindness towards her than she should have done, or maybe … Well, you never know, do you? I expect there's nothing in it at all, but it can't do any harm to check her out.'

'OK. I'll let Sandra know. Anything else?'

'Hector Bayliss, the caretaker. There's been some talk of him stealing from residents' rooms. Nothing of any great value and nobody had enough evidence to make an official complaint, but, if it's true and Olive had found him out, he might have a motive for silencing her.'

'That sounds interesting. He had ample opportunity to administer the lethal dose during the night, assuming that he could get into the drugs cupboard.'

'Which, in view of the generally lax regime here, is very likely. And there's another thing: he was supposed to have been fixing the broken lock on Olive's patio doors weeks before she died. Was he just very slow at getting jobs done, or did he leave it broken deliberately in order to be able to get in?'

'I'll let Sandra know. All the staff will have had DBS[5] checks done before they were employed, so their criminal records can't have much in them, but she may be able to dig out some more about their backgrounds.'

'Of course, the broken lock being common knowledge in the Home means that *any* of our suspects could have used the patio doors to get into Olive's room. And that reminds me: ground floor residents regularly use their garden doors to get from the old part of the building to the new part without going through the hall and dining room. And there's a door into the garden from the kitchen, which someone could use to get outside and then into Olive's room. Ask Sandra about the catering staff. There must be someone cooking the meals, and they could easily have slipped across to Olive's room shortly after dinner that day. I wonder if there have been any food poisoning incidents,' Jonah went on thoughtfully. 'That would provide a motive for the kitchen staff, if Olive had them on her little list. I wish we could find that dossier of hers.'

'Assuming that it ever really existed,' Peter said sceptically. 'It may have been all talk on Olive's part.'

'Yes. I rather fancy she may have enjoyed the feeling of power that it gave her, hinting that she knew people's secrets. On the other hand, would the manager have called the staff together and told them about it, if she hadn't

---

[5] Disclosure and Barring Service: a British government service providing employers with information about the criminal records of potential employees working with vulnerable people.

actually seen the dossier? Perhaps we ought to ask her outright why she called that staff meeting and what evidence she had for saying that Olive was keeping tabs on them all.'

'If she can tell us what was actually in the dossier, that might give us a better idea of who had most to lose by it being made public, but would she tell us the truth? I mean: she's in charge, so she has to take ultimate responsibility for whatever her staff may have done, *and* we agreed that she *could* be our murderer.'

Meanwhile, upstairs in her room, Dot was having a far from satisfactory conversation with her nieces. It was extremely frustrating to know that an investigation was going on, but to be unable to find out what progress had been made – especially when one had been the instigator of their involvement in it.

'I've told you before, Aunty,' Bernie said firmly, 'Jonah is working with the Merseyside Police. He isn't a private investigator hired to exonerate your Jonathan. And that means he can't share what he knows with you. He's here to help find out the truth – even if it turns out that Jonathan is guilty after all. Come to that, for all the police know, *you* could have killed Olive. You were here when it was done and you used to be a nurse, so you wouldn't have any difficulty handling a syringe of insulin.'

'And what motive am I supposed to have had?' Dot asked, sounding interested rather than offended.

'Jealousy,' Lucy answered promptly. 'You thought that Olive was stealing Jonathan away from you.'

'Which does, of course, explain your determination to clear his name,' Bernie added, joining in the joke with a will. 'How ironic if your attempts to clear your rival out of the way, in the end also removed the object of your deranged passion!'

'If you're interested in passion,' Dot replied, 'you would do better looking toward the younger generation. And forget about Jonathan. The two you ought to be worrying about are Ian Wilton and Maxine Shaw.'

'Ian's the guy who met us when we arrived this morning, right?' Bernie was immediately interested. 'But Maxine Shaw?'

'She's the other registered nurse, apart from Jonathan. She isn't on duty today. I don't have any cast-iron proof, but I reckon she's carrying on with Ian.'

'Is that what other people think too?' Bernie asked. 'Olive, for example?'

'Maybe,' Dot shrugged. 'If I'd noticed, I dare say I wasn't the only one.'

'And is it something that they'd want to keep secret?'

'I daresay Ian would be upset if his wife got to hear about it.'

'Aah!' Bernie nodded.

'You mean, one of them might have been worried that Olive would tell her and they could have killed her to stop her?' Lucy asked excitedly. 'Were they on duty that day?'

'I can't remember,' Dot shook her head. 'I *think* it may have been Ian who got me up that day, but ... days all tend to merge into one in here.'

'I'm sure the police will have been given a list of everyone's shifts for the days in question,' Bernie assured her. 'But we'd better let them know about this affair, in case there's anything in your idea that it gives Ian a motive for getting rid of Olive. I must say,' she went on with a grin, 'that, for a harmless little old lady, she seems to have an extraordinarily long list of people who might be pleased to see the back of her.'

'What makes you think that old ladies are harmless?' Dot asked. 'We have a lifetime of grudges to pay back and a lifetime of experience to give us the means to do it. Take Olive, for example, she had no intention of disinheriting her sons, but she didn't like their presumption that they had a right to the family home and I think she teased them with the idea that she was leaving money to Jonathan. I'll bet they knew about the legacy, but didn't know how much – or rather, how little – it was.'

'Jonah had better watch out then,' Lucy said, trying to sound as if she were joking, but deadly serious underneath. 'If any of you take against him, he won't stand much chance, will he?'

'Don't you worry about that!' Dot laughed. 'He's been a great hit with everyone. 'The ladies all think he's a hero – and tremendously dishy with it – and Eric is making a big thing of being pleased to have another man about the place. Even Joan doesn't have a word to say against him, which is something of a miracle in itself!'

15. SLOW WATCHES OF THE NIGHT
But the slow watches of the night not less to God belong
Federick Lucian Hosmer: "Thy kingdom come"

Jonah lay in bed pondering the events of the day. He had made a good start, he decided. He had met almost all the residents and all the staff that were on duty that day, and he had learned several new things about the routine of the Home and the relationships between those who lived and worked there.

It was a pity that Julia had been assigned the task of putting him to bed. He had been hoping that Rebecca, the night nurse, would have done it, giving him the opportunity to get to know her and to gauge how likely it was that she might have crept into this same room two weeks earlier and injected one of her charges with a lethal dose of insulin. These hopes had, however, been based on a miscalculation, Jonah having failed to realise that Julia was working a long shift, which did not finish until nine-thirty at night.

What time was it? There was a clock on the bedside cabinet, but he was lying on his side, facing the other way and could not turn over to look at it. There was no light showing through the narrow gap between the curtains, but that was little indication of how many hours had passed since he had been settled into his bed at nine. Rebecca would have been briefed to come in and turn him over during the night. That would give him the chance to talk to her – provided that she was prepared to stay for long enough. He had better think up a pretext for detaining her.

As he pondered on this, he became aware of a small sound in the corridor outside his room. What was it? Was it footsteps? If it was, they were rather shuffling steps and there was a tapping sound as well, as if something hard was striking against the floor. Then he was startled to hear a rattling at the handle of his door, as if someone were trying to get in.

'Who is it?' Jonah called out, intensely frustrated at being unable to turn over to look in the direction of the sound.

'I've come to give you your medicine,' came back a thin voice. 'Open the door and let me in.'

'Mr Porter?' another voice sounded from the small loudspeaker above his bed. It was Rebecca Anderson speaking from the office. 'Is there something wrong?'

'I'm not sure.' Jonah was surprised how relieved he felt to hear her calm, measured tones. 'There was a noise outside my room, as if someone was trying to get in, and then someone said something about giving me some medicine. It's all very-'

'I'll be along right away,' Rebecca said quickly. 'Don't worry. We'll soon have this sorted.'

There was a click as she switched off the intercom. Outside the door, the woman, whoever she was, continued to rattle the handle and ask for the door to be opened. Then another voice broke in, speaking cheerfully but with a tone of authority.

'Hello Lottie. Off on your travels again? Time to go back to your room now. Let me give you a hand.'

Lottie mumbled a reply, but Jonah could not hear what it was. Then the shuffling sound resumed, this time accompanied by footsteps and reassuring words from the Care Assistant as she guided Lottie back to her own room. After a short while, Jonah heard a lock turning and a door opening, then more shuffling and muffled voices and, finally, a door closing, followed by silence.

Jonah waited. He was confident that Rebecca would be back soon. Once she had settled Lottie in bed, she would surely come to check that he was not alarmed at the incident and to reassure him that he was safe and nobody, apart from the staff, could enter his room uninvited.

Sure enough, it was not long before he heard a key turning in the lock, followed by the sound of his door opening and someone stepping inside.

'Mr Porter?' a voice called softly. 'It's only me. I'm Rebecca. I'm on duty tonight. I'm sorry you were disturbed. Poor Lottie gets confused sometimes. She used to be a District Nurse, you see, and she sometimes thinks the other residents are her patients. Are you OK? Do you need anything?'

'I'd be grateful if you could give me a drink of water,' Jonah replied.

'Of course. No problem. Do you have a glass handy?'

'There's a cup in the bathroom, I think – or if not, there should be one in the bag at the back of my wheelchair; and there's a pack of drinking straws somewhere – on the dressing table I think. Sorry. I can't remember where they left everything.'

'Not to worry. I'm sure I'll be able to find them. Just relax while I have a look around. Do you mind if I put the light on?'

'Go ahead. I'm not keen myself on sitting in the dark.'

A few minutes later, Rebecca was back with one of Jonah's plastic cups, filled with water and with a long straw protruding from the top. She put it down on the bedside cabinet and then came round to the other side of the bed to speak to Jonah.

'What's the best way for me to sit you up?' she asked.

'I know it sounds like a lot of palaver, but the easiest thing to do is probably to get me into my chair. There's a button on the side to make it recline and then you can roll me onto it and put my hand on the controls and I'll take it from there.'

'Don't you think I could just prop you up in bed to have your drink?'

'I'd rather go in my chair, if you don't mind. It's got a place for the cup that adjusts to the right height for me to drink and I always feel so much more control when I'm in it. Sorry to be a nuisance.' Jonah favoured Rebecca with one of his endearing lopsided smiles.

She smiled back, nodded and then looked doubtfully towards the electric wheelchair, which was standing in the corner of the room, plugged into one of the electric sockets.

'It looks like it's charging. Is it OK to use it?'

'It should be, but probably the best thing will be to disconnect it so we don't have wires trailing all over the room. Just don't forget to plug it in again afterwards. And talking about disconnecting things, my urine bag's attached to the bed, so you'll have to undo my plumbing before you get me out.'

Rebecca followed his instructions and it was not long before Jonah was sitting up in his chair with his left hand on the controls and the cup of water standing on the tray attachment.

'I'm sorry to put you to so much trouble,' Jonah apologised. 'I don't usually ask for things in the night, but when I woke up just now I felt so parched that I really didn't think I'd be able to sleep if I didn't have a drink. I suppose it's having to get into a new routine. I don't usually go to bed so early at home.'

'Yes. A lot of the residents find that a bit odd at first,' Rebecca sounded apologetic. 'It takes time to adjust to a fixed routine when you've been used to doing things when you want. We do try to be as flexible as possible, but some residents need a lot of help with getting ready for bed and it all takes time.'

'I know. I'm not complaining. I'm sure you all work very hard to make us all comfortable, and I can't blame the staff for wanting to get off home to their families in the evening. Well – all except you. Do you always work nights?'

'Yes. I like it, because of the kids. It means that I can be at home with them during the day. There's only my dad to look after them, you see. He's fine about being there at night and getting them breakfast in the morning, but he has his own work to go to during the day, so it's good that I can get home in time to take them to school.'

'It doesn't sound as if you get much chance to rest.'

'Oh, I generally doss down for a few hours while the kids are at school, and because the night shift is a long one, I get three nights off every week. So it's not so bad really.'

'It sounds like hard work to me, but I suppose if you need the money …'

'Which I do. My bastard of an ex buggered off and left me with three kids and no maintenance, so getting the extra for working unsocial hours is the main thing that pays the rent and keeps the kids in shoes.'

'You're in the right business anyway. They keep saying that there aren't enough Care Home places to go round. So, at least you're not likely ever to be out of work.'

'I do hope you're right. It doesn't feel like that just at the moment.'

'Oh? Why's that?'

'All the bad publicity we're getting right now, with this suggestion that one of the residents was killed by a member of staff. You must have heard about it.'

'Yes. Miss Fazakerley did tell me. She seemed rather excited about it all,' Jonah gave another smile, 'almost as if a murder or two was just the thing to brighten up an otherwise tedious existence.'

'I expect Miss Fazakerley fancies herself as Miss

Marple, solving the case and proving the police wrong.' Rebecca spoke jokingly, but Jonah thought that he detected an underlying bitterness in her voice. 'She'd love that. I suppose it's good that some of the residents manage to keep all their mental faculties after their bodies start wearing out, but in some cases … well, it can make them quite hard work.'

'What about the woman who died? Was she one of those?'

'Oh yes!' Rebecca said vehemently. 'She was still all there alright. And not above telling everyone else how to do their jobs. Why do you ask?' she added, with a hint of suspicion in her voice.

'I was just wondering if it could have all been an accident. If she was a bit confused and muddled up her medication. That's all. It seems more likely than someone doing it deliberately, doesn't it?'

'I don't know about that. I don't have anything to do with the residents medications. I wouldn't know how to give someone an overdose if I wanted to. I just wish they'd hurry up and get this all sorted before any more residents leave and the Home goes under.'

'I hadn't realised any residents had left. Because of this?'

'Well, I suppose she hasn't actually left – yet, but her daughter has taken her to live with her for a few weeks. I can't see her coming back – not unless this is all cleared up – and then …,' she sighed. 'Well, would *you* put your mum or dad in a place where there might be a murderer on the staff?'

'Put like that … perhaps not. So what about you then? Are you looking for other jobs?'

'Sort of,' Rebecca sighed again, 'but I'm scared to apply in case they turn me down because of working here. In any case, there aren't any at places I'd want to go. I don't drive you see and I'm tied to getting home to take the kids to school. But we can't sit here chatting all night. If you've finished your water, let's get you back into bed and off to sleep, shall we?'

16. I STAND AT THE DOOR, AND KNOCK

Behold, I stand at the door, and knock: if any man hear my voice, and open the door, I will come in to him, and will sup with him, and he with me.
Revelation 3:20

Jonah looked at the time on the computer screen attached to his wheelchair: nine forty-five. That must be late enough to pay a call on one of his fellow-residents to introduce himself. There were still some whom he had not yet met, despite his best efforts at socialising during breakfast. It seemed that some of the inmates preferred to make do with tea and toast in their rooms, rather than face the communal dining room bleary eyed and dishevelled.

The lounge, where Jonah was sitting, was deserted. The staff were all busy with their duties and the residents must be in their rooms. Jonah looked down at his list and decided to visit Charles Melling, the man who had moved into the room formerly occupied by Edna Lomax. He was out of the frame for the murder, having only moved in after Olive was already dead, but for that very reason, he might have valuable insight to offer into relationships between residents and carers. He could have no reason for lying or for glossing over any disagreements and animosities.

Jonah headed off down the corridor towards Room 4. The door was closed. He prepared to knock on it by driving his chair against it. Then he hesitated. He had no idea how physically fit Charles Melling was. It might be a struggle for him to get to the door. What would his reaction be to Jonah's knocking? In all probability, he would merely call out for him to come in and there would ensue a complicated conversation through the closed door to explain why he was unable to do so.

He decided to try another approach. He retraced his steps and returned to the lounge, where he was pleased to see that the glass doors leading to the garden were standing open. He set off across the paving, weaving around the tubs of flowers to reach the wide path that led past his own patio doors and round the back of the building. He passed the window at the back of his room and the fire door at the end of the corridor and came to a halt outside the doors leading from Room 4. Good! They were open. Charles Melling must enjoy fresh air, or perhaps his room had become uncomfortably hot with the morning sun streaming in through the expanse of glass.

Jonah looked in and saw a small man with a goatee beard sitting in an armchair facing the glass doors. His eyes were lowered. He was apparently intent on reading the book that he was holding in bony, blue-veined hands and did not appear to have noticed Jonah's approach.

'Excuse me!' Jonah called out, trying to pitch his voice loud enough to attract the man's attention without startling him. 'I'm new here. Let me introduce myself.'

The man looked up, stared at Jonah for a moment or two and then nodded his acknowledgement of the greeting.

'My name's Jonah Porter,' Jonah went on. 'I'm just here for a week, to give the friends that I live with a bit of a break. I'm in Room 5, just across the way from you.'

'Charles Melling,' the man replied laconically.

'Have you been here long?'

'No. I only came last week myself.'

'How're you liking it?'

'A bit difficult, to be honest.' Melling appeared to be forcing himself to engage in a conversation that he did not relish. 'I'm not used to living in a crowd.'

'Yes. I suppose it must be difficult to adjust, if you're used to being in your own home and not having to suit anyone except yourself. It's not so bad for me. I've already had to come to terms with having people around to look after me. Technology can only do so much, unfortunately. But even so, this communal living is a bit different from being at home.'

'D'you want to come in?'

'If I'm not intruding. I don't want to interrupt your reading.'

'Oh, that was just a front really – to stop the staff feeling sorry for me and trying to take me out of myself. They will keep coming round to check that I'm settling in OK. They don't seem to realise that I've been on my own for eight years, since my wife died, and I'm used to my own company.'

'What made you decide to come here?' Jonah asked, gliding through the doorway and positioning his chair at a convenient distance from where Melling was sitting.

'Force of circumstances. By which I mean, my daughter. I had a fall – not a serious one, but it worried her – and she decided that I wasn't safe living alone any more. Her idea was that I would move in with her, but I knew that would never work, so I found this. I'm giving it two months' trial before I put my house on the market.'

'That sounds like a wise decision,' Jonah agreed. 'Never burn your boats until you're absolutely sure you've made the right decision. My sons tried to persuade me to go into a Home when my wife died – either that or to move up to county Durham to live with my eldest and his family. But I was only fifty-five and not ready to give up my work, which is in Oxford. And in any case, as you say, moving in with your kids doesn't always work.'

'What is it you do?' Melling was evidently trying to make conversation.

'I'm a police officer – a detective inspector.'

'Isn't that rather difficult for you – being in a wheelchair?'

'Well, being paralysed certainly brings challenges that I didn't have before, but I have minions to do the leg work while I agitate the little grey cells in true Poirot fashion. And, as I said, technology helps a lot. This chair, for example. It's got a computer built-in, which gives me internet access and a mobile phone. I can operate everything either using this keypad or via voice recognition. The main problems aren't around doing the job; they're keeping my body in shape: feeding, toileting, exercising. But I've got a personal assistant who sees to all that for me.'

'How did it happen?'

'Someone took a pot-shot at me. The bullet hit my neck and damaged the spinal cord.'

'Why?'

'We've never managed to find out. Someone with a grudge against the police or against me personally, presumably.'

They lapsed into silence. Melling's well of curiosity seemed to have dried up. Jonah looked around the room, studying the place where the first victim – if indeed Edna Lomax was a victim – had died.

'That's interesting,' he said, inclining his head in the direction of a door in the wall that separated this room from the one next door. 'Where does that door go? Pardon me for asking, but I can't help wondering about that sort of thing. Force of habit.'

'It connects this room with the next one. It's kept permanently locked. According to the old girl in Room 3, these two rooms used to be a suite. This one was the living room, with a kitchenette where the bathroom is now, and the other one was a double bedroom for a married couple. Mind you, she doesn't seem to know what day of the week it is most of the time, so I don't know how much you can rely on what she says about it.'

'Oh yes!' Jonah laughed. 'I've met her. Loopy Lottie, one of the others called her. She thinks I'm a sinister character who shouldn't be allowed in the lounge with respectable folk!'

Melling joined in the laughter.

'Yes,' he agreed. 'You have to see the funny side, or else you'd go potty living here with all the old people and their foibles. And the worst is knowing that I'm getting old too and probably have habits that the others find just as strange. I sometimes wonder: am I the one who's going senile and everyone else is quite normal?'

'It's funny that they didn't block up the door properly,' Jonah mused. 'They must have got builders in to put in your bathroom. Taking off the doorframe and re-plastering that wall wouldn't have been much extra work for them.'

'Penny-pinching. That's the management here all over. Always wanting to save a few pounds. That's why they split the rooms. You can charge more for two separate rooms than for a suite.'

'I suppose perhaps they thought a married couple might come along who wanted the suite again,' Jonah continued thoughtfully, 'but they'd hardly want two bathrooms.'

'If you can call mine a bathroom,' Melling spoke as if Jonah had hit a nerve. 'There's no bath, only a small shower cubicle.'

'You said the door is always locked. Presumably Fiona Radcliffe has a key?'

'I suppose so. I never really thought about it. So long as Loopy Lottie, as you call her, can't get through, I'm not bothered. She does try sometimes, you know. She lived here with her husband before he died, and sometimes she forgets that this isn't her sitting room anymore. I hear her rattling the door and calling his name.' He sighed. 'It's a terrible thing getting old.'

'Mmm.' Jonah, grinning mischievously, looked across and caught his eye. 'But would you really opt for the alternative?'

Melling laughed out loud.

'I guess you're right. I ought to count my blessings, getting to eighty-three with nothing worse than a few aches and pains and stiff joints when I get up in the morning.'

They sat for a while without speaking. Jonah mulled over in his mind what he had just discovered about the room layout and wondered how best to encourage Melling to talk about his fellow-residents. In the end it was Melling who broke the silence.

'If you live in Oxford, what made you choose this place for a holiday?'

'Ah! That's all down to Our Bernie,' Jonah said mysteriously. 'She's my Personal Assistant and she's also Miss Fazakerley's niece. She's killing two birds with one stone, so to speak, arranging for us both to be in here while she visits her other relatives up here.'

'Miss Fazakerley? That's the old girl with the iPad who keeps talking about her *street cred* and how bad the WiFi connection is here – right?'

'That's the one.' Jonah grinned. 'Now, imagine what she must have been like forty years ago when she was fully fit, and you've got Our Bernie. Poor old Peter – that's Bernie's husband – doesn't know which of us is more insane. I think he despairs sometimes of keeping us in order!'

'I suppose Dot Fazakerley will have told you all about our little murder mystery, and how, in her opinion, they've got the wrong person under suspicion.'

'She has indeed!' Jonah chuckled. 'And she's got this wild idea that I'll be able to find out who really did it. But I suppose all the residents probably have their own ideas about that. I mean, with nothing much else to do, they're bound to speculate aren't they?'

'I don't know about that. I've been surprised how many of the old dears are convinced that it can't be Jonathan, the nurse that they've suspended. It seems to me he must be the obvious culprit – if it wasn't just some unfortunate mistake.'

'That's a pity! I was hoping you might have some clever theory of your own that I could present to Dot to clear the name of her favourite nurse,' Jonah joked.

'If it's theories you want, you ought to talk to Kath Lowe. She fancies herself as a great friend of the woman who died. She claims that she knows that her family were plotting to bump her off. All nonsense, I'm sure – just a fairy story she's thought up to get attention for herself.'

'Oh, I like a good fairy story. I think I may pay Mrs Lowe a visit later, to introduce myself.' Jonah glanced down at the time on his computer screen. 'Now, it looks like elevenses time. I think I'll trundle round to the lounge for morning coffee. Are you coming?'

Melling declined to accompany him, so Jonah headed off alone out through the patio doors and along the path, pondering upon what he had learned.

As he rounded the corner of the building, he almost collided with Eric Martin who was returning from what he described as his *morning constitutional*. He greeted Jonah as a long lost friend and chatted ebulliently as they weaved their way through the slalom of flower tubs.

'Where've you been hiding yourself?' he asked jovially. 'I came to your room earlier, to see if you'd like to take another turn round the gardens with me, but you weren't there.'

'I've been paying a call on my next-door neighbour, trying to get to know everyone.'

'Charles? I don't imagine you got much joy there. Very standoffish. He used to be a dentist, you know. Can't get used to the idea that someone might actually *want* to come to see him!'

'I think he's finding it rather difficult after living on his own for a long time.'

'No different from me,' Eric dismissed this explanation with a wave of his hand. 'He'd soon fit in if he socialised more and didn't always have his nose in one of those books of his. But, each to his own, I suppose,' he added, propelling his wheelchair over the threshold and into the lounge. 'If he wants to hide away on his own all day, that his funeral, isn't it?'

'What's that about the funeral?' asked a small, grey-haired woman in thick glasses, who was sitting in a chair near the patio doors. 'Is it today? I thought it was tomorrow. Or have I got the days muddled up? It *is* Tuesday, isn't it?'

'No Marge,' Eric replied, putting his hand on her knee. 'It's Wednesday. And it *is* Olive's funeral this afternoon. Don't you worry. We won't forget you. I've been talking to Fiona about it. It's all arranged.'

'That's good. I think we all ought to go. We ought to show our respect.'

'And show those lads of hers that she had friends, even if *they* couldn't be bothered with her,' another voice chimed in.

Jonah looked round to see a plump woman with permed white hair approaching from the direction of the dining room with the aid of a walking frame. She was accompanied by Dot Fazakerley, also walking with a frame. When Dot saw Jonah, she took one hand off her frame and waved to him.

'Come along young Jonah!' she called out imperiously. 'Come over here and sit with us. I want to introduce you to Kathleen. She's dying to meet you.'

Jonah smiled apologetically towards Eric, who

shrugged his shoulders and smiled back.

'Better not disappoint the ladies. We can catch up later.'

Jonah made his way carefully across to where Dot and Kathleen were settling themselves into adjacent chairs, steering skilfully round the many sticks and walking frames that made the room into an obstacle course for the unwary wheelchair user.

As he passed the door from the kitchen, Oonagh appeared with the tea trolley. They both exclaimed apologies as she hastily pulled it to a halt, causing the crockery to rattle alarmingly and a small amount of milk to spill from the jug.

'No harm done,' Jonah said to her reassuringly, seeing the look of horror on Oonagh's face. 'All my fault. Driving without due care and attention again, I'm afraid.'

He treated her to a remorseful smile. She looked back, blinked away the tears that were threatening, and smiled back gratefully. Jonah wondered what reaction she usually got from the residents when such incidents occurred.

'Come along young Jonah!' Dot repeated, pretending to be annoyed. 'Don't hang about chatting to the staff all day. Get out of the poor girl's way and come over here.'

'I'd better do as I'm told,' Jonah said to Oonagh, in the tone of a small boy wanting to avoid a reprimand.

She nodded and smiled again, waiting for him to pass in front of the trolley before moving it into the centre of the room ready to serve the drinks.

'Now then Jonah, let me introduce my next-door neighbour, Kathleen Lowe.' Dot said, putting her hand on Kathleen's arm. 'I've told her all about you.'

'Not all my guilty secrets I hope!'

'She tells me you're a policeman,' Kathleen said, speaking in the unnecessarily loud voice of the hard-of-hearing. 'And you're going to bring the person who killed Olive to justice.'

'Now Dot, you must be more careful what you say,' Jonah said teasingly. 'It's true,' he added, turning back to

Kathleen, 'but I'm on holiday at the moment and I work for Thames Valley Police, not for the team who are investigating Olive's death. However, he continued, seeing her face fall, 'if you have any information about it, I'll be happy to get in touch with them on your behalf.'

'I don't know about *information* but I could certainly tell them a thing or two about those precious sons of hers,' Kathleen replied darkly.

'What sort of thing?'

'Well, there was the argument they had the day she died. At it hammer and tongs they were. The older one – Desmond his name is – he got here first, and talked to the doctor and gave his permission for them to cut her up to see how she died. Then, a few minutes later, after the doctor's gone, the younger brother turns up and starts tearing him off a strip for not putting his foot down and stopping it. Now, I ask you, why would he do that, if he hasn't got something to hide?'

'He could just have not liked the idea of his mother being cut up by the doctors,' Jonah suggested tentatively. 'Some people feel that post mortem examinations are disrespectful to the dead.'

'Disrespectful! He's a fine one to talk about respect! If he'd ever shown any respect to his mother when she was alive, I might have believed it, but …'

'So didn't he get on with his mother?'

'I don't know about that. It wasn't so much that they didn't get on as that he could never be bothered with her. Desmond wasn't much better, but he did at least go through the motions of coming to see her every week. But John! If he remembered to bring a card at Christmas he was doing well.'

'But he and his wife did come to see her the day before she died, didn't they?'

'Yes,' Kathleen said grimly. 'They did. A bit of a coincidence that, don't you think?'

'Are you suggesting that John Carter killed his mother?'

'It would make sense, wouldn't it? More sense than Jonathan doing it. Why would he want to kill the goose that laid the golden eggs?'

'You're saying that Jonathan stood to gain more by keeping Olive alive, because she used to give him presents?'

'That's it. You're quite smart. I'll give you that. The way I see it, John Carter came to see his mother that evening, specially to inject her with the stuff that killed her.'

'Now that's very interesting,' Jonah said encouragingly. 'But it's going to be quite difficult to prove that.'

'I'm sure it was him,' Kathleen persisted. 'He tried to get her to sign one of those, what-do-you-call-them? You know! Those papers that let someone else look after your money.'

'A power of attorney?'

'That's it! He said you never knew when she might have a stroke or something and not able to do things for herself. He tried to frighten her by saying the government might take all her money if she didn't have someone to look after it for her. But she knew better than that. She hadn't lost her marbles, even if her sight was going and her knees kept giving her bother.'

Oonagh came over to them with cups of coffee and a plate of biscuits. For a few minutes, the conversation was halted while they settled to their drinks.

'I see your argument,' Jonah resumed, once Oonagh had left them to see to other residents. 'But, I was wondering if anyone in the Home here might have wanted her out of the way. Someone told me that she used to talk about reporting the Home to the Care Quality Commission. Do you think any of the staff would have been worried about that?'

'They may have been,' Kathleen smiled grimly. 'She did say that sometimes. She told me she only did it to keep them on their toes. She didn't want to get the place closed down and have to find somewhere else to go, any more than any of the rest of us did.'

'So, when someone told me that Olive was keeping a list of all sorts of ... irregularities, shall we say? ... that wasn't strictly true? I mean, she didn't actually have them all written down somewhere?'

'Oh yes! She wrote everything down alright. And she used to tell the people that she was writing about. She'd say: "I've got that down on my list for the CQC. So make sure it doesn't happen again." As I said, she wanted to keep them on their toes.'

'So, the list wasn't a secret? All the staff knew about it?'

'I don't know about *all* the staff. She kept it hidden from Fiona, because she was afraid that she'd try to stop her or take the diary away from her. And any of them who never did anything wrong probably wouldn't get to hear about it, because she'd never need to tell them about it would she?'

'Now that's a very interesting point. You're saying that it's only the people who'd done something that she considered worthy of putting in her dossier, who would know of its existence?'

'That's about the size of it,' Kathleen nodded.

'And did she ever show it to you?'

'Not what she wrote,' Kathleen shook her head. 'She wrote it all in her diary, which she carried around with her in the bag on her zimmer frame. So I saw her writing in it, but I never looked inside myself.'

'I had a strange experience last night,' Jonah said, apparently changing the subject. 'Mrs Goodman, from the room opposite, tried to get into my room. Do you think she could have forgotten Olive wasn't there anymore and have been wanting to talk to her?'

'That's about as likely as any other explanation,' Kathleen answered.

'Poor Lottie does a lot of strange things these days,' Dot added. 'Even before her husband died, she was getting dreadfully forgetful, but since he passed away ...'

'She seems to be in a world of her own most of the time,' Kathleen continued.

'Do you think she could have given Olive an insulin injection, thinking that she was treating her?' Jonah suggested cautiously. 'Someone told me she used to be a nurse and she sometimes thinks the other residents are her patients.'

'I wouldn't have thought so,' Kathleen began.

'But she can be very unpredictable,' Dot interjected.

'And, even if she tried, Olive wouldn't have had any truck with it,' Kathleen said decidedly. 'She'd have pressed her alarm buzzer. No, you mark my words: it was that son of hers, wanting to get his grubby hands on her money.'

'Now Mr Porter, I'm sorry to break up your little party, but it's time for your skin care.' An unfamiliar figure in the blue and white uniform worn by the Care Assistants approached them, smiling benevolently. 'Let's go back to your room and get you ready for it.'

'Sorry ladies,' Jonah smiled apologetically towards Kathleen and Dot. 'A man's gotta do what a man's gotta do, I'm afraid. See you later.'

'I'm Scarlet Jones,' the young woman introduced herself. 'It was my day off yesterday, so we haven't met before.'

'Pleased to meet you.' Jonah remembered the face from the photograph that Charlie Simpson had shown him three days earlier. It had presumably been taken when she was off duty, since the bright, multi-coloured scarf, which had secured her hair in a pile on top of her head in the picture, had been replaced by a plain blue one that matched her uniform.

She took a key out from her pocket and unlocked the door of Jonah's room. She held it open while he went inside and then closed it firmly behind them and turned the key in the lock.

'I have to do that, just in case one of the other residents comes to see you and forgets to knock first,' she explained.

'We don't want them seeing you in the altogether, do we now?'

With a great effort, Jonah forced a smile at this remark, fighting down the irritation that he felt at being treated like an infant.

'I'll get the hoist to transfer you to the bed,' Scarlet said, heading towards the bathroom.

'No need. My chair can sort that. Just watch.'

Jonah brought the chair alongside the bed, put it into its reclining position and then adjusted the height so that he was lying on a level with the top of the mattress.

'Now, all you need to do is to roll me over on to the bed.'

'That's wonderful! I've never seen a chair like that before,' Scarlet said admiringly.

'It *is* rather special,' Jonah told her, taking advantage of an opportunity to build up a rapport with someone who might prove to be a key witness. 'I'm very lucky to have a couple of friends who design this sort of thing for a living.'

Scarlet gently undressed him and examined his skin all over. Satisfied that there was nothing there to warrant medical intervention, she proceeded to apply moisturiser to sooth the skin and protect it from the constant pressure caused by his sedentary life. While she worked, Jonah chatted about life in the Home and her role within it.

'I like having the early shift,' she told him, 'because it means that I can pick the kids up from school on the way home.'

'How many children do you have?' Jonah asked conversationally.

'Two little boys. Well, they're not such little boys now. They're nine and eleven. Joel will be going to High School in September. They grow up so fast! It seems like only yesterday he was crawling round on the floor getting into everything.'

'I know. I've got two boys too, and I sometimes find it hard to believe that they're both grown up with kids of their own now. It makes you wonder where all the years go. How do you manage in the mornings? If you're on earlies, you'll need to be here before school starts, won't you?'

'Fortunately, my husband doesn't have to be in work until nine, so he drops them off at breakfast club on his way. It works out fine, except in the school holidays. We take our leave at different times and look around for holiday clubs they can go to, but it would be nice once in a while to be able to go out together as a family.' She sighed. 'I guess when they're older it'll be easier.'

'The other residents have been telling me about a mysterious death here,' Jonah said, trying to sound as if he did not take it very seriously. 'They said that you were the one who found the body.'

'Yes,' Scarlet admitted reluctantly.

'Do tell!' Jonah said eagerly, pretending not to have noticed her discomfiture. 'What was it like?'

'There's nothing much to say. I just went in and found her there.'

'And everything was just as normal? None of her things disturbed at all?'

'As far as I could tell, but I wasn't really looking. I was more concerned with seeing if there was anything I could do for her. And I don't often get her up. She likes Nurse Bates to do it, and we always try to go along with what the residents prefer – unless there's good reason not to – so when he's on duty, he generally does it.'

'So wasn't he there that day?'

'Yes he was, but he got called away to look after one of the other residents. You've probably seen her around. Her room's just across the way from yours. Dear old Lottie! She does get so confused sometimes. That morning, she was wandering the corridors in her nightie muttering something about a child needing a whooping cough vaccination. I ask you! You couldn't make it up could you? Anyway, Jonathan was busy calming her down and persuading her to go back to her room and get dressed, so I went to see to Olive. It gave me an awful turn, seeing her like that.'

'I'll bet it did,' Jonah agreed. 'But I suppose, working in a place like this, you must have to get used to residents passing away.'

'Not like that. Mostly they go into hospital first, or at least we know there's something wrong with them. It was awful coming in expecting her to be ... well, to be her usually cranky self, and finding her, just lying there like that.' Scarlet sniffed a few times and wiped her eyes with her hand. 'Right!' she said briskly. 'That's you done. We'll get your clothes back on and put you back in your chair and then you can decide what you want to do until lunch time.'

17. BELOVED PHYSICIAN
Luke, the beloved physician, and Demas, greet you.
Colossians 4: 14, King James Bible

'This is my second cousin, Lucy Paige,' Dominic told the supervisor at the hospice where he worked as a volunteer. 'Remember you said it'd be OK for her to come and help?'

'That's right,' Moira Wren smiled at Lucy. 'You're very welcome. Our patients always like to see new faces – especially young faces. Maybe you could start by calling in on Tony Paulson. He's feeling a bit down because his son was supposed to be coming back from America today, but he's had to put it off until next week.'

'When she says "young faces" she means "pretty faces" like yours,' Dominic whispered to Lucy as he led the way along a cream-walled corridor with windows along one side and gaily-painted doors on the other.

'Don't be silly,' she squealed indignantly. 'I thought you'd stopped all that nonsense.'

'I have, but that won't stop other people thinking you're pretty – including Mr Paulson, who is a gentleman of a certain age, as they say.'

'Do you think that's why Aunty Dot thinks her nurse can't have killed that woman? Because she's old and he's young and attractive?'

'I shouldn't think so,' Dominic laughed. 'Aunty Dot doesn't need that sort of excuse to decide that she's going to fly in the face of popular opinion. She just likes to be contrary and to take the side of the underdog. Now, here we are: this is Tony Paulson's room.'

He opened a canary-yellow door to allow them both to enter a bright airy room with a wide window opposite them, through which the morning sunshine was streaming. Outside, Lucy could see beds of flowers and a small pond with a waterfall, whose tinkling sound was faintly audible through the open window.

In the bed, propped up on pillows, lay a man with sparse, steely-grey hair and thick bushy eyebrows. The brows, together with his cavernous eye-sockets, made it difficult to discern the colour of his eyes, which might have been brown or a very dark blue. His skin hung in folds beneath his chin, as if it were a size too large for the face that it covered. Both of his bony hands lay on top of a gaily-patterned patchwork quilt.

Two thin plastic tubes led from his nostrils across his cheeks and disappeared behind his ears. A drip stand, supporting a bag of transparent fluid, stood on the far side of the bed, with its plastic tube trailing across the quilt to his left arm.

As soon as she stepped into the room, Lucy became aware of his laboured breathing. She looked round, and spotted an oxygen cylinder standing on the floor behind the bed. Then she noticed the strange clip on the forefinger of his left hand, which she recognised as a meter to measure his oxygen saturation[6].

'Good morning Mr Paulson!' Dominic called out cheerfully. 'How're you doing?'

'Mustn't grumble,' the man replied in a rasping voice

---

[6] The human body requires the correct ratio of oxygen-saturated and non-saturated haemoglobin in the blood. A pulse oximeter is a non-invasive device for monitoring this ratio.

that Lucy had to strain to understand. 'And how many times do I have to tell you? It's Tony.'

'Sorry Tony,' Dominic replied in a tone of mock contrition, which made it clear that he knew that he was not really being scolded. 'It's that air of authority you have about you. It makes me feel like I'm back at school and you're one of the teachers.'

'And who's this lovely lady you've brought with you?' Tony asked, looking towards Lucy. 'Your sweetheart?'

'No. I'm sorry to disappoint you.' Dominic coloured at the suggestion. 'This is my second cousin, Lucy Paige. She's staying in Liverpool for a few days and she said she couldn't go back to Oxford without coming to see you.'

'You're a good liar, I'll grant you that.' Tony turned his head slightly in order to fix Lucy with his gaze. 'Well now, young lady, what makes you decide to spend your holiday in a cheerful place like this?'

'I – I thought it was good that Dom was doing something useful while he's off.' Unusually for her, Lucy felt somewhat at a loss for words. 'And ... and I'm planning to train as a doctor, so I'm always looking for experience of working with patients.'

'A doctor eh?' Tony wheezed, looking searchingly into her face. 'Well, I suppose you've come to the right place. Stop you expecting to be able to cure *all* your patients.'

'Actually, I'm hoping to become a forensic pathologist, so my patients will mostly be dead already.'

A momentary look of surprise crossed Tony's face. Then he smiled.

'That's the spirit! Pick the ones that can't sue you for negligence. I like your style, young lady. Now, sit yourself down and tell me all about yourself. And don't just stand about there like a spare part, laddie. Go and get us all some tea.'

Dom raised his hand in a salute, to signify that he had heard his orders and was on his way to obey them, before turning to go, closing the door behind him as he left. Lucy sat down on one of the two chairs that stood on either side of the bed. She looked towards Tony, wondering what he wanted her to talk about.

'Go on,' he repeated, 'Tell me about yourself.'

'I'm not sure what you'd be interested in,' Lucy began, wishing that her cousin had not left her alone with this stranger. 'I'm seventeen – just about to go into upper sixth. As I said, I'm applying for medical school. My mam is Dom's father's cousin. We live in Oxford and that's where I'm hoping to go to university too.'

'Any brothers or sisters?' Tony asked, seeing that Lucy was struggling to think of more to say. 'Or are you the only one?'

'No. My mum was quite old when she married my dad, and then he died before I was born, so ... But I've got a stepdad who's just like a real dad,' she added hurriedly, detecting a look of pity forming on Tony's face. 'And we all live together with a great friend of ours, who's a police inspector – a detective. So it's not like ... I mean, we're all perfectly happy.'

'My wife died when my son was a baby. Maybe it would have been better if I'd married again, so he'd have had a mother.'

'Only if it was the right person,' Lucy said earnestly. 'I think it's nice to think that you wanted to stay loyal to your wife. It was different with Mam and Peter. He was my godfather and his wife had been my Mam's best friend. I expect you were like a mum *and* dad to your son.'

Tony smiled.

'Go on. Tell me why you want to be a forensic pathologist. It seems a strange choice for a nice girl like you.'

'My dad and my stepdad and our friend Jonah are all in the police, so I've grown up hearing about murder enquiries and suspicious deaths. And we've got another friend who is a forensic pathologist and he showed me how to do a post-mortem on a dead squirrel that I found.

And it's all dead interesting – and useful too.'

'My, my! The things you girls do these days. My wife would have run a mile at the very idea of touching a dead body.'

'That's what my dad was like – according to Peter. He says he always used to try to get out of being the officer who was there at the PM.'

A knock at the door signalled that Dominic had returned. Lucy got up and opened the door to let him in. He carried in a tray and set it down on the shiny wooden bench that ran along the wall opposite the bed, serving as a desk, dressing table or work surface, as required.

'Here we all are!' he said heartily. 'It's a bit hot, so I'll leave it here for a few minutes before I bring it to you. I hope I've remembered how you like it. Milk and one sugar: is that right?'

'That's the ticket. Now come and sit down. Your young lady is just telling me about her dad's work in the police force.'

'Well, I don't think there's much more to tell you,' Lucy began. Then she broke off at the sound of another knock on the door. Moira's friendly face appeared, smiling a little apologetically.

'I'm sorry to interrupt, but the doctor's here, and he's keen to have a look at your chest.' She looked from Tony to the two young people. 'If you could just come outside for a few minutes?'

'I won't keep you long.' A man of South Asian appearance, dressed in a lounge suit followed Moira into the room. 'I just want to check that there hasn't been any more fluid building up in your lungs and that we've got your oxygen therapy at the right level.'

Lucy and Dominic got up and left the room, with Moira following behind them.

'We're very lucky to have Dr Amandeep,' she told them, once the door was closed. 'He's a GP with a special interest in palliative care for older people. I don't know how he finds the time to call in as often as he does, and he's always so caring and empathetic.'

'He's my Aunty Dot's GP too,' Dominic told her. 'When she moved into the Care Home, she was a bit worried about changing to a new doctor, but they told her it was better to have the same one as all the other residents, and now she wouldn't have anyone else.'

It was not long before Dr Amandeep Bhaskar emerged from Tony's room and signalled to them to go back in. As they did so, Lucy looked at him with renewed interest, remembering that he was one of the people who had been present in the Care Home during the time when Olive Carter must have been poisoned. He certainly looked innocent enough, but then presumably murderers – successful ones, at any rate – usually did.

Dominic helped Tony to drink his tea, while Lucy chatted about her life. Tony was familiar with Oxford from having been stationed at RAF Brize Norton during his time in the Airforce, and was interested to hear how some of the places that he knew had changed.

After the tea was finished, the conversation returned to the subject of families and, in particular, Tony's regret that his own son had been deprived of both a mother and siblings.

'Brothers and sisters can be a mixed blessing,' Dominic joked, trying to raise his spirits. 'Sometimes I wish I was an only child – especially first thing in the morning when there's a massive queue for the bathroom!'

'There's nothing wrong with being the only one,' Lucy backed him up. 'I wouldn't want to share my Mam with other kids. I like things the way they are.'

After an hour or so, Tony's eyelids began to droop and his breathing slowed. Seeing that he was dozing off, Dominic got to his feet.

'Well,' he said, 'I'm afraid we'll have to be moving on now. I'll be in again on Friday, so we can talk some more then.'

Tony did not reply, so Dominic signalled to Lucy to leave. She opened the door for him to go through with the tray of teacups.

'I was expecting to be *doing* more,' Lucy said to her cousin in a low voice as they walked down the corridor to the kitchen to return the cups. 'Not just sitting around talking.'

'Sometimes having someone to talk to is the thing people need most,' Dominic told her. 'But I know what you mean. At the end of the day, I sometimes wonder if I've been much use coming here. And I feel a bit of a fraud when one of the relatives stops me in the corridor and says how grateful they are, when it seems like I haven't done anything.'

When they reached the kitchen, Lucy was surprised to find Dr Bhaskar sitting there drinking a mug of coffee with one of the nursing staff. He looked up and smiled at them.

'You've certainly made a hit with Tony Paulson,' he said. 'I was just telling Andrea here, how pleased he was that you came to see him.'

'Shall we do the washing up?' Dominic asked, to cover Lucy's embarrassment, having noticed the self-conscious smile with which she had responded to the doctor's remark.

'Yes please,' Andrea answered, looking towards the sink. 'I don't know how it is, but we always seem to get through a vast amount of cups and spoons of a morning.'

Lucy stepped forward eagerly and turned on the tap, waiting for the water to run hot before filling the bowl. As she washed and Dominic dried, Andrea and the doctor continued their conversation behind them.

'I've made some small changes to Mrs Johnson's pain relief, but I'm afraid we may still need to get someone from the pain team in to see her. Keep an eye on her and call me at once if you have any concerns.'

'I'll do that. It's at night that she's the worst. Brenda was telling me, she was asking her again last night to end it all.'

'I know. And that's just what we ought to be able to prevent. There's no reason she should be feeling that way, if only we can get her pain management regime right.'

Dr Bhaskar finished his coffee and brought the empty mug over to the sink for Lucy to wash. She took it from him with a muttered word of thanks. Then she plucked up her courage to ask a question.

'Do patients often ask for euthanasia?'

'That's a very direct question,' Dr Bhaskar commented, somewhat taken aback and playing for time.

'Our Lucy doesn't beat about the bush,' Dominic told him, with a grin. 'She believes in calling a spade a spade.'

'Actually, I just called "killing" "euthanasia",' Lucy pointed out.

'To answer your question,' Dr Bhaskar went on, 'no. It doesn't happen very often. Why do you ask?'

'I was just wondering. And I was wondering what you say to them, if they do – as a doctor, I mean.'

'Lucy's planning to train as a doctor,' Dominic added, by way of explanation.

'Exactly what I say depends on the circumstances. It would always include, at some point in the conversation, telling them that I can't do anything to deliberately hasten death; but usually I'd start by reassuring them that there are lots of things that we can do to make things easier for them.'

'You mean like pain relief?'

'Yes, but not just that. Often what people are most worried about is losing their dignity and losing control over what happens to them. So sometimes, it can help to talk about technology that can keep them independent for longer or things such as urinary catheters to stop them wetting the bed.'

'Yes,' Lucy agreed. 'Our friend Jonah, has lots of technology to help him. I think it would drive him crazy if he had to ask other people to do everything for him.'

'And sometimes, what people are really worried about is becoming a burden on other people,' the doctor continued. 'So then, we sometimes need to involve the whole family to ensure that that isn't the case.'

'But, whatever happened, you'd always try to stop them wanting to kill themselves?' Lucy persisted.

'Absolutely! It's my job to give all my patients the very best quality of life, right up to the end of it.'

'So you don't think the law ought to be changed to allow assisted suicide?' Lucy asked innocently.

'I certainly do not. It would undermine trust between doctor and patient. And I wouldn't want that sort of responsibility. People – especially when they're very ill – go through ups and downs all the time. How could you ever be sure that they wouldn't have changed their mind later?'

'But, if their life has become completely unbearable?' Dominic suggested tentatively. 'If there's nothing you can do to stop the pain or …'

'It's our job as doctors to do whatever we can to relieve suffering,' the doctor insisted gently but firmly. 'In extreme cases, it can be necessary to prescribe a level of morphine to a dying patient that you might hesitate to give normally, but with the intention of relieving pain, not of shortening life. It's not a failure for a patient to die, but I do consider that I've failed if they don't die peacefully.'

'Good.' Lucy nodded her satisfaction with his response. 'That's what I think too.'

'Well!' Dr Bhaskar picked up his bag and made for the door. 'I'd better be on my way. It's been interesting talking to you.'

Lucy and Dominic put away the last of the crockery and went in search of Moira. They eventually found her in the patient lounge, talking with two elderly women who were engaged in completing a jigsaw puzzle. She looked up as they entered.

'We were wondering what you'd like us to do next,' Dominic said. 'Mr Paulson is sleeping now.'

'Well, I know it's not one of your usual jobs,' Moira said apologetically, 'but the garden does really need some attention. The grass has been growing so fast these last few days; it's really getting away from our regular gardener. Some of the patients like to go for a stroll out there, and I'm afraid of them tripping up or slipping over on all that long grass, especially in the mornings when it's wet. Do you mind?'

'No, of course not,' Dominic said heartily. 'Just tell us where to find the mower and stuff and we'll soon get it into shape.'

Dominic tackled the expanse of lawn with a power mower, while Lucy did the rounds of the many trees and shrubs wielding a strimmer to tidy the grass at their bases. They worked steadily, each concentrating on their own task and lost in their own thoughts. It was an hour or more before they had an opportunity to converse.

As they returned the machines to the tool shed, Dominic plucked up courage to ask Lucy the question that he had been wanting to put to her ever since her arrival in Liverpool

'Do you see anything of Cameron these days?' he enquired casually.

Lucy pulled a face.

'He's got a place to study drama at Oxford Brookes,' she sighed. 'I just hope he's going there because it's the best course for him and not because …'

'Because you live there?'

'I expect I'm just being silly. It's probably got nothing to do with it.'

'But, at any rate, you and he aren't …?'

'Aren't what?' Lucy couldn't help smiling at her cousin's coy questioning.

'Well. You know … going out together. He seemed rather keen on you last year.'

'I'm afraid perhaps he is.' Lucy sighed again. 'The thing is: I'm not so sure that I'm that keen on him.'

'You could try telling him that,' Dominic suggested brightly, feeling suddenly extremely cheerful.

'But I can't help feeling sorry for him,' Lucy explained. 'He's got a mother who's completely obsessed with her career, and his father wants him to be something totally different from what he is, and is an absolute bastard in any case. And his uncle, who was the only person who seemed to have any idea of where he was coming from, managed to get himself killed[7]. He can't have much of a life. I just wish … I wish he didn't seem to see *me* as part of the solution to his problems. I'm going to be far too busy over the next six years for that sort of thing.'

'Not even if the right person came along?' queried Dominic.

'They'd just have to wait until I qualify,' Lucy replied decidedly.

'And if he wasn't prepared to wait?'

'Then he wouldn't be the right person, by definition.'

'Getting back to Cameron,' Dominic said hastily. 'Why don't you just tell him to get lost?'

'Because it would be a bit unkind, wouldn't it. And he's harmless. I mean he hasn't tried anything on or anything like that. He just keeps messaging me on Facebook and … Well, like I said, I feel sorry for him.'

'You don't feel sorry for *me*, do you?' Dominic asked anxiously. It had suddenly occurred to him that Lucy might be gracing him with her company out of pity or a sense of duty.

'No. Of course not!' Lucy laughed. 'What have you got for me to feel sorry for you about? You've got a mum and dad, who are still married and seem to get on together. And they both seem dead proud of you. You've done your degree and you've got a career all lined up. Your brother

---

[7] See *Death on the Algarve* © Judy Ford 2016. ISBN 978-1-911083-16-0, 978-1-911083-17-7 (E-book), 978-1-911083-27-6 (Large Print)

and sister both seem nice enough. James is a bit of an idiot, but I expect he'll grow out of it.'

'You've got a nerve!' Dominic laughed out loud. 'You're seventeen and he's twenty-nine and you're telling him to grow up!'

'No. I just think he's a bit ... a bit *ignorant* about things like equality and sexism. I expect it's because of going into the business with your dad. He's never had to fit in with people who come at things from a different perspective.'

'Whereas you are a woman of the world, I suppose?'

'I just get to hear a lot of things from my mam and Jonah and people. And things like not saying *male nurse* or *lady doctor* are just obvious. There are actually more women than men training to be doctors now.'

'You ought to be pleased that I'm going into a female-dominated profession. I'll be doing my bit to counteract out-dated gender stereotypes,' Dominic joked.

'Do you think James will start calling you a *male teacher* when you finish your training?' Lucy giggled. 'And I wonder what he would make of Jonathan Bates and his husband.'

'To be honest, I'd be more concerned about what my mum would say if she knew about them.'

'Surely she must know,' Lucy objected. 'I mean, Aunty Dot gave them a wedding present and everything.'

'Yes. I suppose so. Mum never said anything about it, but she's probably being careful not to mention it in front of the children – or Father Nat. She'll be afraid of corrupting us and shocking him.'

'Or maybe she doesn't think it's important enough to comment about,' Lucy suggested. 'It doesn't affect the way he does his job, after all.'

'No. I know Mum. You saw the way she was with Chloë and Chris. She likes to pretend that things are still the way they were when she and Dad were growing up; and she imagines that Father Nat thinks that they still are.'

'I bet she's wrong about that. I bet he knows as much

as anyone about that sort of thing. Peter says that nothing shocks Father Damien. They seem to spend an awful lot of the time when he's supposed to be being instructed in becoming a Catholic, talking about old police cases and ethical dilemmas.'

'And he's really serious about that? I mean, it seems very strange to me. It's all very well for us – me and Mum and Dad and the others – being brought up to it; but why would you choose all that stuff if it wasn't what you were used to?'

'That's exactly what Jonah keeps saying,' Lucy exclaimed. 'He says the reformers went to the stake for the right to get away from all that mumbo-jumbo, so why would anyone choose to go back to it now?'

'Plenty of Catholics went to the stake for the right to keep their mumbo-jumbo,' Dominic observed drily.

'Yes. It's hard to understand isn't it? Killing someone because you disagree with them. I like all the different sorts of churches there are in Oxford. It's fun seeing all the different costumes and music and stuff. But, I suppose it's not that different from Islamic State wanting to kill anyone who doesn't agree with them. Do you really think you'll be able to make things better by being a Religious Studies teacher?'

'I dunno,' Dominic shrugged. 'I don't suppose I'll ever be able to point at one of my ex-pupils and say, "Look at him. If he hadn't come to my comparative religion classes he would have strapped explosives to his chest and blown himself up in the foyer of the Philharmonic Hall." But maybe I will manage to make a few people understand a bit more about other people's beliefs and then maybe they'll be less inclined to want to blow them up.'

After lunch, Lucy got the satisfaction of playing a more active role in caring for the patients. She was asked to help with bringing those who wished to come from their rooms into the lounge for the weekly programme of entertainment.

'There you are, Mrs Bronson,' said the nurse who had transferred one of the cancer patients from her bed into a wheelchair. 'You're all set. Now this is Lucy, who is going to take you to the lounge.'

'Hello, Mrs Bronson,' Lucy greeted her. 'Are you ready?'

'Yes, thank you.'

'It's another nice day,' Lucy said, fixing on the weather as a subject that was unlikely to be upsetting.

'If you like the heat. I'm not keen on it myself.'

'I'm only staying for a week, so it's nice for me that it's not raining. It'll give me a chance to get out and see a bit of Liverpool.'

'Funny sort of holiday.'

'My mam comes from Liverpool,' Lucy explained. 'We're visiting family.'

'I meant it's funny spending your holiday in this place. It's not exactly a laugh-a-minute in here.'

'Oh, I hope it will be this afternoon,' Lucy smiled. 'We've got a comedian coming in to entertain everyone. He's supposed to be very good. And then afterwards, there's going to be a sing-song, like you usually have.'

'Well, I suppose I'd better give him a chance. You never know, he may not be too bad. When I came here, I never thought I'd still be around now.' Mrs Bronson suddenly became expansive as she reminisced. 'I came here because I was tired of all the treatment and I wanted to be left to die in peace. I probably *wouldn't* still be here if it wasn't for Dr Amandeep.'

'Really? Why's that?'

'He talked to the cancer doctors for me and they came up with some chemo that didn't make me so ill as the other lot. And he got them to agree that I could stop any time I liked. That's what's better about being here,' she added. 'People have time to listen to you properly. Not like in the hospital where they're all in such a hurry. Dr Amandeep is the first doctor I've ever known who really acted like it was up to me, not him, what they did to me.'

'So did you have the chemotherapy?'

'I started it, and it wasn't as bad as the other lot, but then it got worse and I said I wanted to stop. The other doctor tried to persuade me to carry on, but Dr Amandeep said, no, it was my decision. I can't fault him. He always listened and he always stuck up for me. And they told me three months ago that I only had six weeks to live, and I'm still here, so I guess the chemo did do some good.'

'Everyone seems to think that Dr Amandeep is very good,' Lucy said, as they turned in at the door of the lounge.

'Course they do!' a man's voice chimed in from one of the seats, which had been arranged in a wide semi-circle ready for the entertainment. 'I don't know what we'd do without him.'

18. FOR WHOM THE BELL TOLLS
Therefore, send not to know
For whom the bell tolls,
It tolls for thee.
John Donne: "No man is an island"

Fiona Radcliffe had given way to pressure from the residents and arranged for a minibus to take all of those that wished to go to Olive's funeral that afternoon. There was something of a holiday atmosphere as they all waited inside the main entrance for the signal that it was time to depart. For most of the residents, it was a rare treat to be going outside the walls of the Home.

Fiona had decided that she ought to attend in person, as the official representative of the Home. Ian Wilton was also drafted in to accompany the residents and see to their needs while they were out, leaving an agency nurse in charge of those who chose to remain behind.

Fiona had taken care not to invite Lottie to attend, in case she proved an embarrassment. Everyone agreed that she might well not have remembered who Olive was, in any case. Joan said that, having never had much time for Olive in life, it would be hypocritical of her to indulge in eulogies over her after she was dead. Charles, who had never known Olive and disliked any occasion where there might be crowds of strangers, had declined the invitation, appearing surprised to have been asked.

This left six residents to make the four-mile journey to Springwood Crematorium. As she stood on the pavement outside the Home, gazing down the road in anticipation of the arrival of the minibus, Fiona reflected how inconvenient it was that the most severely disabled among her charges had all chosen to come. Two staff were not really sufficient, but there was no-one else that she could ask to help.

The bus arrived and she directed it to stop in the parking bay near the bottom of the sloping path that led from the main entrance down to the pavement below. After a few words with the driver to check that the vehicle was equipped, as per her booking, with a lift at the back for wheelchair users, she went back to bring down the residents.

Jonah and Eric both insisted on being allowed to make the descent unaided, leaving Ian free to accompany Dot as she walked slowly down the path with the aid of a walking frame. Fiona guided Margery, gripping her elbow firmly and speaking softly in her ear to warn her of possible hazards.

'You wait here,' she said to Kathleen and Frances. 'I'll come back and help you down when I've got Margery settled.'

Eventually, they were all sitting in the minibus with seatbelts fastened and walking-aids stowed. Fiona nodded to the driver and they set off.

Frances chattered incessantly as they drove through the streets, telling them about funerals that she had attended in the past and bemoaning the fact that they would not be going on to share in the buffet that the family was providing for funeral guests after the ceremony.

Dot looked out of the window, eager to point out features of interest to Jonah as they passed, and disappointed to see that recent redevelopment work had destroyed many of the landmarks that she remembered.

'Liverpool Hope University is down there,' she said, pointing to the left as they crossed a busy junction. 'That's where our Dominic's going to be studying. And now,' she went on, as they progressed along a wide tree-lined road with a grassy central reservation, 'on the right here is the road where Paul McCartney lived when he was a boy.'

'Really?' Jonah replied, doing his best to sound interested, while trying to remember the map that he had studied before they left, and to work out whether they might be close to the Carter family home in Mossley Hill. 'And I suppose Olive and her family must have lived near here too. Is that right?'

'We've passed that,' Kathleen told him. 'Her house was to the right down Queen's Drive.'

'That's the big junction we came past a minute or two ago,' Ian explained helpfully. 'We're nearly there now. In fact – here we are!'

The minibus crossed another wide, tree-lined road and continued between two rows of beech trees. On either side, railings separated the road and its accompanying footways from the surrounding grassed areas. Soon, rows of gravestones appeared beyond the railings on the right.

'That's Allerton cemetery on the right,' Frances told them. 'My parents are both buried there – and our Jack. I don't hold with this cremation business. You ought to have a grave to visit after someone dies.'

'Cilla Black is buried there too,' Dot told Jonah, 'and John Lennon's mam.'

A sign to the crematorium appeared on the left and the bus turned in, following the curving driveway that led to the modern chapel. A hearse and a second black limousine stood in the parking bay outside the entrance door. The bus pulled up in a small car park on the opposite side of the drive. A silver hatchback followed them in and stopped a few spaces further on. Sandra Latham and Charlotte Simpson got out and stood together chatting, apparently ignoring the party in the minibus.

The driver helped the wheelchair passengers out first, to make more room for those with sticks and walking frames to manoeuvre their way to the door. As soon as he reached the ground, Jonah looked round. The Carter family were already there, standing in a huddle outside the closed doors of the chapel, apparently reluctant to go inside.

There were two men – presumably the Carter brothers Desmond and John – both tall and dark, wearing black suits. The two women who accompanied them were very clearly mother and daughter. They both had light brown hair cut in pageboy fashion, and oval faces with almost identical features. You could have imagined that you were looking at the same woman at different periods of her life. The older one was dressed completely in black. Her outfit had a new look that made Jonah suspect that it had been bought for the occasion. Her daughter, evidently making do with clothes that she already had, was wearing a dark grey jacket over a navy blue skirt.

Taking advantage of the delay while the others were helped out of the bus, Jonah glided over and took up an inconspicuous position next to the wall of the chapel, where he could eavesdrop on the conversation.

'I think you might have agreed to split the estate equally between us,' the taller of the two brothers said in a low voice. 'It's absurd that you should get more just because you're married. I did far more for Mum than you ever did.'

'But she wanted to keep her father's legacy in the family,' John growled back in a similar undertone. 'When you die, you've no-one to leave it to. And what do you mean, you did more for Mum than we did? If you'd really cared about her, you'd have moved in with her and saved her having to pay through the nose for that Care Home.'

'Anyway, if you're so bothered about getting your share, why did you encourage that stupid doctor to insist on a post mortem and an inquest?' broke in his daughter petulantly. 'It could be ages before the money's released now, and I need it right away.'

'If you got your finger out and got yourself a proper job, you wouldn't need to keep sponging off your dad the way you do,' Desmond retorted. 'And why Mum should want to reward you for having two illegitimate kids when you can't even support yourself, I can't imagine.'

'That's so unfair!' Priscilla Carter protested, while her mother also leapt to her defence.

'Poor Cilla does her best,' she insisted. 'It's not her fault Jessie and Luke's dad went off and left them. And it's difficult getting a job when you've got childcare responsibilities.'

'Tell it your own way,' Desmond mumbled bitterly. 'But I still say she should've thought about all that before she got herself-'

'Oh change the record, can't you?' John interrupted. 'We've heard it all before.'

They relapsed into an angry silence.

'And if you're so concerned about Mum,' John began again, speaking low with his head close to his brother's face, 'why did you let them go ahead with cutting her up like that? What possible good could it do?'

'As it happened, it showed that someone did away with her deliberately. Isn't that good enough reason?'

'But does it though?' John persisted. 'Why couldn't it have been an accident? Maybe one of the staff thought she hadn't had her daily dose and gave her another one, and then got frightened and was afraid to own up.'

'That's not what the police think.'

'But they always like to think a crime's been committed. It's their job to think that way. *I* heard the doctor was fine about signing the death certificate until you started sounding off about informing the coroner.'

'That's not what it was like at all.' Desmond whispered back angrily. 'You weren't even there. How can you possibly know what the doctor was thinking? Anyway, can't you at least shut up about it until after the funeral? If you're so keen on showing respect to Mum, why not start with a bit of dignity for her last moments with us? And stop showing up the family in front of the old dears from the Home,' he added, looking towards the cluster of figures making their slow way from the minibus.

John followed his gaze. Then he stepped forward with a brave smile on his face, designed to convey a warm welcome to the guests, while suggesting that he was fighting to keep down the emotion that he felt on the death of his mother.

'Thank you so much for coming,' he greeted Fiona. Then, turning to Kathleen, 'Mum would be so glad you were able to come. Let me take your arm and we'll go in. I'm sure Mum would like you to sit with the family; she always said that you seemed as close to her as a sister.'

Kathleen made her way into the chapel, leaning on John with her left arm while helping herself along with her stick in her right. Fiona watched them for long enough to check that they were safely inside and then turned back to see to the other residents in her care. Good! Dot and Margery had remained inside the minibus. She put her head through the open door and told them to stay in their seats until she or Ian could assist them across the drive.

Eric and Frances were deep in conversation as Frances, leaning heavily on her walking frame, plodded alongside Eric's wheelchair. They seemed intent on making their own way to the chapel, so Fiona instructed Ian to see them across the drive together, while she assisted Margery. The bus driver offered to help Dot. Fiona hesitated for a moment and then agreed that this would be very useful.

Eventually, they were all safely across the drive and

making their slow way inside the chapel. A woman from the funeral director's ushered Jonah and Eric to a space for wheelchairs at one side of the room. They sat there chatting and watching the other guests arriving and taking their seats.

'It's a good thing we all turned out for this,' Eric said cheerfully, pointing towards the front row, where the Carter family was sitting. 'Otherwise it would have been a pretty thin audience. There's only those four from the family. Those two in the discrete trouser suits, are police women.' He pointed towards Sandra and Charlie, sitting inconspicuously at the back. 'They came round asking questions about who did what the day Olive died.'

'I wonder what they're hoping to find out from being here today,' Jonah said innocently.

'Watching the family, I shouldn't wonder. I told you I reckon one of them did her in, didn't I?'

The service began. Just as the opening words were being said, Jonah heard the sound of the door opening behind him and then closing again quietly, but he was unable to turn his head sufficiently to see who had come in and did not dare to disturb the proceedings by moving his chair.

Desmond and John Carter each gave speeches about their mother's life. Jonah gained the impression that they were competing to show how much they appreciated her and what a great loss they were now feeling.

Mrs Carter sniffed and dabbed her eyes throughout the short service and appeared ready to break down at the sight of the coffin disappearing through the curtains at the end. She held tight to her husband's arm and leaned her head on his shoulder.

Priscilla remained unmoved. She sat engrossed in something on her mobile phone until her mother nudged her hard with her shoulder and whispered something in her ear. She put it hastily away in her jacket pocket, scowling as she did so, and spent the remainder of the time staring blankly ahead of her, apparently bored with the proceedings.

As the music began to play, signalling that it was time to leave, Jonah swivelled his chair round rapidly and was rewarded with a glimpse of Jonathan Bates and Nigel Hicks as they slipped out. Why had they come? Jonathan presumably wanted to pay his respects to a woman whom he had known and liked and who had left him five hundred pounds and a painting that he had admired. Nigel, on the other hand? Jonah pondered. He must have had to take time off work in order to be there. It was unlikely that he had ever so much as met Olive. He was clearly there to support Jonathan. That was obvious from the protective way in which he had held open the door for him to leave first, barring the way against anyone who might try to accost him. Why? Did he expect recriminations from the family? Or trouble from the staff or residents?

'Get a move on!' Eric's jovial voice interrupted his thoughts. 'Stop holding up the line! Time we were off!'

Jonah made his way to the door and out into the open air. He looked round. There was no sign of Jonathan and Nigel. Then he caught sight of them getting into a yellow Volkswagen Beetle, which was parked next to Sandra's silver Astra. They drove away, disappearing behind the crematorium building on their way round the one-way system to the exit.

The *Park View* residents made their slow way back across the drive to the car park. John Carter assisted Kathleen, talking earnestly to her all the way. Jonah wondered whether he was actually fond of her or if he was merely wanting to impress upon everyone how concerned he was for his mother's best friend. Desmond also came with them, waiting self-consciously by the minibus while they got in, and thanking Fiona very formally for bringing them all. Both brothers repeated the invitation for them all to come to the local hostelry for drinks and sandwiches, but they seemed relieved when Fiona said firmly that this was infeasible.

As the minibus set off, Jonah was reminded of school trips that he had been on as a boy. Now that the solemn occasion was over, everyone appeared to feel free to enjoy the outing openly. Frances chattered away, comparing this funeral with those of her many relatives. Eric speculated cheerfully on what information the police might have gleaned from their observation of the proceedings. Dot tried to persuade the driver to make a detour so that she could show Jonah Sefton Park and the magnificent architecture in the surrounding area. Fiona, more relaxed now that the trip had gone off without any serious hitches, sat next to Ian, discussing with him the distribution of tasks for the remainder of the day, like the teachers planning the best way of settling their pupils back to work after an outing. Only Kathleen appeared subdued. Was she the only person who had truly liked Olive Carter?

19. TENDER CARE
Can a woman's tender care cease toward the child she bear?
William Cowper: "Hark, my soul it is the Lord."

'But why can't I have riding lessons like Ellie?' Pippa whined for what seemed to Sandra the hundredth time.

'I've told you already,' she sighed, looking up from her notes on the *Park View* murder enquiry, which she was studying in preparation for a meeting with Jonah the next day. 'Riding lessons are expensive and we're saving up for a deposit on a house, so that we don't have to stay here with Granny and Granddad forever.'

'Let us pay,' Sandra's father urged from his seat in the bay window of their house in the Liverpool suburb of Knotty Ash. 'We don't mind.'

'No Dad,' Sandra said firmly. 'I know you mean well, but they've got to learn that money doesn't grow on trees. You and Mum have done quite enough by letting us live here. I don't want the girls thinking they can sponge off you.'

'There's no point asking Mum for anything these days,' Sophie told her younger sister. 'She always says "no". Remember the school skiing trip? *All* my friends went.'

'That's not true,' Sandra said sharply and then

immediately regretting having risen to the bait. However, having responded she had to go on to justify her statement. 'What about Caitlyn and Danielle? They didn't go either.'

'All my *best* friends went,' Sophie insisted. 'And you said I could go and then backed out. It made me look really stupid.'

'I'm sorry, love. Things changed. I didn't know I was going to have to find the money to set up a new home for us all when I said you could go.'

'I don't see why we couldn't all have just stayed at home with Dad,' Pippa said. 'There's plenty of room in the big house and he said we could. It's only you who wanted to move out. And then we wouldn't have had to change schools this year and leave all our friends behind and wear that yucky uniform and-'

'You always used to say that your old uniform was the pits,' Sandra reminded her caustically. 'Look, I know you didn't want to come here, but can't you try to see it from my point of view? I simply can't carry on living with your dad when he's shacked up with Mel and they've had a baby together. It just wouldn't work.'

'Anyway, about the riding lessons,' Pippa resumed. 'Ellie says her mum would take us both over there, so it wouldn't be any bother for you.'

'I've already told you,' Sandra said, keeping her temper with some difficulty. 'We don't have money to spare for riding lessons. If you're so keen to go, why don't you ask your dad if he'll pay?'

'I already have,' Pippa told her. 'He said he'd think about it, but it'd be easier for you to do it because you know Ellie's mum.'

'*I* don't think it would be fair to ask him,' Sophie interjected self-righteously. 'He's got baby Ariana to think about now. Babies cost a lot of money. Mel was telling me about all the stuff they've had to buy. There's a cot and a car seat and a buggy and a high chair and-'

'There's your old cot and high chair in the loft if they only bothered to look for them.' Sandra retorted. 'And he should have thought about all the expense eighteen months ago when I was working all the hours God sends trying to put a serial rapist behind bars while he was fooling around with Melanie in the polytunnel.'

'If you weren't working all the time,' Sophie said, still sounding as if she considered herself to be the voice of reason in an unjust world, 'maybe he wouldn't need to-'

'Sophie!' Sandra's father barked abruptly. 'What a thing to say! You just apologise to your mother at once, young lady! I'm surprised at you – and disappointed.'

Sophie clamped her mouth shut and looked sulky.

'Go on,' her grandfather said. 'I'm waiting. Tell your mother that you're sorry.'

'Why should I say *sorry* when I'm not?' Sophie demanded, getting up and heading for the door. 'It's all Mum's fault that we're stuck here instead of being back in the big house with my own room and my old friends and my old school. Dad wanted us all to stay. There's plenty of room and Mel says she wouldn't mind at all having Mum there.'

Sandra took a few deep breaths and fought down the urge to shout at her daughter.

'Sophie,' she said at last. 'Surely you *must* be able to see that it wouldn't work: me in the guest bedroom while your dad and Mel are in *our* bed together.'

'I don't see why not,' Sophie muttered stubbornly, turning round in the doorway and looking directly at her mother. 'It's not as if you'd be there most of the time anyway. You're always out working.'

'I'm here now, aren't I? Sandra kept herself from raising her voice with increased difficulty.

'Oh yeah? With your nose in your laptop and a pile of police files in front of you!' Sophie sneered.

'Sophie!' Sandra's father intervened again, getting out of his chair and advancing towards his granddaughter. 'I've already told you. This is out of order. Apologise to you mother at once.'

'It's alright, Dad. I can handle it,' Sandra waved her father back into his seat and then turned back to address Sophie. 'Look, love. I know I haven't always been there for you, but it isn't for want of trying. It's just that my job isn't one of those nine-to-five ones where you can predict when you're going to be free.'

Sophie still stood there with her hand on the door handle and a sulky expression on her face. Sandra's exasperation grew.

'And if I didn't have my job,' she said bitingly, 'you wouldn't have had any of the holidays or outings or nice clothes that you've enjoyed over the years. I don't know what state your Dad's business is in, but it always seems to be having a temporary cash-flow crisis when the bills arrive.'

'Maybe if you helped Dad properly with the business, it would do better. Mel is still serving in the shop even though she's got a baby to look after.'

'That's her job!' Sandra exploded, no longer able to keep her voice down. '*My* job is catching criminals, and it pays a whole lot more than your Dad's business ever has. My salary has been propping up that ruddy garden centre for years. You'd soon notice it if I jacked it in and spent all day potting up shrubs and watering seed trays. And now, will you please stop arguing and let me finish what I'm doing? You may not like it, but I'd prefer to keep my job, thank you very much!'

'Have you finished now?' Sophie asked rudely, when Sandra paused for breath. 'Only I've got lots of better things to do than stand here listening to you wittering on.' Then, without waiting for a reply, she flounced out slamming the door behind her.

'Couldn't I just have *one* lesson?' Pippa asked immediately. 'To see if I like it?'

'No love. There's no point when you wouldn't be able

to go again afterwards. Now, please! I need to read all these reports, ready for an important meeting I've got tomorrow.'

Pippa pulled a face. Then she took her smartphone out of her pocket, drew her feet up onto the chair and started flicking through texts from her friends, carefully ignoring her grandfather's attempts to catch her eye in order to suggest that she might like to play a board game with him on the kitchen table so that her mother could work in peace.

Sandra tried to concentrate on the list of suspects in front of her, but her daughters' demands kept intruding on her thoughts. It was a pity that she had not been able to let Sophie go on the skiing trip last February, but the deadline had come only days after Gary's bombshell and her decision to move out of the family home. By the time you added in all the necessary clothes and equipment, there would not have been much change from a thousand pounds. That was unthinkable when their finances were so uncertain and, if Gary decided to be awkward, she might have hefty lawyer's fees to pay for a divorce.

She sighed. Children were very expensive these days, especially if they had friends whose parents were well-off and inclined to indulge their offspring. Not that riding lessons were in themselves unreasonable. She was glad that her father had not mentioned that she had herself gone riding as a child. It was so difficult to explain that new school uniforms and making a contribution towards the running costs of her parents' house and finding a way for them to set up home independently were all more important than enabling her daughters to follow every new fad among their friends.

She told herself to think more positively. At least she had a secure and well-paid job. It must be dreadful for single mothers who were unemployed or on the minimum wage. They must always be having to tell their kids that they could not have the things that their friends took for granted. People like ... like the Care Assistants at Park View, for example.

She scanned down the list of staff. Yes, several of them had children – children who would expect the latest computer gadgets and training shoes, dancing lessons and holidays. If they thought that their jobs were under threat, what might they be willing to do to prevent the loss of their meagre wage for the sake of their kids? If Olive was threatening their family's livelihood, that was surely a far more convincing motive for doing away with her than Jonathan's paltry five hundred pounds or even the Carter brothers' far larger legacy. Now, which of these were present during the crucial time when the murder must have taken place? No! That was no longer a relevant question. The broken lock on Olive's patio doors meant that anyone who knew the code to the side gate could have crept in during the night and entered her room.

Everyone seemed to agree that Julia Freeman was likely to feature prominently in Olive's dossier. She had children, but they were grown up and living apparently independent lives. But did that mean that they were no longer a drain on Julia's resources? You heard a lot these days about young people relying on the *Bank of Mum and Dad* when they were starting out.

Rebecca Anderson was not known to have any reason to fear any revelations from Olive's list of misdemeanours, but if she had committed some serious breach of protocol and it had so far not come to light, might she not be all the more anxious to keep it that way? She had three children, whose father was notably absent. She would certainly struggle if she were to lose her job and its out-of-hours enhancements.

Who else was there? Scarlet Jones had children. Her husband also had a job, but that did not necessarily mean that they did not rely on her income to make ends meet. What about Ian Wilton? He was the breadwinner for a family of three kids.

Her thoughts were interrupted by the ringing of her mobile phone. She snatched it up off the table in front of her and looked at the screen. It was Gary. What could he want?

She swiped the screen to answer the call, at the same time getting to her feet and walking towards the door. Whatever her husband had to say to her, she would rather her father and daughter were not listening in.

'Hi Gary! What do you want?' She pulled the door closed behind her and started up the stairs to her small bedroom.

'Sandy?' He hesitated. Sandra knew the signs. He had something to say that she was not going to like. He cleared his throat and started again. 'Sandy? I'm sorry to have to ask you, but ... do you think you could do me a massive favour?'

Sandra did not answer. Let him sweat. If he wanted whatever it was so badly, he would have to come out with it without any help from her. She reached the landing and slipped quickly into her room, closing the door firmly behind her.

'Sandy? Are you still there?'

'Yes.' She sat down on the bed and waited for him to continue.

'Like I said, I wish I didn't have to ask you, but ... but could you lend me a couple of grand?'

'Two thousand pounds! You've got to be kidding. Where am I supposed to get that sort of money from?'

'I know you've got savings in the Building Society. Please Sandy. It won't be for long. It's just to tide the business over a bit of a short-term cash-flow problem.'

'I'm sorry, Gary,' she began. Then she stopped. Why should she be sorry for not giving in to this outrageous demand? 'Look, Gary,' she resumed. 'I really don't have any money to spare. I'm already having to tell the girls they can't have all the things they want. It wouldn't be fair on them if I throw away a couple of thousand propping up your business. If you can't make it pay, you'd better sell up and get a proper job.'

'I can't do that,' Gary protested, 'Dad would turn in his grave. He spent his whole life building it up. Oh come on, Sandy! I promise it won't be for long. Just 'til things pick up a bit. It's just the uncertainty after the Brexit vote. People aren't spending on their gardens. But it won't last – you'll see. Just a couple of grand for a few months – please!'

'No. I'm sorry Gary. I've got to think of the girls, and finding a place for us to go so we can get out of Mum and Dad's hair. Why don't you ask Melanie to help you out?'

'Don't be like that. You know she doesn't have that sort of money. She's been working for me since she left school and goodness knows I can't afford to pay much! Oh please, Sandy! The bank won't increase my overdraft and I'm up to the limit on my credit cards and I just need a few thousand to tide me over.'

'Then I can't see any other way out. You'll just *have* to sell up. Move into a flat with Melanie and the baby and start again.'

'We're mortgaged to the hilt. We probably couldn't even afford a flat.'

'Then try living with her parents.'

'Oh yeah, very funny.' Gary's pleading tone gave way to anger. 'Her Mum's only got one bedroom and her Dad's at the other end of the country with six kids of his own. Oh well! I suppose I shouldn't have expected you to understand. Just remember you're the one who's going to have to tell the girls if the house goes and they can't come to stay any longer.'

He ended the call. Sandra sat for a few moments staring down at the phone in her hand. Were things really as bad as Gary had made out? The garden centre must have been on the rocks for years. How had she failed to realise? Had he deliberately concealed it from her, too proud to admit that he did not have the business acumen of his father? Or had she been too busy with her job and the girls to allow him to share his worries with her?

She went back downstairs and tried to focus her mind on the staff list from the Care Home. At its head was Fiona Radcliffe. By all accounts, she was a weak manager, thoroughly out of her depth, it appeared – like Gary, trying to run a business without the necessary skills. Her husband had set her up, like a benevolent parent giving a child a toy to keep them occupied. He was the businessman and she was supposed to be an expert in healthcare. It would be a humiliation for her if the Home were to fail an inspection, or if clients started leaving because they did not trust her to keep them safe. She stood to lose more than just financially if Olive's dossier were to be passed on to the CQC inspector.

20. THE DARKNESS DEEPENS
The darkness deepens Lord, with me abide
Henry Francis Lyte: "Abide with me"

A distant crash woke Jonah in the small hours of the following morning. He lay there listening, trying to make out what was going on. Had he dreamed the sound of several small items clattering on to some hard surface? Then a door banged and there was a murmur of voices from somewhere in the building. There was a low, calm voice speaking slowly and coaxingly, and a more high-pitched slightly whining voice, not exactly shouting, but loud and determined.

The voices grew louder. Straining his ears, Jonah could make out the sound of footsteps in the corridor outside his room. They approached slowly. He could now distinguish the soft padding of bare feet and the tapping of shoes on the parquet flooring. He strained his ears to make out what the voices were saying, but could only catch a few phrases.

'Come along now,' said the calm voice. 'Everything's alright.'

'Let me go!' came the high-pitched voice. 'I've got to …'

Got to do what? Jonah wondered, unable to make out what followed.

'It's alright,' the calm voice repeated, right outside Jonah's door now. 'It's all done. You can go to bed now.'

'But Mrs Foster's dressing needs changing.'

Who was Mrs Foster?

'No, no. That's all been done. Don't you worry. Come back!' With more authority now, and a little louder: 'Not down there. Here we are.'

The footsteps, which had passed Jonah's door, apparently heading for the fire exit, now stopped.

'Come along,' the calm voice urged. 'You'll wake Mr Melling. Come back and we'll get you into bed, nice and snug.'

The bare feet padded back past Jonah's door and stopped again. There was the sound of a key turning in a lock and a door opening. That must be Lottie's room, and the high-pitched voice presumably belonged to her.

'In you go,' came the calm voice. 'And let's get you-,' it stopped abruptly as the door closed.

They must have gone inside Lottie's room. Presumably she had gone wandering again and Rebecca, who was on duty overnight, had brought her back. What had she been doing to cause the crash that he had heard?

There was the sound of the door opening again and another soft murmur from the calm voice. Jonah could not discern the words, but he imagined that Rebecca must be saying *goodnight* to Lottie and encouraging her to go back to sleep. Then the door closed and she headed back down the corridor. Her footsteps were brisker now as the tapping of her shoes receded.

Jonah lay in silence, listening for any sounds that might indicate what had gone on. He thought he heard a clinking, as of broken glass being swept up, but he could not be sure. Then it was all quiet again. He closed his eyes. Did Lottie's nocturnal roaming have anything to do with Olive's death? Someone had said that she used to be a nurse, hadn't they? Could she have gone into Olive's room, imagining her to be one of her patients, and injected her with insulin, believing ... believing ... what exactly? He drifted off to sleep, still pondering on the possibilities.

A gentle but firm hand gripped his shoulder and rolled him over on to his other side. Immediately Jonah was awake.

'What time is it?' he asked.

'Three thirty. I'm sorry, Mr Porter, I was trying not to wake you.'

'Don't apologise. I'm used to it. I'll be off again as soon as you've gone; don't you worry.'

'We ought to get you one of those automatic beds that turns you by itself; then we wouldn't need to disturb you in the night.'

'Oh! I've tried one of them. It was no good. It made such a row that it kept me awake all night. Besides, my concubines would feel scorned if I exchanged them for a pneumatic mattress.'

'Concubines?' Rebecca asked with a puzzled frown.

'Like King David in his old age,' Jonah explained, grinning up at her. 'He had a beautiful virgin who slept in his bed to keep him warm at night. I've got Our Bernie and Our Lucy, who take it in turns to sleep in my room and turn me at night.'

Rebecca still looked puzzled.

'I'm only joking. Actually, they have a rota of three, but old Peter can hardly be described as a concubine, can he? I only meant that Lucy might be offended if she thought I didn't need her any more. Now, tell me what all that noise was about earlier.'

'What noise?'

'All the crashing and banging, and doors slamming, and people walking about.'

'Oh! Did that wake you? I'm so sorry. It was only Lottie having one of her fantasy trips. Did I tell you she used to be a District Nurse? I found her in the office rummaging through the drawers. Goodness knows where she got hold of the keys from! I suppose I ought to have locked the room when I went upstairs to answer Mrs Lowe's buzzer, but I never thought, and I was *sure* the drawers were all locked. You won't tell anyone about it, will you? Mrs Radcliffe's in one of her moods at the moment, with this business with Mrs Carter, and I'm afraid she might dismiss me to show how tough she can be and how it isn't her fault if anything goes wrong.'

'I won't say anything,' Jonah assured her, 'but don't you think it might be better to log it all as a "near miss" in the accident book? Then you're squeaky clean if anyone notices anything wrong and it might mean that something gets done to stop it happening again.'

'You don't know Mrs Radcliffe.'

'No, I suppose not,' Jonah conceded. He debated whether to press her further, knowing that covering up the incident was unwise, both for the safety of the residents and for Rebecca's own long term future. He decided not to do anything that might antagonise his witness.

'She won't want something like that written down where the inspectors might see it. And *I* don't want the inspectors finding out either. The last thing I need is for this place to get closed down.'

'I don't think that's likely,' Jonah tried to reassure her. 'From what I've seen, it seems very good. Everyone's been very helpful and friendly to me.'

'We do our best,' Rebecca sighed, 'but it isn't easy sometimes. Mrs Radcliffe is so penny-pinching! With all the residents getting older and needing more help with everything, there aren't enough staff on duty half the time.'

'It must be very worrying for you, having Lottie so confused at night and you all on your own.'

'Yes,' Rebecca sighed again. 'To be honest, I think it's time she was moved somewhere else. She needs to be somewhere that's properly geared up for dementia patients.'

'Is that what she's got?'

'I don't know that she's actually been diagnosed, but

that's what it looks like, isn't it?'

'I suppose it does. Has anyone asked the doctor about her?'

'I don't think so. I don't know if you can. I mean it's all supposed to be confidential, isn't it?'

'Yes. I suppose so, but–'

'Right!' Rebecca pulled the covers back over Jonah's body and tucked in the sheet, 'I'll leave you to get back to sleep.'

'Can't you stay and talk for a while?' Jonah pleaded. 'I'm wide awake now. I'd enjoy the company. Tell me about your family. How many children did you say you had?'

'Three – a girl and two boys. I've got some pictures on my phone. Would you like to see?'

'Please!'

Rebecca sat down on the bed and got out her phone. She flicked through to find a photograph of three children: a girl in a blue checked dress and two boys in white shirts and grey trousers.

'This is Ben's first day at school. He's five and Alex is seven and Olivia is nearly ten.'

'They look a bright crowd. I bet they keep you on your toes.'

'Yes – especially Alex. He's got Asperger's and that means I've got to keep exactly to his normal routine or he goes ballistic. That's why it's so good to have this night job. It's impossible to get childcare for him. Even my dad can't cope with him during the day. But he's a lovely boy so long as you let him do things in his own time and don't get offended when he says what he thinks. Here he is arranging his collection of Liverpool memorabilia.'

Jonah looked down at a photograph of a boy in a red football shirt surrounded by items bearing the familiar Liver bird logo of Liverpool Football Club.

'My dad's got a season ticket at Anfield for him and both boys. Alex has to buy something in the shop every time he goes. It gets awfully expensive, but if we don't, he's liable to have a meltdown. He insisted on having his room painted red,' Rebecca went on. 'He's got red walls, a red carpet, a red bed, and I only just persuaded him not to have a red ceiling as well.'

'It must be exhausting for you during the school holidays,' Jonah said sympathetically. 'If you're working all night and then you've got the kids at home all day.'

'Yes,' agreed Rebecca. She paused for a moment and then went on. 'Though, actually, it's not been so bad these holidays, because my dad lost his job back in June, so he's been around to help. I don't know how we're going to manage though, once his redundancy money's used up.'

She turned the phone off abruptly and got up to go.

'And now, you really ought to try to get some sleep. Julia tells me you're going out with your friends tomorrow morning. You don't want to be too tired to enjoy it, do you?'

21. HAIL MARY
And the angel came in unto her, and said, Hail, thou that art highly favoured, the Lord is with thee: blessed art thou among women.
Luke 1:28

Dot came back to Jonah's room after breakfast, and they sat talking together while they waited for Peter and Bernie to arrive to take them out. Ostensibly, this was a generous gesture on Bernie's part, providing a rare opportunity for her aunt to leave the confines of the Home and spend some time out in the open air getting the benefit of the summer weather (not that good weather was guaranteed in this exceptionally changeable August). In reality, it was a meticulously planned scheme for enabling Jonah to report his findings to DCI Latham well away from any prying eyes at the Care Home.

'I haven't been to the Festival Gardens since they were restored,' Dot told Jonah. 'If they're anything like they were before, you're in for a treat. Bernie tells me you're quite a gardener yourself.'

'Well, only in a managerial capacity these days,' Jonah

grinned back at her. 'I leave all the hard graft to Bernie and the others. And that means that when the plants grow well, it's down to my expert advice, and when they fail it's the fault of the workers!'

'I looked out the photos I took when I went to the Garden Festival back in '84. I've got them here, if you'd like to see them. Dot placed her capacious handbag on her lap and started to rummage inside it. 'I'm sure they're here somewhere.' She took out a telescopic umbrella and a smartphone, placing them on the table in front of her before returning to her search. 'Here they are!' she said triumphantly, then, 'No,' she corrected herself, recognising that the envelope that she was holding was merely an appointment from her optician for an eyesight test. 'They must be in the other compartment.'

She bundled the umbrella, phone and envelope back into the bag and zipped it up. Then she turned the bag round on her lap and opened another section of it. After a few moments of fruitless searching, she tipped the entire contents out on the table. Jonah saw a handkerchief, two tubes of peppermints, a diary, a tablet computer and a rosary of black beads.

'Never mind,' he said as Dot, shaking her head in exasperation, returned each item to the bag. 'I'll see it in the flesh soon enough and there'll be plenty of time, after we get back, to compare it with what it was like back then.'

Dot picked up the rosary, pausing for a moment to kiss the crucifix and mutter some words that Jonah could not hear, before placing it carefully back in the bag.

'Do you take your prayer beads with you everywhere?' he asked, struggling to reconcile Dot's fascination with new technology and lively interest in the world about her with religious practices that he associated with credulous mediaeval peasants.

'I do. At, my time of life, you do a lot of waiting around for things to happen and they give me a way of using the time productively.'

'Productive? Reciting Hail Marys and stuff?'

'Praying, and meditating on the Mysteries of the Rosary. At my age, praying is about the only contribution I can make to the benefit of mankind.'

'I suppose so,' Jonah said grudgingly, thinking of the prayer meetings that his father had expected him to take part in, when he was a teenager. To his young mind, they had felt interminable, and he had not been sorry that, after he started work, his police duties had often prevented him from attending. 'But why Mary? Why not go direct to God?'

Dot did not answer, so Jonah continued. 'I suppose it's only natural if that's the way you've been brought up. The thing I can't understand is why Peter should decide to go in for all that at his time in life and when he's never had anything to do with it before.'

'I'm glad you're willing to make allowances for me being an ignorant old woman,' Dot remarked drily.

'I didn't say that. I just meant that, when you've been doing it all your life, presumably these things are meaningful to you, even if they don't make logical sense. Whereas, with Peter it's different. If he was brought up to any sort of religion it was the Methodist Church and that's where he went for years with his first wife. So why choose something so completely different?'

'To prove to himself that he isn't doing it just *because* it makes him feel closer to his first wife, perhaps?' Dot suggested mildly.

'I can't see why that matters.' Jonah refused to be convinced. 'It just seems like madness to me. One moment he doesn't even believe in God, and the next he's chattering away with the Virgin Mary and taking lessons from some Catholic priest and going into a daze every time he sees a statue or a picture of "our Lady". It doesn't make any sense to me. If he's had this wonderful conversion experience, why can't he just start coming along to church with the rest of us?'

'Our Bernie told me that you're good at your job because you've got the imagination to put yourself in the shoes of the criminals and see things from their point of view. Why don't you try to think what it must be like for your friend? Think about it: a motherless boy growing up in a children's home. The first experience he's going to have of parenthood is when he becomes a father himself; and the nearest he's going to get to a mother's love is going to be his wife. Imagine what it's like when she dies a horrible death and-'

'I don't see what all this has got to do with-,' Jonah interrupted tersely, but Dot refused to be deflected from setting out her proposition.

'And then, just when things seem perhaps to be going right again at last, his son's baby girl is snatched from her pram, and he's helpless to do anything for him. If, in that moment of despair, he snatches at the possibility that maybe there is *Someone* in charge of this mess, don't you think that God would show him compassion?'

'Yes. I do, but I still don't see-,' Jonah tried again.

'I know your father was a man of the cloth, so I expect you know a whole lot more clever theology than I do. But when *I* think about what God could do for a motherless boy who wants more than anything to comfort his grieving son, I can't help thinking that He might decide to turn it all over to His own mother to sort out.'

'Peter's mother? But-'

'No. The Mother of God: Mary.'

'There you go again. Why do you call her the Mother of God? God can't have a mother.'

Before Dot could reply, the door opened and Oonagh entered, pushing a trolley of cleaning equipment in front of her. She stopped short when she saw them and her face went very red.

'I'm so sorry,' she apologised, sounding very flustered. 'They said you'd gone out for the day. I didn't mean to disturb you.'

'That's alright,' Jonah said kindly 'No harm done.'

'It's just that I'm so behind with the cleaning this week,' Oonagh continued, evidently feeling obliged to justify her actions. 'I should have done your room yesterday. I do Rooms 1 and 2 on Monday,' she went on as if reciting a memorised list of instructions, 'and 3 and 4 on Tuesday. So I should have done 5 and 6 yesterday. That's why I thought I'd come early and try to catch up.'

'Tell you what,' Jonah suggested. 'Why don't you give this room a miss for one week? I'm only here until Saturday and then it'll probably be empty for a while after that, so it really isn't necessary.'

'But Mrs Radcliffe-,' Oonagh began.

'I won't tell on you,' Jonah said, with an impish grin, which only served to make Oonagh all the more agitated.

'But if she asks …?'

'If she says anything to me, I'll just tell her how impressed I've been at the spotlessness of the rooms and how conscientious the cleaning staff must be.'

'Really, Oonagh,' Dot added. 'It's alright. And, my room is fine too. Why don't you give both of them a miss this week, and then you'll be able to catch up and be back on track by the end of today.'

'I'm not sure …,' Oonagh still sounded anxious.

'It's simple,' Dot insisted gently. 'You go and do Room 6 this morning and Room 7 this afternoon. Miss out Room 8, and then tomorrow you can do 9 and 10 and nobody need ever know that you got behind.'

Oonagh stood for a few moments frowning in concentration, counting off the rooms on her fingers. Then her face cleared and she smiled round at them both.

'Yes! Thank you so much – if you're both really sure?'

'We're quite sure,' Dot said firmly. 'Now run along and get started on Margery's room.'

'She worries too much, poor child!' Dot said to Jonah, once Oonagh had closed the door behind her. 'She's very willing, and Fiona exploits her shamefully. The trouble is:

she has to keep to her routine or she goes to pieces. If anything interferes with it she gets anxious and then she starts making mistakes.'

'She told me that Jonathan sometimes helps her when she gets behind schedule.'

'That's right. He's very understanding. He's knows it's not her fault. She's too obliging and, as I said, not good at working round things that interfere with her schedule.' Dot sighed. 'It's a dreadful nuisance that Frannie Ray has Room 1. That always gets poor Oonagh's week off to a bad start.'

'Is Mrs Ray difficult then?' Jonah queried. 'She seems very pleasant and easy-going to me.'

'Oh yes,' agreed Dot. 'She's always very kind to Oonagh and never criticises. No. The problem is that she's such a gossip. She never stops talking, and Oonagh's too polite to tell her that she doesn't have time to listen to her tittle-tattle, which means that cleaning Frannie's room always takes far longer than it ought to.'

'And she's in Room 1, so that's always the one that Oonagh cleans first?'

'That's right. I did try suggesting that she might start with Room 2 and leave Frannie to last, but that only got the poor girl totally confused. She has to stick to the same routine every week and every room has to be cleaned in the same way. It's no good telling her that the bath doesn't need cleaning this week or that I've already wiped the dressing table myself. She has a list of jobs in her head and she has to do them all in the same order every time.'

'Do the residents complain if she doesn't get things done on time? She sounded very dubious about agreeing not to clean our rooms.'

'Most of them are OK about it, but one or two aren't very sympathetic. Joan, for example. She can be very cutting, but it's more what she says to Oonagh herself than complaining to the management. She always says there's no point complaining, because Fiona wouldn't know how to do anything about it anyway. Mind you, I don't think she's any worse to Oonagh than to any of the other staff; it's just that poor Oonagh takes it more to heart than they do. And then there's Betty Hunter – or rather Betty's daughter, Helen. She's a dreadful one for complaining to the management about everything. And when she complains to Fiona about Oonagh, Fiona shouts at her – more to show the residents that she's listening to them than anything else – and poor little Oonagh quite goes to pieces.'

'What about Olive?' Jonah asked, trying to sound casual. 'Was she sympathetic?'

'Up to a point. She was usually quite nice to Oonagh's face if she got things wrong, but she was always writing things down in that little diary of hers. I don't know if she wrote anything about Oonagh, but I wouldn't be surprised.'

'And did Oonagh know about Olive's little book?'

'Probably.' Dot said shortly, as if she had grown tired of the subject. 'Now, to get back to what we were talking about, I'd like to know why you're so against Our Lady.'

'I'm not against anyone,' protested Jonah. 'I just can't understand people taking all this stuff seriously anymore. How can some woman who's been dead for the best part of two thousand years speak to people here and now!'

'As I said before, I'm sure you know more about it than I do,' Dot replied equably, 'and, of course, you young people are always right, aren't you?'

'I'm not trying to get you to change *your* beliefs.' Jonah smiled at the way in which Dot was treating him like a self-opinionated teenager. 'I just can't fathom why old Peter's swallowed it all the way he has.'

'Might I suggest that you consider why it is that you are so resentful of his change of heart?' Dot said quietly. 'I think that might be quite an instructive exercise.'

'I'm not resentful,' Jonah protested.

'I think you are.' Dot's voice remained calm and even.

'Why? What makes you say that?'

'Your demeanour. The way you can't seem to let go of it and admit it's none of your business.'

Jonah said nothing. He sat staring at his computer screen, pretending to be engrossed in something there. Dot watched him for several minutes and then resumed.

'I think it's all to do with Our Bernie.'

'That's nonsense. How d'you make that out?'

'Well, it seems to me that you are very reliant on her-,' Dot broke off as Jonah leapt to protest.

'No more than on Peter and Lucy. They all take a hand equally, except during working hours and that's different: it's a job.'

'I'm not talking about who wipes your bum and brushes your teeth,' Dot said smoothly. 'I mean that anyone can see that Bernie's a lot more to you than just a Personal Assistant.'

'As are Peter and Lucy,' Jonah put in quickly.

'I'm sure you know best.' Dot refused to be perturbed by his protestation. 'But perhaps I could finish? As I was saying, you are very reliant, emotionally, on a woman who is another man's wife.'

Jonah opened his mouth to dispute this statement, but Dot held up her hand to silence him.

'Up until now, you and Bernie have shared one thing from which her husband was excluded, namely your religious faith. But now, all of a sudden Peter has a change of heart. If he had merely dropped his agnosticism and come into the fold with you and Bernie, it wouldn't have been so bad. You would have been in the position of an old hand who could show the new boy the ropes. It might even have enhanced your standing with Bernie. But no! He, inexplicably, hits on Roman Catholicism, which symbolises to you a part of Bernie's past that you can't understand and that you were hoping she had put behind her. Now there is the danger that she will revert to her childhood religion – Lucy has been talking about how they will all be able to go to Mass together – and you will be the one left on the outside looking in. And that, I think, is why you resent Peter's decision to become a Catholic.'

They sat together without speaking, eyeing one another. Eventually, Dot broke the silence.

'It might help you to know that my niece is quite extraordinarily stubborn. Now she's got you, there's no way she's going to let you go.'

'I don't need you to tell me that,' Jonah muttered disagreeably, 'and you've got no business suggesting that I resent old Peter becoming a Catholic. I don't see why you're so-'

He broke off at the sound of a knock on the door. It burst open and Bernie strode in, followed closely by Lucy, with Peter bringing up the rear.

Lucy ran over to Jonah and put her arms around his shoulders.

'We've missed you,' she murmured in his ear, kissing him on the cheek. 'I hope you solve this murder mystery soon: we want you back.'

'How're you doing, Aunty? Are you ready for the off?' Bernie asked. Then, without waiting for an answer, she turned to Jonah 'Where's the manual chair? We'd better check that Aunty Dot's comfortable in it.'

'In the bathroom.' Jonah inclined his head towards the door. 'Better check it before she gets in. It may still be wet from when they gave me my shower this morning. They're short-staffed with Jonathan suspended and I'm not confident they dried it properly.'

Peter disappeared into the bathroom returning a few seconds later with the wheelchair.

'Your chariot awaits!' he announced dramatically, pushing it over to where Dot was sitting. 'Let me help you in and then we can adjust the footrests and so on.'

It took several minutes to prepare Jonah and Dot for their day out, but eventually Peter was satisfied that Dot was safe and comfortable in the wheelchair, propped with cushions to protect her brittle spine and with a blanket across her knees to keep her thin limbs warm. Meanwhile, Lucy and Bernie had been checking that Jonah was correctly positioned in his chair and adding a few necessary items to the storage space at the back, while Jonah waited impatiently, eager to be on their way. Bernie caught his eye and smiled, recognising the signs that he was intent on solving a case and resented any delay.

'Lead on, Macduff!' she commanded, holding the door wide. 'Let battle commence!'

22. COME INTO THE GARDEN

There has fallen a splendid tear
From the passion-flower at the gate.
She is coming, my dove, my dear;
She is coming, my life, my fate;
The red rose cries, 'She is near, she is near;'
And the white rose weeps, 'She is late;'
The larkspur listens, 'I hear, I hear;'
And the lily whispers, 'I wait.'

Alfred, Lord Tennyson: "Come into the Garden Maud"

Sandra and Charlie were waiting for them in the car park when they arrived at their rendezvous in the Festival Gardens. Lucy undid Jonah's fastenings while Bernie set up the ramp and Peter lifted Dot out of her seat and into the folding wheelchair. By the time they were all safely out of the car, they had been joined by Dominic, who had arrived on his bicycle. He chained it up and came over to them.

'I'll push you now, Aunty,' he said. 'We can't have Peter straining his back, can we?'

Peter smiled as he relinquished the handles of the chair and gave a sidelong glance towards Lucy. If Dominic had been hoping to impress her with his thoughtfulness towards her aunt and stepfather, he had been wasting his time, because she was still busily checking that Jonah had everything that he needed, quite oblivious of her cousin.

Jonah introduced Dominic and Dot to Sandra and Charlie. Dot, who had been disappointed not to have been interviewed as a key witness when they visited the Home to view the death scene and speak to the staff, attempted to give Sandra a detailed account of everything that had gone on during the day leading up to Olive's demise. Jonah politely explained that there was limited time available and he needed to speak with his police colleagues confidentially. He assured her that he had taken notes of his conversations with her and would ensure that everything that she had told him would be included in the file of evidence.

They agreed that Dominic and Lucy would take Dot for a stroll in the gardens, while the police contingent compared notes and made plans for taking forward the investigation. Lucy hugged Jonah around the shoulders by way of goodbye before falling in beside her cousin, who set off at a brisk pace, pushing Dot ahead of him.

'The Chinese garden is the best,' he told them. 'The rest hasn't really been properly restored, just tidied up a bit. I'll take you there first.'

The others settled themselves around one of the picnic tables that were provided for visitors. Charlie got out a laptop computer and set it up in front of her. Sandra cleared her throat and began.

'We've followed up on those leads that you suggested,' she told Jonah. 'Thank you for telling me about Oonagh Conlon. She'd somehow escaped our notice altogether. Her name wasn't on the list of staff that Fiona Radcliffe gave us. Neither was Grace Massey, who comes in twice a day to cook meals. I don't know why Fiona left them off. She said that she'd made the list from the duty rota of care staff and forgotten to add them to it. That may be true or I suppose there could be a reason that she deliberately left them off.'

'It's difficult to see what that could have been,' Peter

observed. 'One of you could easily have seen them around when you visited and wanted to know who they were. She couldn't hope to hide them from you, and why would she want to?'

'We wondered whether there could have been anything wrong with their employment,' Charlie told him. 'But neither of them is an illegal immigrant or paid cash-in-hand; and both have had DBS checks done. It all looks completely kosher.'

'Anyway,' Sandra continued. 'While everyone was out at the funeral yesterday, one of our guys went round and took their fingerprints, which means that we now have the complete set that we thought we'd already got. We matched up Oonagh's prints with some that we'd lifted from the bedside cabinet in Olive's room.'

'The cabinet where the empty syringe and vial were found?' Bernie asked excitedly.

'That's right.'

'So what?' Peter was not convinced of the significance of this discovery. 'She was the cleaner wasn't she? Why wouldn't her prints be all over the place?'

'Yes. You're quite right,' Sandra agreed. 'It doesn't prove anything, but it does seem quite interesting that those were practically the only prints that we found in the room, when we know that at least four people had been in there between when Olive retired to bed and when PC Thomas saw the syringe. Jonathan Bates put her to bed; Scarlet Jones went in to wake her in the morning; Dr Bhaskar examined her body and her son Desmond went in to see his mother's body and to talk to the doctor. None of them appear to have left any fingermarks.'

'What about John and Valerie?' Jonah asked. 'Didn't they go in too?'

'I don't think so,' Charlie said, looking down at her notes. 'They seem to have spent the time between when they arrived at the Home and when Rob Thomas got there, in the office arguing with Desmond about the post mortem. But that's not the point. The strange thing is that we know that several people did go into the room and yet they didn't leave any traces.'

'So what are you saying?' Bernie asked. 'That Oonagh cleaned the room *after* they'd all come out of it that morning?'

'It certainly looks as if someone probably went round wiping all the surfaces,' Sandra agreed, 'unless they all wore gloves or were very careful not to touch anything.'

'Which is entirely possible,' Jonah said. 'Let's think about it. Jonathan, Scarlet and the doctor *could* all have had gloves on. Remember, they were there to handle an elderly person in their care. Jonathan was assisting her with taking her medication. Wouldn't it be fairly standard infection-control procedure to wear gloves? That only leaves Desmond, who has been called in to see his dead mother. Apart from the handle on the *outside* of the door, I reckon he might well not touch anything in that room. The natural thing would be to go straight over to the bed to see her and to talk to the doctor.'

'So those fingermarks don't really tell us anything,' Charlie said regretfully.

'Only that, now we know they belong to Oonagh, we don't need to keep looking for some mysterious interloper whose prints we can't trace,' Sandra pointed out. 'So it is progress of a sort. Now, moving on to your other suggestions, Jonah: we've re-checked Hector Bayliss's police record and he definitely doesn't have form of any kind; and we've also checked out Oonagh Conlon and Grace Massey, the cook. Both of their records are clean as a whistle; and there are no reports of any food poisoning incidents in the Home either.'

'It looks as if we're back to the care staff being the most likely suspects,' Peter observed. 'They were surely more likely to have been the targets of Olive's dossier; and they would have had more to lose too, if it meant that they were blacklisted from working with elderly people.'

'Yes,' Sandra agreed, 'and I've had a few thoughts about that, but first, to finish bringing you up to speed on what we've been doing at our end. We've been through the police notes on the contents of Olive's room again. By the time our people got there to check over her possessions, there was nothing there that could have constituted a dossier of information about the Home. No diary, no notebook, not even so much as a shopping list. It looks very much as if, either the dossier didn't exist or else someone took it.'

'Or it wasn't in her room,' Jonah added. 'Various people talked to me about her carrying around a notebook or a diary and writing in it wherever she went. Could she have left it in the lounge or the dining room or somewhere?'

'I suppose she could,' Sandra admitted. 'We didn't search the whole Home. For one thing, it wasn't until you told us about the dossier that we'd have known what to look for.'

'Unless she hid it very well, someone will surely have found it by now,' Peter said.

'I don't know,' Jonah disagreed. 'A notebook or diary wouldn't necessarily be that obvious – if she shoved it in among the books on one of the shelves, for example.'

'OK,' Sandra cut in. 'Charlie – make a note to get that checked out. Now, the other thing I wanted to tell you about is my interview with Fiona Radcliffe yesterday evening. I asked her about the staff meeting the day Olive died and about the dossier. She basically agreed with Jonathan's assessment of the meeting. She had been aware for some time that staff were not always being as meticulous as they might have been about reporting adverse incidents and she was taking the opportunity to warn them that there could be consequences if they continued to be so lax.'

'How did she find out about Olive's dossier?' Jonah asked.

'She overheard Olive talking to Desmond when he came to take her out for the day. Fiona was in the office with the door ajar. Olive and Desmond were on their way out. Olive was talking about Mr Martin's fall and how she had a good mind to report it, but she was saving it up for the next CQC inspection. According to Fiona, Desmond tried to talk her out of it, but she insisted that she was going to hand over her list to the inspector next time they came.'

'Do we have any idea who else was around when she said all that?' Jonah wanted to know.

'The staff on duty at that time were Maxine Shaw and Oonagh Conlon,' Charlie told them. 'Depending on the exact time, Julia Freeman may have been there too. She came on duty at ten that morning.'

'It must have been after she came on duty,' Bernie interjected. 'Aunty Dot said that that Olive told her off about the incident with Eric Martin and threatened to report her to the manager.'

'Wasn't that the night before?' Peter suggested. 'When the incident actually took place. That's what *I* thought she meant.'

'Either way, there's a very good chance that Julia knew about the record that Olive was keeping,' Jonah said. 'How about this as a possible scenario? Olive tells Julia off on Monday evening. Julia goes home, feeling guilty about the accident and anxious that Olive may go through with her threat to report her, but not all that concerned, because Olive has made such threats before. Then, just as she walks in the door to start her shift, she hears Olive talking to Desmond, threatening to take a list of incidents to the CQC. Suddenly, it isn't just Olive trying to make people squirm, it's deadly serious and it could lose Julia her job.'

'Yes, I agree that Julia is one of the suspects with the biggest motive,' Sandra said, 'but let me finish what I was telling you about my interview with Fiona. I asked her if she'd actually seen the dossier and she said "no". She went on to admit that she had gone looking for it in Olive's room. In fact, she tried twice. The first time was while the residents were all in the dining room having lunch and the second time was when they were having dinner – after we thought Fiona had already gone home that day.'

'But, I take it she didn't find the dossier?' Jonah asked.

'No. The second time, she didn't even get to look for it, because Oonagh was there, supposedly cleaning the room, but according to Fiona, she was actually sitting on the bed mooning over a photo of Jonathan that Olive had on her shelf. Fiona told her it was time she went home and they both came out of the room and went off. Oonagh went to put away her cleaning things, and Fiona went home.'

'It's odd that Oonagh was in Olive's room on a Tuesday,' Jonah said, frowning. 'Apparently she has a very rigid cleaning schedule in which she cleans two of the residents' rooms each day, starting with Room 1 on Monday morning. She should have been doing Room 4 on Tuesday afternoon and Room 5 on Wednesday morning. And Dot says that she tends to fall behind, rather than getting ahead of schedule.'

'Are you suggesting that she may have had some other reason for being in Olive's room?' Charlotte asked eagerly.

'I don't know,' Jonah sighed. 'I can't honestly see little Oonagh killing anyone – least of all managing to do it in a way that makes it almost impossible to tell who was responsible. I'm sure she wouldn't know one end of an insulin syringe from the other. But it does seem odd.'

'Wasn't Room 4 empty at that time?' Peter asked. 'That was Edna Lomax's room, wasn't it? And the new person – Charles something, was it? – didn't move in until after Olive died. So maybe Oonagh didn't need to clean that room. She could have done rooms 3 and 5 on Tuesday, instead of 3 and 4.'

'OK. Let's park that for the time being,' Sandra said. 'The main thing is that Fiona admits to having been in Olive's room *after* the time that we thought she'd left that evening and well within the window for administering the lethal dose of insulin.'

'But Olive wasn't there,' Bernie pointed out. 'She was in the dining room with all the other residents.'

I know, but what's to stop Fiona hiding in her room – in one of the wardrobes, say – waiting until she was settled in bed and then coming out and taking her by surprise? Afterwards, she could slip away, unnoticed through the patio doors and round to the side gate. There's nobody in Room 4 to see her passing its patio doors, and the window of Lottie's room is high enough that she could creep along under it and not be seen. Then off she goes home to her hubby, telling him what a nightmare the traffic was that evening and how she'd begun to think she'd never get home.' Sandra looked round triumphantly.

'OK,' Jonah said slowly. 'I can see where you're coming from. I suppose your idea is that she *did* in fact find the dossier at lunchtime, and it worried her so much that she decided to silence Olive once and for all. The timings sound reasonable. The only thing I'm *very* sceptical about is the idea of leaping out on Olive and attacking her with a hypodermic. Surely Olive would have pressed the emergency alarm button, either right away or, if Fiona somehow prevented her from doing so, as soon as she'd left.'

'He's right, you know,' Peter agreed. 'Insulin doesn't make someone go unconscious instantly. She'd have had plenty of time to summon help.'

'But, suppose she didn't attack Olive,' Charlie suggested. 'Suppose she just came up to her and told her that the doctor had phoned to say that he'd been reviewing her case and she needed an immediate change in her medication. If she was half asleep after taking her sleeping pill, she might just accept that – coming from a trusted member of staff.'

'Hmm,' Jonah still sounded sceptical. 'I'm not totally convinced, but on the other hand, *whoever* gave her the insulin must have had her co-operation.'

'Unless the extra sleeping tablets had zonked her out so much that she didn't notice them doing it,' Bernie hazarded.

'In which case, we then have to work out how, whoever it was, persuaded her to take *them*,' Jonah pointed out. He turned back to Sandra. 'Was there any other reason that you think Fiona may have done it?'

'Only that she has a strong motive, because, whatever the dossier has in it, it's bound to reflect badly on her management of the Home.' Sandra hesitated before adding, 'and I thought that she might not want her husband to know that she wasn't making a success of his investment.'

'You're right,' Peter agreed. 'It would be quite humiliating for her to have to admit that she couldn't hack it, after he'd invested money in her little project.'

'But she's not the only person with a motive,' Bernie objected. 'I think we ought to be a bit more systematic about this. How about making a list of everyone who had access to Olive's room during the crucial time and going through them one at a time?'

Charlie looked down at her computer screen and manipulated the mouse to locate the necessary information.

'If we're being pedantic,' Sandra said wryly, 'that broken patio door catch means that we'd have to include absolutely anyone capable of getting through, or over, the side gate and into the garden. However, it seems reasonable to restrict ourselves to people who could reasonably have known that they could get into Olive's room that way. So, I suppose we're talking about all the staff and residents plus Olive's family.'

'Let's start with the staff,' Jonah suggested. 'We seem to be agreed that it's irrelevant whether they were on duty that evening, because any of them could have come back during the night. Have you done anything about checking their alibis for that time?'

'Not really,' Sandra shook her head. 'When we interviewed them, we asked them where they spent the night, but most of them were at home either alone or with only their close family. We haven't tried to follow up on any of their statements yet.'

'OK,' Jonah turned to Charlie. 'Who's first?'

'Starting with the carers, and working alphabetically, the first is Rebecca Anderson. She's a Care Assistant and she was on the night shift the day Olive was killed.'

'On the face of it, she has the best opportunity of anyone,' Sandra said. 'And she also has a big motive for not wanting to lose her job, because she's got a family to support.'

'Not just that,' Jonah added. 'She told me that her father has just been made redundant, which is going to make money even tighter for them, and one of her kids has special needs.'

'That must make her our number one suspect, surely?' Charlotte said excitedly. 'If she knew – or even suspected – that Olive was planning to reveal something that would lose her her job, she'd be desperate to prevent it.'

'On the other hand,' Peter cautioned, 'attempting to kill one of the people in your care has got to be a dismissible offence. Unless she's done something really serious, and believes that Olive knew about it, would it be worth the risk?'

'Maybe not,' Sandra shrugged, 'but she does have a motive, and it would be easy for her to go into Olive's room, late at night when Olive is too sleepy to argue, and give her some more of her sleeping tablets, disguised in a drink or a midnight snack maybe. Then, later, after they've sent her into a deep sleep, she comes back with the insulin and gives her the fatal dose, leaving the syringe and vial behind in the hope that we'll think it was suicide.'

'Yes,' Bernie said. 'I wanted to ask about that vial. It's been worrying me. You said that you couldn't tell whether it came from the stock in the drug cupboard?'

'That's right,' Sandra nodded.

'But why not? I mean, medicines usually have batch numbers and dates on them. It suddenly struck me when we were packing Jonah's things to take to the Home with him. All his medical supplies have labels on them that would enable them to be traced. And a lot of them have his name on them too.'

'The vial that was found in Olive's room didn't have any label on it,' Charlie confirmed, after checking her notes. 'Are you saying that there must have been one that was removed?'

'Yes. You couldn't possibly have vials of drugs lying around with no labels. How could you tell what was in them?'

'Presumably you did get the vial checked?' Jonah asked sharply. 'It *was* insulin that it had contained?'

'Oh yes,' Sandra assured him quickly. 'There were traces of rapid-acting insulin in both the vial and the syringe.'

'I think we can assume that it was the murderer who removed the label,' Peter said thoughtfully, 'but why? Presumably they didn't want anyone to know the source of the insulin.'

'You mean they didn't want us to be able to tell that it came from the drugs cupboard in the Home?' Charlie queried.

'Or that it didn't,' Jonah remarked. 'Either way, it could be significant. However, let's get back to our list of suspects. I think we're agreed that Rebecca Anderson has to be a strong possibility, although she seems a thoroughly decent person and quite good with the residents. She was very patient with Lottie Goodman, for example. Who's next?'

'Jonathan Bates,' Charlie reported, looking down her list. 'As we've been through before, he gave Olive her insulin and sleeping tablet before he put her to bed. He could have told her that her insulin pen was broken and she'd have to use a syringe instead. And he could have got her to take the extra sleeping tablets somehow. Maybe he could have put them in her dinner or brought her a bedtime drink or something.'

'Why did he need to give her the sleeping tablets?' Peter asked. 'We said that Rebecca might have done it to make Olive compliant when she came along later to inject her with insulin, but if Jonathan was doing it disguised as her normal dose, why bother with sleeping tablets as well?'

'Belt and braces, maybe?' Sandra suggested. 'He knew that the insulin might not kill her, so he tried to give her a fatal dose of sleeping tablets as well?'

'Or could he have come back later?' Jonah suggested. 'The same as you said Rebecca might have done.'

'No,' Charlie shook her head. 'If he did it, it must have been before he left that evening. His partner claims that they were together all night. Even if he's lying, we have independent witnesses who say they were in a gay bar until gone ten and there's a concierge at their apartments who saw them come in not long after that, and there's a camera over the entrance to the apartment complex, which would have shown him leaving if he'd gone back out again.'

'Well that's a relief!' Bernie joked. 'It looks as if Aunty Dot may have been right about him after all. I wasn't looking forward to having to break it to her if he'd turned out to be guilty.'

'Next please!' Jonah said briskly. 'We haven't got all day.'

'Julia Freeman,' Charlie said, scrolling down the list. 'She was on duty until nine-thirty that night, so she could have worked things the same way as we said for Rebecca, except that she had less time to do it, and she would have had to make sure that Rebecca didn't see her going into Olive's room.'

'Or she could have given Olive the sleeping draught before she left, and then come back during the night,'

Sandra suggested. 'She lives alone, so there's nobody to say that she didn't go out again after she got home.'

'Everyone seems to agree that she's the one with most to worry about if ever Olive's dossier came to light,' Jonah said. 'According to everyone I've spoken to, she's inclined to be careless and lazy. You could imagine that she might be the one that Fiona would pick on if she decided that she needed to make an example of someone. Right! Now who've we got next?'

'Scarlet Jones.' Charlie told him. 'The Care Assistant who found the body. It was her day off on the Tuesday, so-'

'So I'd say we could rule her out,' Peter cut in quickly. 'She wasn't at the staff meeting, so she wouldn't know about the dossier, and she had no opportunity to give Olive either the sleeping tablets or the insulin injection.'

'But we just said that *anyone* could have got in during the night to do it,' Charlie pointed out. 'So we can't be absolutely sure.'

'If she wanted to do away with Olive, why would she come back during the night like that?' Peter persisted 'It would make much more sense to manufacture some sort of accident the following day, when she was back on duty.'

'Except that whoever did it seems to have been intent on putting the blame on to the staff who were there in the evening and night,' Sandra reminded him. 'What about the way the syringe appeared during the morning.'

'If it *did* appear and wasn't there all the time, but nobody noticed it,' insisted Peter.

Bernie looked at the photograph of Scarlet Jones that was displayed next to her name on Charlie's computer screen and smiled to herself. Trust Peter to leap to the defence of a black woman, who probably reminded him of his first wife. It just went to show how difficult it was to remain objective in an investigation.

'OK,' Jonah said a little impatiently. 'Let's leave her and move on. Who's next?'

'Maxine Shaw. She's the other qualified nurse. She worked the early shift, leaving at three in the afternoon, before Olive got back from her day out.'

'So, on the face of it, her only chance to do away with Olive would have been to come back during the night,' Jonah murmured. 'She's got kids, which would make that tricky, and unless she hung around for a long time, we've got the same question as we had with Jonathan about why the sleeping tablet *and* the insulin injection.'

'She was there in the staff meeting,' Sandra pointed out. 'So she knew about the dossier and she may have had reason to believe that she featured unfavourably in it.'

'Didn't Aunty Dot say that Maxine is rumoured to be having an affair with Ian Wilton?' Bernie asked. 'She seemed to think that might be a motive for one or both of them to get rid of Olive, to prevent her spilling the beans. I can't see it myself, because, if it's common knowledge, Olive can't have posed much of an additional threat.'

'I suppose she might have had some proof that the others didn't,' Charlie suggested tentatively.

'More importantly,' Sandra said, 'it means that they could have been working together. For example, one of them could have given Olive the sleeping tablets and then the other could have crept in during the night-'

'No good,' Charlie shook her head. 'Their shifts don't work for that. Maxine went home before Olive got back and Ian wasn't on duty at all that day. Neither of them was even around the following morning to plant the syringe.'

'OK,' Jonah said briskly. 'I think that's all the Care Staff. Then we've got Hector Bayliss, who lives in and so had ample opportunity for getting into Olive's room. He's suspected of petty pilfering, which could give him a motive, if he thought that Olive had evidence to prove it. On the other hand, she would be very unlikely to allow him to give her an injection if she was conscious when he did it.'

'Which could be the point of the sleeping tablets,'

Charlie suggested. 'Could he have somehow slipped them into her bedtime drink or something?'

'Or into her dinner?' Bernie added. 'Didn't Jonathan say that she seemed sleepy when he put her to bed?'

'OK,' Jonah said again. 'We'd better keep Hector Bayliss on the list of suspects. Who've we got left to consider?'

'There's just Grace Massey, the cook,' Charlie informed them. 'She lives a few minutes' walk from the Home and comes in for a couple of two-hour shifts each day to prepare the meals.'

'I went round to her house and interviewed her,' Sandra added. 'She's a friend of Fiona Radcliffe's. I get the impression that she doesn't particularly need the money and is just doing the job out of interest and to help Fiona. She used to be a school dinner lady and she told me that this was better because she was more in control.'

'It doesn't sound as if she has any motive for killing Olive,' Peter said, 'unless she wanted to protect Fiona. But I suppose she would be best placed to put sleeping tablets in her food.'

'So then the only other person on the staff is Oonagh,' Charlie said, seeing that Jonah was once again looking impatient to move on, 'but we've already discussed her.'

'Yes,' he agreed. 'And I really don't think she could be our murderer. If she's mixed up in it at all, it'll be because she's being manipulated by someone else.'

'I'd say that Julia is the most likely,' Charlie said, looking down the list. 'We know that she had at least one incident against her that she wouldn't want being made more widely known and everyone seems to think that there were plenty of others; and she was there at the right time. She could easily have brought Olive a bedtime drink laced with sleeping tablets and then come back just before she left to give the injection, after Olive was asleep.'

'I'm not so sure,' Jonah disagreed. 'She strikes me as one of those careless happy-go-lucky types who never anticipate things going wrong and then, when they do, they just shrug them off and carry on. I can't see her being sufficiently concerned about what Olive had in her dossier to go to the trouble of bumping her off. No. Killing is more like an act of desperation from someone who had a lot to lose.'

'Like Rebecca Anderson,' Sandra put in. 'I was thinking about it last night. I think the ones who are most likely to kill in order to avoid the risk of losing their jobs are the ones whose families depend on them. She needs the money – all the more so now, given what you told us about her father losing his job – and she had the whole night in which to go into Olive's room and administer the insulin.'

'And being on duty alone all night would give her plenty of time to imagine what might be in that dossier,' Jonah agreed, 'and to worry about what would happen if it got out.'

'Yes,' Bernie chipped in. 'And she must be dead tired all the time, working nights and looking after the kids during the day. It would be no wonder if she wasn't thinking straight.'

'It's going to be difficult to nail her for it, though,' Sandra said glumly. 'There's nothing concrete to single her out from the others – especially not from Jonathan and Julia.'

'Which may be because she didn't do it,' Peter pointed out. 'You say that she's got the biggest motive, but that's only if she's convinced that Olive's dossier contains something that will make her lose her job. I'd say that the person who ought to have been most worried about Olive's revelations is the manager. The buck stops with her. So *everything* that goes wrong is ultimately her responsibility. Even if the place doesn't get closed down, she's going to lose a lot of face with her husband if it gets a critical report from the CQC or if residents start moving elsewhere. My money would be on her having found the dossier at lunchtime that day, read it, realised how damning it was, and then gone back to deal with Olive that evening. It was bad luck for her that Oonagh was in the room, but she shooed her out, made a play of going home herself and sneaked back in, ready to attack Olive as soon as Jonathan had finished putting her to bed. She somehow persuaded her to allow her to inject her on some sort of pretext and then left, taking the syringe and vial with her, because she didn't want Rebecca or Julia to see it in time to save Olive. She then returned it to the room the following morning to make it look as if the deed was done overnight, when she was at home with her husband. That explains why nobody saw it until after she arrived at work that morning.'

There was a contemplative silence after this uncharacteristically lengthy speech from Peter.

'You know, Peter,' Jonah said at last. 'I think you may have something there. It does seem to cover all the main points.'

'But it isn't going to be any easier to *prove* than the case against Rebecca,' Sandra sighed.

'Unless she still has the dossier in her possession,' Jonah said eagerly. 'Could you get a search warrant for her home d'you think?'

'Maybe, but what are the chances she's still got it? She's had more than a fortnight to dispose of it. And why would she take it home, where her husband might see it?'

23. SITTING IN THE SHADE

Our England is a garden, and such gardens are not made
By singing:-" Oh, how beautiful," and sitting in the shade.
Rudyard Kipling: "The glory of the garden"

'What about the residents?' Charlie asked. 'We said that it could have been one of them. Do any of them have a good enough motive do you think?'

'There was certainly no love lost between Olive and Joan Pickles, by all accounts,' Jonah answered. 'Apparently Olive came to live there a few months before Joan and set herself up as some sort of Leader of the Gang – organising the social programme, that sort of thing. Joan was used to being in charge of things and didn't like playing second fiddle to Olive. I'm sure that she will find her life a lot more satisfactory with Olive gone, but that's a long way from saying that she would kill her.'

'I agree,' said Sandra. 'If Joan wanted to get away from Olive, she could always have moved to another Home. She surely wouldn't be stupid enough to risk murdering her, just because they didn't get along.'

'How about Mrs Goodman?' Charlie suggested tentatively. 'I mean, she doesn't seem to be all there. Might she have got confused and …'

'Loopy Lottie?' Jonah laughed. 'No. I don't think so. She did try to get into my room last night, thinking I was one of her patients, but Rebecca was there right away to take her back and calm her down.'

'But you had the intercom switched on all night,' Bernie pointed out. 'At least, I *hope* you did,' she added, giving Jonah a warning look to show that she was aware of his tendency to ignore simple safety rules when it suited him. 'So the person on duty would hear immediately if something was going on in your room. What if Olive didn't have time to press the emergency button?'

'Or the night nurse may have been out of the office dealing with another resident,' Charlie suggested.

'A bit of a coincidence.' Jonah was reluctant to give way. 'However, you're quite right. Lottie could have got it into her head that Olive needed an injection of insulin and gone in to give it to her. That's assuming that her door was left unlocked. I *can't* believe that Lottie would have gone outside and in through the patio doors. But what about the sleeping tablets? She surely couldn't have given her those as well?'

They all sat in silence, thinking.

'Let's be systematic about this,' Sandra said at last. 'We must at least be able to rule out some of the residents, because they would simply be incapable of administering the drug. Read out the names, Charlie, and let's see how far we can get.'

'In Room 1, we have Frances Ray.'

'Too scatty,' was Jonah's opinion. 'And she can only just about hobble around with her walking frame. I can't see her managing to reach up to get the syringe out of the drugs cupboard or to carry syringe and vial from the office to Olive's room.'

'Then in Room 2, there's Eric Martin. He's in a wheelchair, so presumably the same would apply to him.'

'Possibly,' Jonah agreed. 'On the other hand, he's the only other resident with a legitimate reason for having access to insulin. If he had any reason to do away with Olive – which I don't think he did – then he might have managed to secrete a syringe and vial in his room somehow, and nobody would have thought anything much of it. He'd been used to managing his own medication before he came to the Home and rather resented having to ask for it to be brought to him.'

'OK,' Sandra conceded, 'we'll have to keep him on the list of people with means and opportunity. However, with no motive, I don't think he's a very likely suspect.'

'Room 3 is Lottie Goodman,' Charlie continued, 'and Room 4 was empty. That's all of the ground floor rooms. Could someone have come down from upstairs without being noticed?'

'I doubt it.' Jonah shook his head. 'They'd have had to go right past the door of the office, where Rebecca was sitting all night.'

'Just run through the list quickly,' Sandra instructed, 'to make sure we don't miss anything.'

'The first floor residents are Margery Cooper, Elizabeth Hunter, Dorothy Fazakerley, Kathleen Lowe and Joan Pickles,' Charlie told them. 'If we're ruling out everyone on the first floor, then that's Joan gone.'

'Keep her on,' Jonah said. 'I've just remembered! There's a door from the kitchen into the lounge, as well as one to the dining room. So someone from the old part of the house could get through to Olive's room without going past the office after all, by going through the kitchen.'

'Wonderful!' Sandra sighed. 'Are you saying that we can't rule out any of the residents after all?'

'No,' Jonah smiled. 'It's not quite as bad as that. Kathleen's Parkinson's would prevent her from handling a syringe; and so would Margery's eyesight. I don't know anything about Betty Hunter, I'm afraid.'

They all fell silent, nobody liking to mention the one remaining resident's name. Then Bernie took a deep breath and began.

'You ought to know that Aunty Dot used to be a

nurse,' she told Sandra. 'She knows all about giving injections and the dangers of an insulin overdose. I don't know any reason why she would want to kill Olive Carter, but if she had one, she'd be jolly careful not to let on to me, wouldn't she? In her defence, she went out of her way to try to clear Jonathan's name, but that could just be a clever bluff to put you off her scent. Probably the biggest factor in her favour is that she finds it very hard to get about unaided and she has arthritis in her hands that would probably make it difficult for her to manipulate the syringe.'

'Hmmm,' Sandra mused. 'You know, on reflection, I think it's unlikely that the murderer was one of the residents. They're all frail and elderly, and questions would be asked if they were seen going into another resident's room at night; and none of them has sufficient motive to justify the enormous risk that they would have been taking. I'd say that it has to be one of the staff.'

'There's one person that we've forgotten,' Bernie said suddenly. 'He's not a resident and he's not exactly on the staff, but what about Dr Bhaskar? He was there that evening, and who else would be better placed to convince Olive that she needed to have an injection of some sort?'

'Ah yes!' Jonah murmured. 'I have to say that I have my suspicions of him. For a busy GP, he seems to have spent a surprising amount of time at the Home in the days immediately surrounding Olive's death.'

'But what would he stand to gain?' Charlie asked. 'Or are you suggesting that he was another Harold Shipman[8]?'

'Of course we can't be sure why Shipman killed his patients, but I wasn't thinking that,' Jonah replied. 'I was thinking that he might have been carrying out Olive's own wishes.'

---

[8] Harold Frederick Shipman was a GP who practised in Hyde, Greater Manchester. In 2000, he was convicted of killing 15 of his patients and sentenced to life imprisonment.

'Like Mrs Lomax's daughter said?' Sandra suggested, suddenly remembering their conversation in the Day Centre. 'She thought that Olive was frightened of going blind and could have asked him to help her to die before it came to that. Do you have other evidence for that?'

'Well, yes and no. Oonagh told me that Olive wanted to die because she was in so much pain and the painkillers weren't working for her anymore. I don't know how reliable that is, though, because Oonagh is dead set on exonerating Jonathan, so she may be exaggerating in order to provide a solution that doesn't incriminate anyone else. And, she said that Olive had complained that the doctor wouldn't increase the dose of the painkillers because it might kill her, which doesn't suggest that he would be willing to assist her if she wanted to commit suicide.'

'She may have worn him down,' Sandra suggested. 'If she kept badgering him to prescribe more painkillers or else to help her to die – maybe even threatening to kill herself in some other way – he could have decided that the least worst option was to help her to do what she wanted in a painless way.'

'Can we be sure that it *wasn't* suicide?' Peter asked. 'That seems like an obvious solution. Olive takes the syringe and vial from the drugs cupboard at some point during the day – or even maybe the day before – and waits until she's been put to bed and the staff have gone. Then she injects herself with the entire contents of the vial, takes several of her sleeping tablets, which she's also purloined from the office cupboard, and settles down to sleep … and never wakes up again.'

'What about the way the syringe wasn't there when Scarlet Jones came in the next morning?' Bernie asked.

'It was there. Nobody noticed it until later because they were all much more concerned with checking whether Olive was still alive or not and ringing for the police and the ambulance.'

'And that would make a very satisfactory solution all

round,' Sandra agreed, 'unless you're wrong and we end up letting a serial killer get away with it and go on to kill again.'

'Do you still think that Edna Lomax could have been killed too?' Jonah asked. 'Her daughter seemed to think it was unlikely.'

'I do too,' Sandra agreed with another sigh, 'but we can't completely rule it out — especially if it could have been the doctor who did it. He was the one who confirmed that Edna died from her existing heart condition and signed the certificate.'

'Hi there!' At the sound of this cheerful greeting, they all turned to see Dot waving to them from her wheelchair as Dominic pushed it across the grass to join them. 'How're you doing? Have you solved the case yet?'

'Alas, no!' Jonah replied, grinning back at her. 'We still have a disheartening number of suspects and no clear way of proving which of them was responsible for Olive's death.'

'Am I still on the list?' Dot asked eagerly, as if being tried for murder would be an interesting experience that she was rather looking forward to.

'Yes Aunty,' Bernie laughed. 'I think you probably are, but way down near the bottom, on the grounds of lack of motive and quite probably lack of stamina and manual dexterity.'

'You mean I'm past it?'

'In a word, yes,' Jonah confirmed, bestowing one of his most charming smiles upon her, 'like several of your fellow residents. However, as you know, we can't discuss it with you.'

'I realise that. We came back to see if you were ready for lunch. Lucy tells me there's a hamper in the car.'

'Yes.' Bernie grimaced. 'I don't know what will be in it. I mentioned to the hotel reception that we were going out for a picnic and they insisted on packing one up for us.'

'Well, what's keeping you?' Dot demanded. 'Let's get it

out and have a look.'

Charlie closed the lid of her laptop and she and Sandra moved round to make room for Lucy and Dominic to sit down. Bernie and Peter went to the car to get the hamper.

'Dominic has been telling me about the work he's doing at the hospice,' Dot said, conversationally. 'Getting ready to look after me in my last days, no doubt. And Lucy here has been helping him. It's a funny way to spend your holiday, that's all I can say!'

'It was good,' Lucy insisted. 'Everyone's very nice there. We met Dr Amandeep while we were there. He's your doctor too, isn't he Aunty?'

'That's right,' Dot nodded. 'Did you hear that?' she added turning to speak to Bernie who had arrived back and was unpacking paper plates and cups from the hamper. 'Lucy has been hob-nobbing with Dr Bhaskar. Well now, Lucy, tell us what you think of him.'

'He's very nice,' Lucy said cautiously, frowning a little, wondering what this was all about.

'You don't think he might be a serial killer who enjoys bumping off old women?'

'No! Of course not!' Lucy exclaimed, then, more uncertainly, 'You *are* joking, aren't you, Aunty?'

'I might be.' Dot's eyes twinkled as she grinned round at them all. 'Tell us what you really think of Dr Bhaskar.'

'I just did. He's very, very nice. He comes round to the hospice every day to check that the patients are doing OK, and they all say how much he does for them.'

'Lucy's right,' Dominic backed her up. 'He's very good, always prepared to go the extra mile if one of the patients needs it.'

'That's a pity,' Jonah said, straight-faced, 'when you consider that he was just shaping up to be the prime suspect for this murder of ours.'

'That's ridiculous!' Lucy exclaimed indignantly. 'He's not like that. I'm sure he isn't. And why would he want to?'

'We thought that Olive might have asked him to,' Jonah told her.

'He still wouldn't. He doesn't believe in assisted suicide. Dom asked him outright, and he said that patients had to know that their doctor would never do anything to shorten their lives, even if they asked him. You tell them Dom!'

'Lucy's right,' Dominic confirmed. 'That's why he's interested in palliative care. He's seen patients dying in pain and wants to make their last days better – not shorter.'

'The trouble is,' Bernie said, watching her daughter closely and picking her words carefully, 'those are all the sorts of things that he would say if he was hoping to get away with … assisting a patient in euthanasia. As the law stands, he couldn't risk *admitting* that he would help them to die if he couldn't prevent their suffering any other way.'

'But he said that he didn't want the law changed,' Lucy argued. 'Why would he say that, if he believed in assisted suicide?'

'Under the current circumstances, to make certain that nobody starts joining the dots and coming to the conclusion that he could have *assisted* Olive Carter to die,' Peter told her.

'Everyone used to say what a wonderful GP Harold Shipman was,' Charlie added. 'He was very attentive to all his patients – lots of home visits and that sort of thing – but it was all part of his wanting to be in control of them and getting a kick out of having the power of life and death over people. At least, that's what I read.'

'Anyway,' Bernie said, trying to bring the conversation to a conclusion, 'when Jonah said that Dr Bhaskar was our prime suspect, he was exaggerating a bit. We've actually still got about a dozen suspects and no obvious way of distinguishing between them. So don't you worry, Lucy, there's no question of an imminent arrest of your favourite doctor! Now, how about some lunch?'

For several minutes no-one spoke, except to ask for

plates to be passed or drinks poured. Jonah chomped thoughtfully on the sandwiches that Lucy fed to him, while Bernie chatted with her aunt about the places that she had visited the day before and how they had changed since her childhood. Sandra glanced down at her watch and thought that she ought soon to return to the police station with Charlie to consider their next move.

'I think we should try to smoke the killer out,' Jonah said suddenly.

Bernie hastily swallowed the piece of Bakewell tart that she had just bitten off and gave Jonah a hard look.

'And what exactly do you mean by that?' she asked sternly.

'We need to provoke them into doing something that will give them away.'

'Such as?' Bernie asked suspiciously.

'If they thought that someone had found evidence that proved that they killed Olive, then they might try to silence that person before they could tell the police.'

'And that someone would be you, I take it?' Bernie's tone had changed from disapproval to outright hostility.

'You can't be serious!' Lucy exclaimed, horrified at the thought of Jonah being at the mercy of a desperate killer. 'You'll get yourself killed. You mustn't let him do it,' she added, turning to Sandra. 'It's mad idea. Tell him he can't.'

'I really don't think we could go along with that,' Sandra began, addressing Jonah with just a hint of regret in her voice. 'It would be far too dangerous and-'

'Why would it?' Jonah demanded. 'I've got my two bodyguards, haven't I?'

'Oh yeah,' Lucy said sarcastically. 'Aunty Dot told me about them. Two constables playing at gardeners! What use are they going to be if someone tries to smother you in the bedclothes?'

'We could have some officers hiding in my room at night,' Jonah answered promptly. 'That should be straightforward enough. There are two big walk-in wardrobes and the bathroom. And during the day, I'll be in my chair and well able to look after myself.'

'Or so you think,' Bernie said scathingly. 'But you'd still be a bit of a sitting duck. It's not worth the risk.'

'You'd be far better letting me do it,' Dot said calmly, as if she were an adult interrupting a children's quarrel to inject some words of common sense. 'I'm far more expendable than you, Jonah. At ninety-eight, I can't have much longer left and I'd rather like to go out with a bang. And there's no reason why *I* couldn't have discovered this important evidence that you're talking about.'

'No, Miss Fazakerley,' Sandra said firmly, when she had recovered from hearing this unexpected suggestion. 'We couldn't possibly sanction that. We wouldn't be able to guarantee your safety.'

'You can't guarantee Jonah's safety either,' Lucy broke in angrily. 'Tell him he can't do this.'

'I don't think DCI Latham can stop me,' Jonah said stubbornly. 'It's up to me what I tell people. I want to try letting slip that I know who did it, but I haven't told the police yet and just see what happens. I'm sure DCs Foster and Ransom will keep me safe, but if not, as Old Peter was saying only the other day, I'm coming to the end of my useful life-'

'That's nonsense!' Bernie interrupted. 'Peter never said anything of the sort.'

'Yes he did. He said that, now I'm fifty-nine, I ought to be thinking seriously about retiring. Those were his very words.'

'It was your birthday. People always joke about retirement when you get to our age. He didn't mean-'

'He did, though,' Jonah insisted, 'and he had the nerve to say that I ought to do it for your sake, because you can't retire until I do.'

Bernie realised that Peter's innocent remarks had upset Jonah far more than it had appeared at the time. She tried to joke her way out of the awkward situation.

'That's nonsense! I'm already retired. Being your PA is just a hobby of mine.'

'And what has you retiring got to do with inviting a serial killer to do you in?' Lucy demanded, almost beside herself with anxiety.

'Only that if everyone thinks I'm past it, I won't be much loss to the world. But that's all beside the point. I don't think it's such a big risk as you're all making out, and if it is, that's up to me, isn't it?'

'No!' Lucy and Bernie both shouted at once.

'No it isn't,' Peter said more calmly a moment later. His voice carried a tone of authority that made everyone else fall silent. 'You ought to think about all the people who are going to be upset if you get yourself murdered in your bed. What about Nathan and Reuben, and your grandkids?'

'And what about us?' Lucy added indignantly.

'Yes,' Bernie backed her up. 'You don't think we've looked after you all these years just so that you can throw your life away in some dramatic gesture, do you?'

'It's not a gesture,' Jonah argued, determined not to give in without a fight. 'It's a serious plan to catch a killer and to remove the cloud that's hanging over Jonathan Bates and all the other staff at the Home. And it's not that dangerous, provided Sandra can spare the manpower to give me proper protection. *And* it may prevent any more people being killed, if the murderer *is* a serial killer.'

'No,' Peter said again. 'It's not worth the risk, and you know it.'

24. WILL YOU WALK INTO MY PARLOUR?

'Will you walk into my parlour?' said the Spider to the Fly.
Mary Howitt: "The spider and the fly"

It was a very subdued group of people who made the journey back to *Park View* that afternoon. Peter drove, with Lucy sitting next to him, so that Bernie could have the seat facing Jonah in the back of the car.

'It really is time you stopped thinking that your job is the only thing that makes you worth anything,' she said earnestly in a low voice, leaning across towards him. 'Retirement isn't a dirty word, and you're going to have to accept sooner or later that even you can't go on forever.'

There was a long pause. Then Jonah looked back at her with a wistful smile.

'Yes. I do know that, but I can't help part of me thinking that it would be nice to die with my boots on.'

'And *all* of *me* is hoping that, whatever you're wearing, it's going to be a good while off yet.' Bernie lowered her voice still further, regretting that there would be no opportunity for her to speak with Jonah alone before they left him in the Care Home and returned to their hotel. 'You must have seen how Lucy was feeling. You owe her an apology after all this.'

'I know,' Jonah muttered, glancing towards Lucy to

check that she could not hear what they were saying. 'I know I upset her, but I still think ... look, I know I put it badly, but I really am sure that the danger would be absolutely minimal, and it might just work. And wouldn't it be worth the risk to know for certain who really did it? For Jonathan and for all the other innocent people who will have that cloud hanging over them for the rest of their lives if we never find out. And tell me honestly, would you all be making the same objections if I wasn't a cripple in a wheelchair?' he added, allowing his voice to rise enough for Peter and Lucy to overhear.

'Possibly not,' Bernie admitted, 'but only because the risk would be so much less.'

'Are you sure?' Jonah pressed her.

'Yes! And even if you were able-bodied, I wouldn't be happy about it.'

'But you wouldn't try to stop me?'

'Yes – no – I don't know!'

'He's right, you know, Bernadette,' Dot said. 'Are you quite sure that you're not being overprotective because of Jonah's condition? The same as you were doing with me? Can't you give us both the dignity of allowing us to make our own decisions?'

Bernie closed her eyes and put her head in her hands. Nobody spoke for the remainder of the journey ... or while they got Jonah and Dot out of the car ... or as they made their way up the path to the entrance of the Home and swiped Dot's resident's card to open the doors.

'Did you have a nice day?' Scarlet Jones greeted them, smiling round at them all as they entered.

'Yes, it was very pleasant,' Dot told her. 'Very interesting seeing how the gardens have changed since I saw them last.'

Scarlet helped Dot out of the wheelchair and escorted her upstairs to her own room. The others went with Jonah to Room 5, Peter pushing the manual wheelchair and Lucy hurrying ahead to open the door. They went inside and

Bernie closed the door behind them. They stood looking at one another.

'Well, I suppose we'd better be going,' Bernie said at last. 'Do you want us to leave the door open, or will you call for assistance if you want to get out?'

'Close it, please. I need to think and I don't want any interruptions.'

'Right! Well, we'll be off then.'

They still hesitated. It felt as if something more needed to be said, but nobody knew what. Then Lucy went over to Jonah and put her arms around his neck from behind, nestling her chin on his shoulder.

'If you really have to do it,' she said quietly, 'then you'd better ring DCI Latham and ask her for some more backup.'

Jonah leaned his cheek harder against hers.

'Are you sure?' he whispered.

'Yes. Now you'd better go ahead before I change my mind,' Lucy said bravely. She kissed him on the cheek and walked quickly to the door without looking back, so that he would not see the tears coming.

'As I said, time to go,' Bernie repeated, hastening after her daughter.

Peter followed them, looking back at Jonah with an expression that somehow managed to combine admiration with exasperation.

'I hope you know what you're doing,' he remarked as he closed the door.

'Mrs Radcliffe says you've spilt something and need it wiping up,' Oonagh said, coming into Jonah's room later that afternoon.

'Yes, that's right. It's that African violet that was on the table. I barged into it in my wheelchair and the whole thing went over.'

Oonagh got down on her knees and started sweeping

the compost, which had spilled out of the pot, into a dustpan.'

'It's lucky the pot didn't break,' she said. 'I can just put all this back in and then clean the floor and it'll all be good as new.'

Jonah watched her as she painstakingly collected all the compost, poured it carefully back into the pot and pressed it down around the plant.

'I'm sorry to be a nuisance and make extra work for you.'

'It's no bother. I'm all caught up now. Thank you for saying your room didn't need cleaning this morning.'

'Well usually I would say that I can't make much mess, being stuck in this chair,' Jonah joked, 'but, as you see, that's not always true.'

'There you are!' Oonagh put the pot back in its place on the table. 'Now I'll just get the hoover to do the carpet.'

'Thanks. But before you do, can you tell me – you usually clean this room on a Wednesday morning; is that right?'

'Yes. Rooms 5 and 6 are Wednesday.'

'Did that include the Wednesday when Mrs Carter died?'

'Yes,' Oonagh answered. Then, a little defensively, 'Nobody told me not to.'

'It's alright. I'm not saying you shouldn't have. I'd just be interested to know whether you saw anything or moved anything.'

'What sort of thing?'

'A diary or a notebook, for instance.'

'Why do you want to know?'

'Miss Fazakerley asked me to look out for anything that might help the police to find out who killed Olive, so that people will stop thinking that it was Jonathan Bates,' Jonah explained. 'There's been some talk going around that she kept a diary of things that went on here that shouldn't have, and that someone might have killed her to stop her showing it to anyone. If we could find that diary, it might help us to know who was afraid of what was in it. Do you understand?'

'You mean: if it doesn't say anything about Jonathan, he couldn't have killed her?'

'Not quite, but you're getting the idea.'

Oonagh thought for a few moments. Then she sat down heavily on the bed. For several minutes, she sat there without speaking, twisting her hands together in her lap and frowning in thought.

'I knew about the diary,' she said at last. 'I'd seen her writing in it – nasty little notes about everything that went wrong. And I knew where she kept it. It was in that drawer there.'

She looked sideways at the bedside cabinet.

'That Wednesday morning, when I came in to clean, I went in there and got it out. I didn't know anyone had killed her. I just thought that, now she was dead, nobody needed to see those nasty notes. So I took it.'

'I see. And where is it now?'

Oonagh looked at him nervously and bit her lip.

'It's alright. You won't be in trouble,' he assured her. 'I'm guessing you got rid of it somehow, so that no-one would ever read it. Is that right?'

'Yes! I – I tore up the pages and flushed them down the toilet.'

'I see. Now tell me: what sort of book was it? I mean, was it a notebook or a diary? Did it have a hard cover?'

'It was a little diary, with a plastic cover.'

'You couldn't flush that away, could you? What did you do with that?'

'I just threw it in the bin.'

'Here? Or at home?'

'At home. The bin men come on Fridays, so it's gone now. But there wasn't any writing on that.'

'And did you look inside at all, to see what she wrote? *I'd* have been curious to know if she'd written anything about me.'

'No. I don't know anything about what she wrote.' Oonagh sounded suddenly defensive. It seemed that Joan Pickles had been accurate in describing her as *practically illiterate*. Pages of handwriting in a style dating back to Olive Carter's youth would be completely unintelligible to her.

'Never mind. At least you've cleared up that little mystery. Now, just one more thing. They found a syringe with a needle sticking out of it by Olive's bed that morning. Did you see it, when you came in?'

'Oh yes!' Oonagh nodded vigorously. 'It was lying there on top of her diary. I had to move it to get it out.'

'You're sure about that?' Jonah asked eagerly. 'You're telling me that it was in the drawer and you took it out and left it out on top?'

'Yes. There was a syringe and a little glass bottle. I picked them up to get at the diary. I meant to put them back in the drawer, but I forgot. Does it matter?'

'Well, it certainly explains a lot. We'd been wondering how it was that nobody saw it until the police got there. Thank you, Oonagh, that's another little puzzle that you've solved for us. Now, I'm going to have to tell the police about what you've told me. Don't worry!' he added quickly, seeing her look of alarm. 'You're not in trouble. They'll just be very grateful to you for clearing these things up. They'll be able to stop hunting for that diary and trying to think up reasons for nobody noticing the syringe.'

'You're sure they won't be cross about me tearing it up?'

'I'll make sure they aren't. After all, you were only trying to stop people getting hurt, weren't you? And you didn't know that Olive didn't die naturally.' Jonah treated Oonagh to one of his most beguiling smiles. 'Really, you mustn't worry,' he repeated gently. 'I'll ring DCI Latham tomorrow and I expect she'll want to talk to you, but she won't be cross. She'll just be pleased that they can stop looking for that diary.'

Oonagh smiled back apprehensively. Then she picked up her dustpan and brush and stood up to leave.

'Before you go, do you think you could just do one more thing for me? Do you see that piece of paper sticking up there, behind the bedside cabinet?'

Oonagh nodded.

'Could you get it out for me? I left it there last night and it's slipped down the back.'

Oonagh reached over and pulled the paper out. It was a single sheet folded over.

'Open it up, please,' Jonah instructed,' and put it down on my tray, where I can see it.'

Oonagh did as she was told, spreading out the paper on the tray attached to the arm of Jonah's wheelchair. She ran her hand over the handwritten page, smoothing it out beneath her fingers.

'Is that OK?' she asked anxiously.

'Yes. Thank you. That's splendid. I won't keep you any longer. You can go now – and don't worry about anything.'

'I shouldn't really be telling you this,' Dot said to Frances, leaning towards her across the table as they ate their dinner together in the Residents' Dining Room, 'but it's so exciting and I'm sure you won't pass it on. You know Jonah Porter?'

'The friend of your niece who's in Olive's old room?'

'That's right. Well, he told me that he knows who killed Olive.'

'Really? How? And who is it?' Frances opened her eyes wide and leaned closer, to hear what Dot had to say.

'He wouldn't tell me who it was,' Dot said regretfully. 'He said the police ought to know first. He's going to tell them in the morning. And then, presumably, they'll make an arrest! It's exciting, isn't it? I'm sure I won't sleep a wink tonight for thinking about it.'

'But how does he know?' Frances asked again.

'You know the way Olive always used to write things down in that diary thing of hers?'

'Yes?'

'Well, Jonah reckons she must have mislaid it and used a scrap of paper instead. He found it, slipped down behind the bedside cupboard. He saw it there, with just a corner sticking up. It was Olive's diary entry for the night she died and, according to Jonah, what it says makes it clear who killed her and how they did it.' Dot leaned back in her chair with a look of triumph on her face. 'Now you won't tell a soul about this, will you, Frannie? I don't want to be in trouble for passing on police secrets.'

'Dot! Can you spare me a minute or two?' Kathleen accosted Dot on the landing outside their rooms.

'Of course,' Dot followed Kathleen into her room. 'What is it you want?'

'Do you know anything about this story that Frannie's been telling everyone?'

'Which story?'

'About your Mr Porter knowing who killed Olive.'

'Oh that!'

'Is it true? Does he know?'

'So he told me. But he wouldn't say who it was, so it's no good you asking.'

'And what happens now?'

'He said that he was going to ring the police in the morning and they'd take it from there.' Dot paused, as if thinking. Then she continued, 'I suppose perhaps the family ought to know that an arrest is imminent. I mean, it'll come as a bit of a shock to them won't it?'

'I could ring Desmond,' Kathleen suggested. I've got his number, and he could pass it on to John.'

'There's a weird rumour making the rounds,' Julia told Rebecca when she arrived that night. 'That new resident, Jonah Porter, is supposed to have found out who did in Olive! I've no idea who started it, but it's all any of the old dears are talking about this evening.'

'I suppose it gives them *something* to talk about. It must be dead boring for them all, just sitting around here all day.'

'I don't suppose there's anything in it. It's probably just Dot Fazakerley wanting to show off her famous *police connections*!'

'Yes. Or else Frannie Ray getting hold of the wrong end of the stick and passing it round to the others – like that time she got it into her head that they were all going to be put on a vegan diet!' Rebecca laughed.

'Oh yes! That was a good one!' Julia agreed, joining in the laughter. 'And what about when she was convinced that Mr Bayliss was taking photographs of them all in the bath!'

25. A HAMMER IN HER HAND

Then Jael, Heber's wife, took a nail of the tent, and took an hammer in her hand, and went softly unto him, and smote the nail into his temples, and fastened it into the ground: for he was fast asleep and weary. So he died.
Judges 4:21

Jonah lay in bed. The dim nightlight above the headboard cast deep shadows, making it hard to distinguish anything clearly. He was facing towards the patio doors, which were hidden behind thick curtains falling from ceiling to floor. He thought that he detected a movement in them. Was a draught through the doors stirring them?

It was very quiet. He became conscious of the low rasp of his own breathing. Then another sound came to his ears. Was it footsteps out in the corridor? Was that scratching noise someone attempting to put a key in the lock of his door? He wished fervently that he had been left lying on his other side so that he could have watched to see if the handle was turning.

Everything went quiet again. Perhaps he had been mistaken. But he had been so sure that he had heard someone approaching. He gradually became aware of a low murmur of voices – or was that just his imagination? No. There they were again. They must be right outside his room, but they were speaking in whispers so low that, try as he might, he could not distinguish any words.

There was a click and the room grew lighter. Jonah deduced that the door must have been opened, allowing light to come in from the corridor. The striped pattern on the curtains was clearer now and he was sure that they were, indeed, moving slightly. Still unable to turn to see what was going on, Jonah remained staring at the curtains, while his mind raced to imagine the scene behind him. Someone was definitely there. He could hear breathing – rather laboured breathing, shallow and wheezing. It was coming closer and there was a shuffling sound of feet on the carpet.

Then everything seemed to happen at once. The curtains flew apart and Peter appeared from behind them, hurling himself towards Jonah and gathering him protectively in his arms. There was a crash as the wardrobe door banged open, followed by sounds of a scuffle behind Jonah's back.

'I'll take that,' Sandra's voice said firmly from the direction of the bathroom.

Jonah felt Peter's arms relax and saw him lower his eyes from where they had been fixed, staring over Jonah's prostrate body at whatever was happening behind him. He opened his mouth to ask what was going on, but Peter gently rolled him over so that he could see for himself. There was Sandra Latham, standing a few feet away, in the act of sealing a hypodermic syringe into an evidence bag. It appeared that the killer had been planning to use the same modus operandi as when Olive Carter was dispatched. Then he raised his eyes and stared in amazement as he recognised the figure that was standing there, looking round wildly and struggling vainly, gripped firmly in DC Ransom's arms.

'Lottie!'

26. UNTANGLING THE WEB
O, what a tangled web we weave when first we practise to deceive!
Sir Walter Scott: "Marmion"

'Rebecca Anderson, I am arresting you on suspicion of the murder of Mrs Olive Carter and the attempted murder of DCI Jonah Porter. You do not have to say anything; but it may harm your defence if you do not mention, when questioned, something which you later rely on in court. Anything you do say may be given in evidence.' DC Foster's voice could be heard clearly through the open door.

A moment later, she entered, pushing a white-faced Rebecca ahead of her.

'This is all stupid!' Rebecca protested. 'I haven't hurt anyone. Can't you see?' She gesticulated towards Lottie with her two hands, which Jonah now saw were handcuffed together. 'I was trying to get the syringe off her.'

'That's not what I saw,' Bryony Foster said calmly. 'I was watching from the utility room. I saw you going past carrying the syringe.'

'And I've just been checking in the office,' Charlie added, coming up behind them. 'There's an empty vial of rapid-acting insulin, labelled as prescribed for Mr Eric Martin, lying on the desk.'

'Of course there is!' Rebecca shouted, turning from white to red in her agitation. 'That's what I'm telling you. I came back from checking the upstairs rooms and found Lottie there, filling the syringe. I managed to grab it from her, but not until we were both out of the office; so of course I was still carrying it when I went past the utility room.'

'Nice try,' Bryony said sarcastically. 'The only problem with that story is that I was watching all the time and Lottie never went past in either direction all night.'

'You're wrong,' Rebecca insisted doggedly.

'I don't understand,' Lottie moaned, subsiding into a chair now that Oliver Ransom had released her from his grip. 'You told me that Mr Porter needed his medication. Did I get something wrong?'

'It's alright, Lottie,' Jonah said kindly. 'You didn't do anything wrong. Things have just got into a bit of a muddle, that's all.'

'I think you'd better take Mrs Goodman back to her room,' Sandra said to Charlie. 'Help her into bed and stay with her until she's settled.'

Charlie obediently helped Lottie up and assisted her out of the room. Oliver closed the door firmly behind them. Bryony sat Rebecca down in the chair that Lottie had vacated and took up a position standing over her.

'It looks as if this could be a long session,' Peter murmured to Jonah. 'I'd better get you into your chair.'

Jonah nodded gratefully and smiled up at Peter, who was already positioning the chair and preparing to roll Jonah into it. As soon as his hand was back on the controls and Peter had fastened the strap that held it in place, Jonah took charge. He brought the chair up from its reclined position so that he was once again able to look round freely in all directions. He turned the chair to face Rebecca and smiled across at her.

'It's no good,' he told her. 'You might as well come clean. There are too many witnesses for you to hope to convince a jury that your story holds water. It was a clever idea, getting Lottie to do your dirty work for you. If we hadn't taken the precaution of stationing officers in the kitchen and the utility room, watching the path from the office to my room, you might have got away with it. We might have bought the idea that it was all just Loopy Lottie imagining that she was a District Nurse again and that Room 5 was on her rounds. We might even have believed that *she* killed Olive Carter.'

'She probably did,' Rebecca muttered. 'I certainly didn't.'

'Oh, but I think you did,' Sandra put in. 'I think you heard that Olive was planning to report various goings on to the CQC and you were afraid about what might happen then. I don't know whether you thought that you would be named or if you were just worried that the Home would be closed down. Either way, you were in danger of losing your job. And you couldn't afford that, with three children to support – including one with Special Needs – and your dad having been made redundant.'

'*You* told her about that!' Rebecca exclaimed, rounding on Jonah accusingly. 'There was I thinking you were being nice. Thinking how sympathetic you were, asking about the kids and wanting to see their photos, and all the time you were just trying to get me to say something that you could use against me. Of *course* I was worried about losing my job, but that doesn't mean I killed her.'

'No,' Sandra agreed. 'Lots of people were worried. That's why we had to resort to setting a little trap to force the real murderer to show themselves. We've taken that cup of hot chocolate that you gave to DCI Porter earlier – he didn't drink it, by the way – and we're going to get it analysed. I have a funny feeling that they'll probably find some sort of sleeping drug in it – like the one that you used on Olive Carter, so that she wouldn't wake up when you injected her with a lethal dose of insulin.'

'Of course, you didn't need Lottie that time, did you?' Bryony added. 'Or at least, you thought you didn't. You didn't expect anyone to question a diabetic dying of an insulin overdose. You thought that it would look like a tragic accident.'

'It must have put the wind up you when the doctor informed the police and the coroner ordered a post mortem,' Oliver put in, 'but you'd taken the precaution of wearing gloves, so we couldn't pin down for sure who administered the insulin.'

'And it was a bit of a godsend Olive's sons taking against Jonathan Bates the way they did,' Bryony resumed. 'You must have thought you were safe when he was suspended and everyone was pointing the finger at him.'

'However,' Sandra took control of the conversation again, 'in the police service, we don't work on the basis of prejudice and hunches. We look for evidence. And there was no evidence to support the idea that Jonathan Bates was any more likely to have killed Olive Carter than any other member of staff who was on duty that day. In fact, from the very start, you were the person with the greatest opportunity for committing the crime.'

She signalled to Rebecca to get to her feet.

'Now, we could all do with getting a bit of sleep before the night's over, so we'll just take you down to the station and put you in a police cell. We can carry on in the morning, when we've got the lab results on that drinking chocolate.'

'No!' Rebecca burst out. 'You can't! What about my kids? I've got to be there.'

'We'll get on to Social Services right away,' Sandra told her. 'Don't worry. They'll see that your dad has all the support he needs to look after them. And if he can't cope, they'll be able to find temporary foster care for them.'

'But you don't understand! I have to be there to see that things are done the way Alex likes them. He'll have a meltdown if anything isn't just right. He has to keep to the same routine every day. You can't just send in some woman from Social Services.'

'You should have thought of that before you decided to go around drugging and killing little old ladies,' Bryony cut in unsympathetically.

'I'm sorry,' Sandra said gently, flashing a warning look towards Bryony. 'We really will do everything we can to see that your kids don't come to any harm, but you must appreciate that we can't let you go home. You have to come with us now and answer our questions in the morning. If you co-operate, there's a chance you may be allowed out on bail until your case comes up.'

'But that's no good! I've got to be there,' Rebecca insisted, tears welling up in her eyes, as she looked round from one face to another desperately seeking a way out of her plight. 'You can't do this to them. Can't you see?'

'I'm sorry,' Sandra repeated. 'I really am. But there is no alternative. We have two witnesses who saw you preparing to attack DCI Porter, and quite sufficient evidence to charge you with the murder of Olive Carter. We *have* to take you into custody. So now,' she went on more briskly, 'let's cut to the chase and get you off down to the station right away. DC Foster! I want you and Ransom to take Mrs Anderson in, while I finish tying off a few loose ends here. Tell the custody officer that I'm dealing with Social Services, so they don't need to worry about making arrangements for the kids.'

Bryony took Rebecca by the elbow and pulled her to her feet. Oliver opened the door for them to leave and discovered Charlie on her way in.

'Mrs Goodman is asleep,' she reported. 'I think she'll be OK. She seemed surprisingly calm about it all. I don't think she knows what's going on at all, poor old dear.'

'Good.' Sandra waited until Rebecca had left, walking with head bowed between the two police officers, and then continued. 'Now Charlie, I want you to stay in the office here for the rest of the night, in case any of the residents call for assistance. You'd better get on to the manager to let her know that one of her staff has been arrested. She may want to get here before the early shift clocks on, so that she can be the one to break it to them. I'm off to rouse someone in Social Services and then I want to call personally on Rebecca's father to tell him what's going on before he starts worrying about her not getting home on time.'

'Her shift ends at seven thirty,' Jonah told her helpfully. 'So I reckon he'll be expecting her by eight, maybe a few minutes earlier.

Sandra looked at her watch. 'Three fifteen. No point disturbing his sleep. I'll see what I can organise in the way of help with childcare and then call round at seven-thirty to break the news. Well, that about settles everything. I'll leave you to get some rest for what's left of the night. Thanks for your help. I'll be in touch to let you know how things go.'

'Could you turn off the intercom?' Jonah said to Peter, as soon as the door closed behind her. 'We don't need DS Simpson listening in on our conversation.'

Peter did as he was asked, and then started smoothing down the sheets in preparation for returning Jonah to his bed.

'And now, tell me how you came to be skulking behind my curtains instead of tucked up snug in bed with your wife.'

'I promised Lucy I'd see to it that no harm came to you. Now, let's get you back into bed while there's still time for you to have some sleep before things kick off again in the morning.'

'It hardly seems worth bothering, now that it's so late. I'm wide awake now, so I might as well stay in my chair until they come to get me dressed.'

'No,' Peter said firmly. 'I know it makes you feel that you're in control, but you spend too much time in that chair as it is, and you know how tired you get if you miss out on your sleep. You'll be better off in bed; and it'll be easier to get you dressed from there; *and*, even if *you* can go on forever without a rest, the chair can't! It needs to finish charging or we'll have it running out of juice by tomorrow evening.'

'Oh alright,' Jonah grumbled. Although he knew that Peter was right, he nevertheless resented having to give way. 'Let's get on with it then.'

He manoeuvred the chair alongside the bed and reclined it so that Peter could roll him back on to it. Peter carefully positioned him, checking that there were no creases in his pyjamas, which might damage his skin, and that there was no danger of his pillow obstructing his breathing. Then he drew up the covers around his neck and stood looking him up and down for a moment or two, before turning his attention to the chair. Jonah watched as he moved it over to the wall and plugged it back into the electric socket.

'OK. You can get back to the bosom of your family again now. Tell Lucy that I'm touched by her concern, but it really wasn't necessary to keep you up like this. DCI Latham and her team were quite equal to the task.'

'No point me going back and disturbing Bernie now. I'll just settle down in one of those armchairs. Then I'll be on hand to get you up and dressed. They'll most likely be all at sixes and sevens when the staff get in and hear what's happened. Stop talking and try to get some sleep. I'm going to switch the light off now.'

'Just a minute! Don't I detect a bit of hypocrisy here? If I've got to go to bed, how come you're OK sitting up in a chair all night?'

'I can sleep perfectly well in a chair.'

'Not as well as on the bed. Come along! If you're here as my PA-cum-bodyguard, you can do the same as Bernie does when we find ourselves overnighting in a room with only the one bed. There's plenty of space for two, if you shove me up a bit.'

'Very well,' Peter sighed, sitting down on the edge of the bed and bending down to untie his shoelaces. 'I can see we'll be up all night arguing about it if I don't do as you say. Just don't blame me if we get some very funny looks from the staff if they walk in on us in the morning.'

27. THE LEAVING OF LIVERPOOL
It's not the leaving of Liverpool that grieves me,
But my darling when I think of thee.
Traditional song.

'Jonah!' Lucy burst into the dining room, where Peter was giving Jonah his breakfast. She was followed by Bernie at an only slightly less precipitate pace. 'What's been going on? Peter rang to say that someone's been arrested.'

Peter replaced the spoon in the cereal bowl and leaned back out of the way, smiling as his stepdaughter hurled herself towards Jonah and put her arms around him. She hugged him tight, resting her chin on his shoulder and pressing her cheek against his.

'I'm afraid that, contrary to my expectations, Jonah's trap worked,' Peter told her. 'The Care Assistant who was left in charge overnight got scared and tried to prevent him passing on his imaginary piece of evidence to the police by doing away with him the same way as she despatched Olive.'

'Well, at least she didn't succeed this time,' Bernie said heartily, 'which is something of a relief. Although,' she added, grinning across at her husband, 'it isn't going to help me in my quest to make Jonah less irresponsible about his own safety.'

'Or mine to make him less bumptious and full of himself!' Peter grinned back.

'We're taking you out of here, as soon as you've finished your breakfast,' Lucy told Jonah, ignoring her parents' banter. 'We've only got one day of our holiday left to show you the sights.'

'Tell you what,' Bernie suggested. 'Why don't Lucy and I go to your room and start packing, while you and Peter finish breakfast?'

They turned to go and almost collided with Dot, who was making slow progress across the room, leaning on her walking frame.

'Hello Aunty! We've come to collect Jonah.'

'So I heard, but you're not to steal him away until he's given me all the gen on last night. It's the least you can do after all the work I put in, spreading false rumours to all and sundry.'

'Come and sit down here,' Peter said, moving chairs to make a space for Dot to sit at their table. 'I'll tell you all about it, while Jonah finishes his food and Bernie and Lucy do the packing.'

An hour or so later, they were standing by the sliding doors in the entrance lobby, saying their final farewells to Dot. Fiona Radcliffe came out of her office and delivered a rather stilted little speech about how grateful she was to them for helping the police to find the real culprit, and how surprised she had been to discover that any member of her staff had acted in such a way. She finished by saying that Jonah would be welcome to stay at *Park View* any time in the future that he was visiting Liverpool, provided that there was a room free.

They nodded and smiled politely, thanking Fiona and saying that they would not keep her any longer, since she must be very busy organising new staffing rotas and calming the residents after the excitement of having a murderer unmasked in their midst.

They had just stepped through the doors and started their descent to the road, when a voice behind them caused them to turn back. It was Eric Martin, propelling his wheelchair at great speed across the lobby, eager to see them off.

'Maxine told me you were going. And she also told me that your stay was all part of a covert police operation to smoke out the murderer! Well, well, well! You had *me* fooled and no mistake! Still, we live and learn, don't we?'

'Yes, we certainly do,' Fiona agreed, in the tone that adults adopt when humouring a precocious child.

'I couldn't let you all go without something to remember us by,' Eric continued. 'So I've brought these for you two lovely young ladies.'

He put his hand into a brown paper bag, which lay next to him on his chair, and brought out two lace-edged handkerchiefs, embroidered with gaily-coloured flowers. Bernie and Lucy accepted them politely, murmuring insincere expressions of delight in the gifts.

'And to think that it was Becky Anderson that did Olive in!' Eric said to Jonah. 'I must say I hadn't got her marked down as the most likely suspect. But come to think of it, who else had a better chance to do it? I suppose you were on to that right way, eh?'

'Well, it certainly did make me wonder,' Jonah agreed with a smile. 'But there wasn't any proof that it couldn't have been someone else.'

'Until you tricked her into having a go at you,' Eric chuckled. 'That was a clever move. I have to admit, you had me fooled last night. I swallowed that story that Frannie was passing round, hook, line and sinker!'

'Well, I'm afraid we have to be off now,' Bernie intervened, conscious of Lucy's impatience as they stood on the path, poised to depart. 'It's been lovely meeting you. Maybe we'll see you again next time we come to Liverpool.' She turned to Dot, giving her a quick peck on the cheek. 'Good bye Aunty. Take care!'

'You'll notice the difference when you see the other one,' Bernie told Jonah that afternoon, as they left the sandstone magnificence of Liverpool Cathedral and turned into Upper Duke Street. 'It's not on such a grand scale, but at least it's not trying to pretend it's something it's not.'

'How d'you mean?'

'I mean they're both twentieth-century buildings, but one looks like it and the other is pretending to be a genuine mediaeval gothic masterpiece. *And* it was built to be the largest cathedral in Europe, or something like that, to symbolise the importance of Liverpool, but by the time it was finished, Liverpool was very much in decline. It all seems a bit phoney to me. And think how much it must have cost, at the same time that people like my dad were losing their jobs.'

They crossed the road and turned to the left.

'This is Hope Street,' Bernie told Jonah. 'It famously runs between the two cathedrals. You'll be able to see Paddy's Wigwam in a minute. Then you'll understand what I mean about it looking forward into the future, while the other one is all about looking back into some magnificent past.'

The road bent slightly to the right and the Metropolitan Cathedral of Christ the King came into view.

'There you are!' Bernie declared. 'The Mersey Funnel!'

Jonah looked up to see the cathedral's distinctive shape rising above the surrounding buildings. The pinnacles around its circular crown stood out against the brightness of the sky. Beneath this structure, which did indeed have the appearance of a large funnel, the roof spread out in a cone shape. Facing them, apparently almost as wide as the road down which they were looking, Jonah could see a massive concrete slab inscribed with words or symbols that he could not read.

'What's that on the front?' he asked.

'That's the bell tower,' Bernie told him. 'The bells are in

that line of holes near the top.'

'I'm afraid I do think the other one looks more like a cathedral,' Jonah said, a little apologetically. 'This is all a bit concrete-y. It reminds me of those awful nineteen sixties housing estates.'

'It's better inside,' Lucy assured him. 'That round bit at the top is full of coloured glass. It's all about the light shining in from outside and making the colours change as the sun moves round.'

'And being circular is more democratic,' Bernie added. 'I would have thought you'd like that better than having the high altar up behind a screen half a mile from the congregation.'

They started to ascend the long slope that wound upwards through the cathedral gardens, providing alternative access for those unable to climb the long flight of wide steps at the front of the building. Just as they reached the top, Jonah's mobile phone rang. It was Sandra Latham.

'I thought you'd like an update on Rebecca Anderson.'

They all crowded round Jonah's chair, listening in.

'The lab's got back to us with the analysis of that drinking chocolate she gave you last night,' Sandra continued. 'It had been laced with a very substantial amount of a strong sedative, which could have been fatal, even without the insulin injection.'

'Lucky you intercepted it then,' Jonah said, with a smile.

'And it goes to show how foolhardy you were putting yourself in harm's way like that,' added Bernie drily.

'And we've also had some new evidence from Hector Bayliss,' Sandra continued

'The caretaker?'

'That's right. After Rebecca was arrested, he came forward and told us about an incident that happened a few weeks before Olive died. Rebecca was on duty overnight, as usual. Round about midnight, she knocked him up in his flat and persuaded him to man the office while she went back to her kids. Her dad had been taken ill, or something, and one of them had rung her. According to Mr Bayliss, none of the residents needed any help and Rebecca got back before the other staff arrived in the morning, so nobody else knew about it, but …'

'But when she heard about Olive and her dossier, she must have been afraid that she'd got wind of it somehow and was going to tell on her,' Jonah finished for her.

'Yes. She wasn't at the staff briefing, but she got to hear about the dossier by a process of Chinese whispers, during which it got blown up into a definite intention on Olive's part to send the document to the CQC.'

'And Rebecca was guilty of defrauding her employer, as well as neglecting her duty of care to the residents,' Jonah pointed out. 'No wonder she felt she had to stop her.'

'That one incident was a dismissible offence,' Peter agreed.

'I've just come from interviewing her,' Sandra went on. 'We told her what Hector had said, and she broke down crying and admitted that he was telling the truth, but she still denied having killed Olive and trying to kill you. So then we showed her the analysis of the drinking chocolate. She had a half-hearted attempt at claiming that she didn't know how the sedative got into it, but her fingerprints were the only ones on the cup and she couldn't come up with an explanation of how anyone else could have done it. So, in the end, she gave in and admitted everything.'

'What happens now?' Lucy asked.

'We're going to push to get an in initial hearing ASAP. They wouldn't normally grant bail on a murder charge, but we'll see if we can persuade the judge that she isn't a threat to anyone. I'd like to give her a chance to get her kids sorted out before she gets sent to jail.'

'It's going to be pretty grim for them, whatever happens in the end,' Peter observed.

'Yes,' Sandra agreed. 'It's all a bit of a mess, really. That husband of hers, who ran off and left her to bring up three kids on her own, has a lot to answer for!'

She ended the call and they all continued inside the cathedral. Jonah had to admit that the interior was more impressive than the outside had been.

'It's like the Tardis,' he whispered, 'more inside than out.'

They wandered round, looking at each of the small chapels that led off the main circular auditorium. Predictably, Peter stood for some time gazing up at an unusual statue of the virgin and child, featuring the boy Jesus standing in front of his mother, both of them with arms outstretched as if welcoming onlookers into their embrace.

In another of the alcoves, Jonah's attention was caught by a painting on wood of Jesus working in his father's carpenter's shop. Elsewhere, he noticed a sculpture of the adult Jesus surrounded by children. Children and families seemed to feature a lot here.

They walked on. Then Peter stopped again. They were in front of what seemed to Jonah to be a strange contraption made of wrought iron. It comprised several circles, one above another, large at the base, smaller nearer the top. Around each of the circles there were arrayed tea-lights – some unlit, others flickering brightly, yet more burnt out. Peter reached out towards a shelf that was built into the wall close by, picked up a wax taper that lay there, and used it to light one of the candles. Then he blew out the taper and stood for a few moments with his head bowed.

As he moved off again, Bernie slipped her arm through his and leaned her head against his shoulder.

'I wanted to do something for Rebecca Anderson's family,' Peter said, in response to her unasked question. 'She's bound to get Life. I can't see how that can be avoided. The trouble is: it's the kids who are going to suffer the most.'

Lucy waited patiently for Jonah to follow them, but he

remained silently contemplating the circles of flickering tea lights. Then, all of a sudden, he seemed to make up his mind about something and he looked up at her.

'Could you get me that taper?' he asked, speaking in a low voice, as if wanted to avoid being overheard.

Surprised, Lucy picked it up.

'Do you want me to light it for you?'

'No. I'll do it. Just put the end in my mouth for me.'

Lucy did as she was told, still puzzled at Jonah's strange behaviour. He adjusted the height of his chair so that his head was level with one of the rows of tea-lights. Then he moved the chair closer and craned his neck in an attempt to light the taper. Lucy watched his efforts, wondering how long to wait before repeating her offer of assistance. At last, he succeeded in lighting the taper and, a few moments later, in using it to light another of the tea-lights. The look of concentration on his face relaxed and he looked up at Lucy again.

'Thanks,' he grunted through teeth still clenched around the taper. 'Can you blow it out now?'

Lucy took the taper, blew it out and replaced it on the shelf.

'Did I do this candle-lighting business right?' he asked her.

'Yes,' she smiled. 'But you could have let me. It would have been just the same.'

'You told me once that it was all about *doing* something,' Jonah argued. 'Isn't that the point? Doing *something* when there doesn't seem to be anything you can do to help a situation?'

'Mmm. It's just *you* needed to make more effort than everyone else.'

'Will that make it work better than Old Peter's candle, say?' Jonah asked mischievously.

'No, of course not!' Lucy laughed. 'Who was it you were lighting it for? Or don't you want to say?' she added hastily, afraid that she might embarrass her friend.

'Sandra Latham and her family. Things are all a bit–'

'Hi there!' Dominic's voice interrupted their conversation. 'I saw you'd checked in here on Facebook, so I thought I'd come and find you. It's on the way home – well, sort-of – from the hospice.'

'Hello!' Jonah smiled at Dominic. 'We're having a second attempt at seeing round Liverpool before we head off home tomorrow morning. Of course, we'd get on better if people didn't keep committing murders every time we come!'

'Or if you didn't insist on gate-crashing the investigation every time a murder is committed!' Lucy reproached him.

'You'll just have to come again,' Dominic suggested hopefully.

'Oh, I shouldn't think there's any doubt we'll be coming again,' Jonah assured him. 'Dear old Dot will be expecting us to. Now, you'll have to excuse me: it looks as if Bernie's wanting to show me something.'

He headed off towards where Bernie was standing, still arm-in-arm with Peter, looking in their direction. Lucy made to follow him, but Dominic put out his hand to hold her back.

'Tell me what's been going on,' he urged. 'I assume Jonah must have unmasked the murderer or he'd still be in *Park View*, but what happened? And who was it?'

'Don't you know? Well, you remember he'd come up with this mad scheme for pretending he knew who'd done it and that he was going to tell the police?'

'Yes, but I thought you and Bernie had talked him out of it.'

'We had ... or at least we'd persuaded DCI Latham not to let him do it. But he was so keen ...,' Lucy sighed. 'Anyway, he went ahead with it in the end. He pretended to have found a note that Olive had written that proved who it was who killed her. And he got Aunty Dot to spread the word around among the residents.'

'I bet she enjoyed doing that.'

'Yes,' Lucy giggled. 'I'm sure she did. Anyway, the upshot was that the killer did exactly what he was hoping they would and tried to kill him too.'

'Unsuccessfully, obviously,' Dominic added excitedly. 'And who was it?'

'One of the Care Assistants. The one who works nights. Rebecca something.'

'I don't think I've met her. I suppose I wouldn't have if she's always on nights. Why did she do it?'

'As far as I can make out, she was worried that Olive's dossier was going to get the Home closed down and she'd lose her job.'

'She's lost more than her job now. She must have been a bit ... I dunno ...'

'Desperate?' Lucy suggested. 'That's what Peter says. She's got three kids and an ex-husband who won't pay maintenance,'

'I was going to say *crazy*. It doesn't make any sense, risking life imprisonment just on the off-chance-'

'I suppose she worried and worried about it and got to the stage where it didn't seem like just an off-chance to her. A bit like me and Mam not wanting to let Jonah go through with his idiotic entrapment scheme. I mean, we knew that Sandra Latham would do everything she could to make sure he was safe, but I was still convinced that he was going to die. I was awake all night last night, wondering what was happening to him'

'It was a bit mean of him still going ahead with it, knowing how you felt,' Dominic said indignantly.

'No. It wasn't like that. I had to let him do it. I just wish he didn't keep wanting to ...,' she sighed. 'It's bad enough knowing ...'

'Knowing what?'

'Having a spinal cord injury reduces your life expectancy considerably. Ever since I found that out, I've felt we might lose him any time – without him going out of his way to take risks.'

'But that's how it is, isn't it?' Dominic struggled to understand. 'The older generation dies and new ones are born. Like my two granddads and my other gran. They've all died, but life goes on. I suppose it was sad at the time, although I don't really remember now, but ...'

'But I love Jonah,' Lucy said in a small voice. 'I can't imagine ever being ready to let him go.'

Dominic ventured to put his arm around Lucy's shoulders and felt immense relief when she did not shrug it off. They stood together, watching as Jonah, Peter and Bernie continued on their walk around the cathedral, chatting together in low voices.

'I suppose,' Dominic said at last, 'that's why it matters that Olive's killer didn't get away with it. However old and frail she was, someone won't have been ready to let her go either.'

EPILOGUE

'Rebecca Emily Anderson,' the judge said solemnly, fixing her deep brown eyes firmly on the figure in the dock, 'you have pleaded guilty to the charges of murdering Mrs Olive Carter and of attempting to murder DCI Jonah Porter. It now falls to me to pass sentence.'

Journalists in the public gallery leaned forward, pencils poised.

'The heinous crime of murder carries a mandatory life sentence. In setting a minimum term, I have taken into account certain mitigating factors put forward by your defence counsel. I have also considered a number of aggravating factors, including the duty of care that you owed to both of your victims, their vulnerability and your premeditation and planning of the crimes.'

Bernie and Jonah exchanged glances. It was not looking good for Rebecca and her family.

'You have heard the victim impact statement from the family of Olive Carter, in which they express their deep sorrow at the loss of their mother and their conviction that, but for your intervention, she might have had a long and happy life ahead of her despite her advanced age.'

All eyes turned to the Carters, who were sitting on the opposite side of the court from Bernie and Jonah. Desmond was leaning on the rail, looking intently at the judge, eager not to miss a word. His brother sat with his head bowed, as if he did not want anyone to see his emotions as the sentence was read out. Valerie's face was obscured by a large purple hat. Priscilla seemed to be ignoring the proceedings, intent on pressing buttons on the mobile phone in her lap.

'For the attempted murder,' the judge continued, 'I sentence you to ten years imprisonment.'

The prisoner in the dock gave a little gasp and turned very white.

'For the murder, I sentence you to Life imprisonment, with a recommendation that you serve a minimum of twenty-two years. The two sentences are to be served concurrently.'

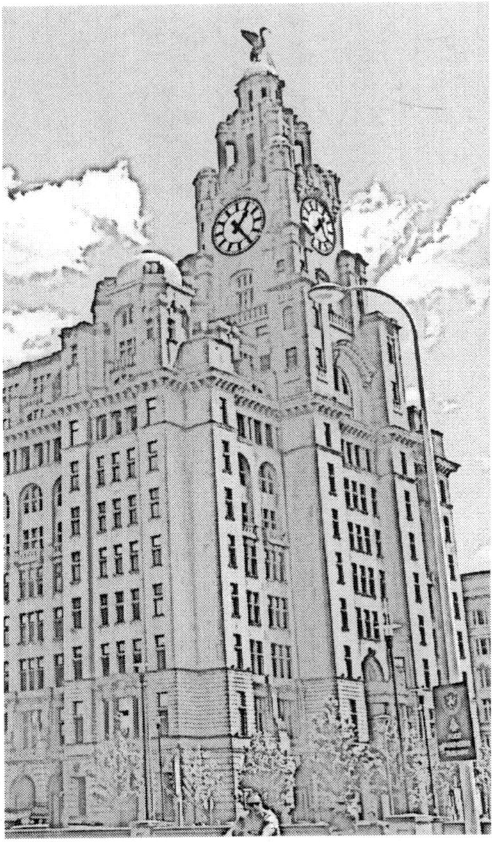

THANK YOU

Thank you for taking the time to read In My Liverpool Home. If you enjoyed it, please consider telling your friends or posting a short review. Word of mouth is an author's best friend and much appreciated.

Thank you,

Judy.

DISCLAIMER

This book is a work of fiction. Any references to real people, events, establishments, organisations or locales are intended only to provide a sense of authenticity and are used fictitiously. All of the characters and events are entirely invented by the author. Any resemblances to persons living or dead are purely coincidental.

Most of the locations and institutions that feature in this book are real. Their inhabitants and employees, however, are purely fictional. In particular,
- *Park View* Care Home does not exist, and it is not based on any existing Care Home in Liverpool or anywhere else;
- There is no Catholic Church of Our Lady of Grace in Toxteth, and the church portrayed here is not based on any existing church in Liverpool or anywhere else;
- None of the police officers mentioned in this story are based on real members of Merseyside Police or of any other police service.

MORE ABOUT BERNIE AND HER FRIENDS

Bernie features in ten other books.
- **Awayday**: a traditional detective story set among the dons of an Oxford college.
- **Changing Scenes of Life**: Jonah Porter's life story, told through the medium of his favourite hymns.
- **Despise not your Mother**: the story of Bernie's quest to learn about her dead husband's past.
- **Two Little Dickie Birds**: a murder mystery for DI Peter Johns and his Sergeant, Paul Godwin.
- **Murder of a Martian**: a double murder for Peter and Jonah to solve.
- **Death on the Algarve:** a mystery for Bernie and her friends to tackle while on holiday in Portugal.
- **My Life of Crime**: the collected memoirs of DI Peter Johns.
- **Mystery over the Mersey**: a murder mystery set in Liverpool.
- **Sorrowful Mystery**: Jonah investigates a child abduction and Peter embarks on a new journey of faith.
- **Grave Offence**: Peter investigates an assault and a suspicious death, while Jonah acts as a backseat driver from the rehabilitation ward of the spinal injuries centre.

You can find them all on Judy Ford's Amazon Author page: https://www.amazon.co.uk/-/e/B0193I5B1M

Read more about Bernie Fazakerley and her friends and family at https://sites.google.com/site/llanwrdafamily/

Visit the Bernie Fazakerley Publications Facebook page here: www.facebook.com/Bernie.Fazakerley.Publications.

Follow Bernie on Twitter: https://twitter.com/BernieFaz.

ABOUT THE AUTHOR

Like her main character, Bernie Fazakerley, Judy Ford is an Oxford graduate and a mathematician. Unlike Bernie, Judy grew up in a middle-class family in the South London stockbroker belt. After moving to the North West and working in Liverpool, Judy fell in love with the Scouse people and created Bernie to reflect their unique qualities.

As a Methodist Local Preacher, Judy often tells her congregation, "I see my role as asking the questions and leaving you to think out your own answers." She carries this philosophy forward into her writing and she hopes that readers will find themselves challenged to think as well as being entertained.

Made in the USA
Columbia, SC
14 March 2018